DEAD RINGER

The last time Thanet had seen this face the eyes had been sightless, the features slack in death. Intellectually, of course, he had been prepared for the resemblance, but emotionally the impact was both unexpected and disconcerting; it was eerie, positively uncanny, to see the dead man standing before him in apparent good health.

DEAD ON ARRIVAL

Bantam Books offers the finest in classic and modern British murder mysteries.
Ask your bookseller for the books you have missed.

Agatha Christie

Death on the Nile
A Holiday for Murder
The Mousetrap and Other Plays
The Mysterious Affair at Styles
Poirot Investigates
Postern of Fate
The Secret Adversary
The Seven Dials Mystery
Sleeping Murder

Dorothy Simpson

Last Seen Alive
The Night She Died
Puppet for a Corpse
Six Feet Under
Close Her Eyes
coming soon: Element of Doubt

Sheila Radley

The Chief Inspector's Daughter
Death in the Morning
Fate Worse Than Death
Who Saw Him Die?

Elizabeth George

A Great Deliverance
coming soon: A Payment in Blood

Colin Dexter

Last Bus to Woodstock
The Riddle of the Third Mile
The Silent World of Nicholas Quinn
Service of All the Dead
The Dead of Jericho
The Secret of Annexe 3
Last Seen Wearing

John Greenwood

The Mind of Mr. Mosley
The Missing Mr. Mosley
Mosley by Moonlight
Murder, Mr. Mosley
Mists Over Mosley
What, Me, Mr. Mosley?

Ruth Rendell

A Dark-Adapted Eye
(writing as Barbara Vine)
A Fatal Inversion
(writing as Barbara Vine)

Marian Babson

Death in Fashion
Reel Murder
Murder, Murder Little Star
Murder on a Mystery Tour
Murder Sails at Midnight

Christianna Brand

Suddenly at His Residence
Heads You Lose

Dorothy Cannell

The Widows Club
coming soon: Down the Garden Path

Michael Dibdin

Ratking

Dead on Arrival

DOROTHY SIMPSON

BANTAM BOOKS
TORONTO · NEW YORK · LONDON · SYDNEY · AUCKLAND

*This edition contains the complete text
of the original hardcover edition.*
NOT ONE WORD HAS BEEN OMITTED.

DEAD ON ARRIVAL

*A Bantam Book / Published by arrangement with
Charles Scribner's Sons*

PRINTING HISTORY
*Scribner's edition published 1986
Bantam edition / March 1989*

To Pat and Ailsa

Dead on Arrival

one

_____

The house was unnaturally silent. Thanet stood in the hall, head cocked, listening: no sound from the television in the living room, no movement or clatter of pans from the kitchen, no muffled, rhythmic thump of distant pop music from Ben's room . . . He glanced at his watch. Ten to six. Where were they all?

He moved to the foot of the stairs. "Anyone in?" he called.

No reply.

He shrugged, went into the kitchen and put the kettle on, feeling disgruntled. Not so many years ago he would have arrived home to a rapturous welcome. Bridget and Ben would have rushed to greet him, faces aglow, reaching up to kiss him, competing for his attention. Unconsciously, he sighed. He certainly wouldn't expect such behavior of an eleven- and a thirteen-year-old, but he had to admit that he sometimes regretted that they were growing up so quickly. In just a few years they would be independent, leaving home . . .

The front door slammed.

"I'm home!" Bridget's voice.

Thanet rose with alacrity, went into the hall. "So I gather," he said, smiling.

"Dad! Hi! What are you doing home?" The wind had whipped color into her cheeks, tousled the fine blonde hair which recently (to Thanet's regret) had been cut fashionably short.

"Finished early for once."

"Wonders will never cease." Bridget shed her coat, hung it in the cupboard under the stairs and followed Thanet into the kitchen. "It's nice to get into the warm."

It was a Tuesday in late November, and since early morning an icy wind had been blowing from the east, bringing a warning of early snow and the prospect of a long, hard winter.

Thanet handed her a steaming mug of tea. "I was beginning to wonder where you'd all got to."

"Thanks." Bridget cupped her hands around the mug and sipped appreciatively. "Mum'll be a bit late tonight. She forgot to tell you."

Joan, Thanet's wife, was a probation officer, and her working hours were sometimes inconveniently unpredictable.

"So I went round to Susan's. And Ben's at Paul's, watching a video."

"What video?" said Thanet sharply. He was only too well aware of the ready availability of the pornographic and sadistic video films which, despite every attempt to stem the flood, continued to pour into the high street rental shops in a seemingly never-ending stream.

Bridget grinned. "Cool it, Dad. It's nothing unsuitable. Just some documentary on photographic techniques that Ben missed because he was at Scouts." She put her mug on the draining board. "I must get on. I want to try another way of decorating that lemon flummery."

Thanet hid his dismay. Much as he enjoyed that particular pudding, a fluffy concoction halfway between a mousse and a cream, this would be the fourth night in a row they'd had to eat it.

"Still not satisfied? I thought last night's looked terrific."

Bridget frowned at the dish she had taken from the fridge. "I've got to get it just right."

About a year ago Bridget had developed an interest in cooking. Her mother was an excellent cook, but ever since Joan had started working full-time she had had neither the time nor the inclination to expend much energy in the kitchen. Thanet had watched with approval as Bridget rapidly developed an astonishing degree of expertise. On Saturday she was to take part in the regional heats for the Junior Chef of the Year, her first competition.

"Nervous?" he asked, watching with admiration as she whipped cream, carefully selected the appropriate nozzle for the piping bag and began to decorate the pudding with minute, glistening whorls.

"A bit, I suppose."

"You're going to win, I know it."

"You're biased, Dad. But thanks for the vote of confidence, all the same."

The front door slammed again and Ben appeared in the kitchen doorway. "Oh no, not yukky lemon flummery again." And he stuck out his tongue and pretended to retch.

"That's enough, Ben. If it'll help Sprig to win we'll eat it until it comes out of our ears."

"It's already coming out of mine!"

"Good program?"

"Great. Dad, when *are* we going to get a video? *Everyone's* got one."

"Not everyone. *We* haven't. And as I've said before, there's no point in going on about it, we've no intention of getting one."

"But why? It's so useful. Just think, when you got home late from work you could watch all the things you've missed earlier on in the evening."

"When I get home late from work all I want to do is go to bed. Apart from which, so far as I can see, there's never anything on worth watching, these days."

"That's not true," they chorused. "There's . . ."

Thanet held up a hand. "No. I don't want to hear, thank you. As far as I'm concerned, kids nowadays have far too much potted entertainment, and I'm not going to provide you with the potential for yet more."

"But if we don't see it here, we only go and see it at someone else's house," objected Ben.

And this, Thanet had to admit, was the one potent argument for having a video recorder of their own. Here, at least, he and Joan would have some control over the sort of material the children watched. But he wasn't going to strengthen Ben's case by saying so. "In that case, what are you complaining about?"

The front door slammed once more, and Thanet went to greet Joan, his heart lifting, as always, at the sight of her. Tonight, fueled by the memory of the emptiness which had marred his return home, his kiss was even more enthusiastic than usual.

Joan pulled away a little, laughing. "Hey, what did I do to deserve that?"

He kissed her again. "Do I have to have an excuse?"

Her arms tightened around his neck for a moment, then she wriggled out of his grasp, began to unbutton her coat. "I must get on with supper. I'm all behind."

"I was wondering if you'd like to go out for a change. Nowhere elaborate. Pizzaland, for instance?"

"Luke! That would be lovely. With the children?"

"Why not?"

"What are we celebrating?"

He came closer, put his mouth against her ear. "Sprig

is decorating yet another lemon flummery. I don't think I can face it."

Joan laughed. "That makes two of us."

They all enjoyed the unusual treat of a family outing midweek, and it was not until a quarter to eleven, when Thanet and Joan were thinking of going to bed, that the telephone rang.

Joan pulled a face. "Guess who that's for."

Thanet went reluctantly to answer it.

"Thanet here."

"It's Bentley, sir. We had an anonymous phone call, at ten twenty-five, reporting a murder at number three, Hamilton Road. We sent someone round, and it's just been confirmed. Young man in his twenties. Head bashed in."

And Lineham's not here . . . "Better get everything laid on. You know what to do. Has Doc Mallard been informed?" *I'll have to get Lineham back, as soon as I can. Hines isn't going to like this one little bit.*

"Yes. He's out on a call apparently, but a message was left on his answerphone."

"Let's hope he won't be too long. I'll be over there as soon as I can."

Thanet rang off. He'd better get on to Hines right away. No, he'd wait until he'd seen what the position was for himself.

Joan was in the kitchen, pouring boiling water into a thermos flask.

"Coffee," she said. "It sounds as though it might be a long night."

" 'Fraid so. Thanks, love."

Outside, the wind tore at Thanet's raincoat. It was beginning to rain and by the time he turned out of his driveway on to the road heavy drops were hurling themselves against the windscreen in gusting sheets.

"That's all I need," he muttered as he switched on the

windscreen wipers. It was at times like these that he paid lip-service to the idea that it would be nice to have a comfortable, nine-to-five office job with weekends off and plenty of guaranteed leisure. But underneath he knew that such work would have bored him stiff. He loved his job, enjoyed its unpredictability, the constant challenge, the thrill of the hunt, the unique satisfaction of victory. There were disadvantages, of course, and he was grimly aware that one of them was imminent, something far more difficult for him to cope with than the inconvenience of being called out at an hour when most people were thinking of getting comfortably tucked up in bed.

For the truth was that, despite all his years on the force, Thanet had never been able to harden himself against his first sight of a corpse. He had tried every trick in the book, from disassociation to levity, but nothing had worked, ever. In the early years he had told himself that familiarity would breed if not contempt, then at least indifference, but it had never happened and by now he began each case with resigned dread and an acceptance that those few moments of acute discomfort were the necessary prelude to the work in which he found such satisfaction.

Hamilton Road was a wide, tree-lined street leading down to the river. The houses were huge Victorian red-brick monsters, built by prosperous tradesmen in the days when servants were plentiful and labor cheap. They had long ago been converted into flats and their original owners would have been appalled to see the dirty windows, peeling paint, sagging gutters, and overgrown gardens. Tonight the façades were punctuated by uncurtained oblongs of yellow light against which were silhouetted the heads and shoulders of neighbors curious to know what was going on. At least the weather should prevent the usual crowd of ghouls, Thanet thought with satisfaction.

It was easy to pick out number three by the police cars parked outside. Thanet cursed as the wind tore the door-handle from his grasp, straining the hinges. He ran through the pelting rain along the short, curving drive to the front door, where a uniformed PC in a waterproof cape was stamping his feet in a fruitless attempt to keep warm.

"Evening, Johnson. Filthy night."

"Certainly is, sir."

"Where's the body?"

"First floor back, sir."

Thanet pushed open the stained-glass inner door and stepped into a spacious hallway which ran the depth of the house to a rear door at the far end. It was cluttered with prams and bicycles and only the curving hand-carved banister and the ornately patterned ceramic tiles on the floor spoke of the gracious way of life for which it had been designed. An unshaded, low-wattage overhead bulb cast a sickly yellow light on flaking plaster and grubby, distempered walls.

Head bashed in. Conscious of the tightening muscles in his abdomen, Thanet ran up the wide, uncarpeted stairs, trying not to think of all the other head injuries he had seen, some of them stomach-churning by any standards. *Another few minutes and the worst will be over.* A door immediately in front of him was ajar and from within came the unmistakable sounds of police activity. Thanet took a deep breath and walked in.

Carson was standing just inside the door, keeping out of the way of the photographers. The room was stiflingly hot.

"Evening, sir."

Thanet nodded a greeting. "Where is he?"

"Over there, sir. On the floor in front of the settee."

Avoiding what looked like a smear of blood on the carpet, Thanet walked around the side of the settee, which stood with its back to the door halfway across the room. Then he took another deep, unobtrusive breath and looked.

The dead man lay face down on the floor in front of the settee, his knees curled up, one arm outflung. He was wearing jeans, a dark blue sweater and shabby sneakers.

After the familiar rush of compassion, the pang of anger and regret at this wanton waste of human life, Thanet's first emotion was one of relief. Often, with head injuries, there is a great deal of blood, but in this case there was only a small, glistening streak in the man's hair.

"A single blow?" he murmured to Carson.

"Looks like it, sir."

"And with something pretty blunt, by the look of it. Flat, even."

Which made this case a little unusual. Thanet knew that in the majority of cases of death by head injury more than one blow is struck—which results in a lot of very quick bleeding and much splashing of blood. If, however, the victim is hit by something flat, the impact is distributed over a large area. There may be local damage to the brain under the point of impact, the skull may be fractured and there may be a large area of bruising, but the skin may not even necessarily split and there may thus be no external scalp bleeding.

Thanet was beginning to sweat. The gas fire was on full blast.

Carson followed Thanet's glance. "Thought I'd better leave the fire on until the doc's been."

Room temperature is an important factor in estimating time of death.

"Quite right . . ." Thanet shrugged out of his coat and slung it over his shoulder.

One of the Scenes-of-Crime officers approached. "All right if I take samples now, sir? I wanted to leave him *in situ* until you'd seen him."

"Finished the photographs?"

"Of the body, yes, sir."

"Fine. Carry on, then."

Thanet began to wander around the room. The shabby settee, sagging armchair, cheap table scarred with innumerable cigarette burns and white rings on its once-glossy veneered surface, all spoke of a room which had been rented furnished to countless careless tenants. And yet, Thanet noticed, attempts had been made to brighten the place up. There were new, brightly colored cotton curtains at the tall window, matching cushions on the settee and armchair. A wife, then? Or live-in girlfriend? If so, where was she? There were two birthday cards on the mantelpiece and he crossed to look at them. One, with a sentimental verse, was signed Sharon, the other, a bawdy, humorous one, was from someone called Geoff.

Carson had been following Thanet about, walking a pace or two behind like a faithful retriever.

Thanet glanced back at him. "Do we know anything about him?"

"Not much. I had a quick word with a Mrs. Bence, who lives in one of the downstairs flats, the one below this. She's a sort of caretaker, and has spare keys to all the flats in case of emergency, so it was her who let us in. She's a funny old bird. She says his name is Steven Long."

"Married?"

"Yes."

Sharon, perhaps?

"But they split up recently. Not surprising, according to Mrs. Bence. She was quite friendly with the wife, but didn't have much time for him."

"Why not? No, it doesn't matter, I'll have a word with her myself, later. How old is she?"

"Mrs. Bence? Early sixties, I'd say."

"Good. Time on her hands to be nosy, then." Thanet was missing Lineham. It wasn't that Carson had been crass, or inefficient, quite the contrary. He was careful, solid, reliable, where the sergeant was eager, impulsive, volatile. But Thanet was so used to working with Lineham that it was almost as if a part of himself were missing. Was this what it would be like if Lineham got his promotion to Inspector? Thanet wondered. Would it be impossible to adjust to working efficiently with someone else, after all these years?

"Tell me what you think happened here, Tom."

"Well, I was thinking about it while I was waiting for you to arrive, sir, and I reckon he was sitting on the settee when it happened. I think he was bashed from above and behind."

"What with, do you think?"

Carson shrugged. "Doesn't seem to be anything likely lying about. Chummy must've taken it with him. I was wondering . . ."

"Yes?"

"Well, that smear on the carpet, halfway between the door and the settee . . . Looks like blood."

"Yes, I'd noticed. What about it?"

"Well, I reckon he must have dropped the murder weapon, after hitting the victim, sir, then decided it was safer to take it away with him."

"Could be." Thanet already had a theory about what that weapon had been but he did not comment, simply gestured at the object which dominated the room, a huge color television set, complete with video recorder on a shelf below. "He can't have been too hard up."

Carson grinned. "It was probably on the HP."

"Even so . . ."

There was a flurry of movement on the stairs. Reinforcements had arrived. Thanet gave Carson the thankless task of tracing and notifying the next of kin and then went out on to the landing and set about deploying his men. He had just finished when the stained-glass front door opened again and Mallard came in, taking off his hat and shaking it, spattering the floor with raindrops which made dark circles in the dust.

Usually the lateness of the hour or the inclemency of the weather would have elicited some sarcastic comment from the little doctor, but tonight he merely glanced up at Thanet and said, "Up there?"

Thanet nodded. "Evening, Doc. Sorry to drag you out on such a filthy night." He ushered Mallard into Long's room.

The SOCOs had finished with the body for the moment and after Mallard had examined the head wound, he and Thanet gently turned Long over.

It was the first time Thanet had seen the dead man's face, and he studied it while Mallard made his examination.

Steven Long had been in his mid-twenties, with a narrow face, beaky nose and dark blue eyes beneath straight brown hair brushed back from a bony forehead. In his lifeless sprawl he looked, Thanet thought fancifully, as pathetic as a dead sparrow abandoned at the roadside. But this had been no accident, and Steven Long no sparrow. Thanet's fists clenched involuntarily. At moments like this he invariably experienced a painful mixture of anger and compassion.

"Can't give a final verdict until after the PM, of course," said Mallard, "but there doesn't seem to be much doubt about cause of death."

"The blow to the back of the head?"

Mallard nodded.

"Any guesses about the murder instrument?"

Mallard heaved himself to his feet. "Something flattish, by the look of it, heavy, with a rim around the base which broke the skin and caused that slight bleeding."

"An ashtray, perhaps?"

Mallard shrugged. "Possible, if it was weighty enough. One of those heavy glass or pottery ones. Why, have you found it?"

"No, but come and look at this."

Thanet led Mallard to the battered oak sideboard which stood against the wall to the right of the door. In the thin layer of dust which covered it was a clean, circular patch about five inches in diameter.

"I can't see anything in the room to match it. Could have been a heavy vase, I suppose," Thanet added.

"It's about the right size, certainly."

"I'd like several shots of this," Thanet said to the photographer. "Make sure you give a clear impression of its size."

"Right, sir."

"You can turn that fire off, too," said Mallard, mopping at his forehead and running his handkerchief over his bald head. "Place is like a tropical greenhouse."

"We left it on because . . ."

"Yes, yes." Mallard waved a dismissive hand. "But I've finished, now. Turn the damned thing off, for God's sake."

Thanet did so, then returned to Mallard, who had finished packing his things away and now closed his bag with a snap.

"Where's Lineham?" he said. "Unusual not to see him here. Still on maternity leave, so to speak, is he?"

Lineham's wife Louise had just given birth to their second child, a daughter this time, and the sergeant had taken ten days of his annual leave to help out.

"No, he's been back at work for a week now." Thanet scowled. "He's on loan to Chief Inspector Hines for the investigation into that murder over at Coddington Woods on Sunday night."

"Ah yes. Nasty business, that. You realize she was still alive when they found her, on Monday morning?"

Thanet grimaced. "So I heard. Died in the ambulance on the way to hospital. I understand they think she was thrown out of a car and cracked her head on a big stone at the side of the road."

"Having been half-strangled first," said Mallard.

"I didn't know that. Anyway, Mr. Hines is rather short-handed at the moment, and as things were very quiet here, I agreed to let him borrow Lineham. I'm kicking myself now, of course."

"You'll get him back, though, surely."

"I certainly shall," said Thanet. *With difficulty.*

Mallard was putting on his coat.

"There's just one more question, Doc."

Mallard frowned at Thanet over his half-moon spectacles. "Don't tell me. The usual. Time of death."

"Well . . ."

"Impossible to be accurate, in the circumstances. The temperature in here would have affected the cooling of the body considerably, and as it's lying right in front of the fire . . . Well, you can see the problem for yourself."

"Could you hazard a guess?"

"Not really. I'm sorry, Luke, I'm usually prepared to stick my neck out, as you know . . ."

Normally, Thanet would have left it there, but Mallard's unusually amiable mood encouraged him not to give up just yet. "Some time this evening, anyway?"

Mallard gave a mischievous smile. "Some time today, I'd say. And I refuse to commit myself any further."

Thanet had to leave it at that. He had expected something of the sort and it certainly wouldn't help. But it wasn't the doctor's fault and he simply nodded his thanks and escorted him to the front door, wondering why Mallard had been so relatively civil this evening. The police surgeon's ill-humor was a legend in the force. Thanet did his best to ignore it, having known Mallard in the days before his wife had died a slow, lingering death from cancer, many years ago. The little doctor had never managed to come to terms with his grief and his irascibility was his way of venting upon the world the anger and despair he still felt at her loss. Lineham would certainly have noticed this change in Mallard's behavior, and together they would have speculated as to its significance. Once again Thanet wished that the sergeant were present, and decided that he would make that phone call his first priority.

They had just reached the front door when it burst open: Brent, one of the new young DCs.

Mallard staggered a little and Thanet put a hand under his elbow to steady him. "For God's sake, man, be careful."

"Sorry, sir. Sorry, Doc. Sir . . ." Brent's eyes were sparking with excitement.

"Take a deep breath and count to five. Then tell me."

Brent did as he was told, but even so the words tumbled out in his haste. "Sir, there's a car parked just along the road. It's been there all evening, I gather. We were just checking it, as a matter of routine, and we found a man inside, half sozz . . . pretty drunk, sir. He's mumbling threats against Long. And he's crying."

two

Until now the other inhabitants of the house had reluctantly obeyed orders and stayed in their rooms, but DC Brent's precipitous entry had created a new surge of curiosity. Thanet was aware of doors opening, of murmured conversations, and of people peering down into the hall.

He and Mallard exchanged glances.

"You want me to hang on for a few minutes?" said the little doctor in a low voice.

"Thanks, yes. Just till we see what sort of state this man's in. Where is he, Brent? Still in the car?"

"At the moment, yes, sir. We didn't know if you'd want him brought in here or taken back to the station."

"From what you say it doesn't sound as though I'll get much sense out of him, but I'd better have a quick word with him, then you can take him back to the station." But where to talk in privacy, that was the problem? He couldn't conduct an interview here, in the hall, it was much too public, and Long's room was out of the question.

Thanet glanced around. The door to the right of the stairs remained shut, but a middle-aged couple was peering curiously from the one on the left and at the back of the hall, arms akimbo, wrapped in a brilliant scarlet kimono with a gold dragon emblazoned from shoulder to hem, stood a squat little figure squinting at them through the smoke from the cigarette hanging from her lower lip; Mrs. Bence, presumably.

There appeared to be no choice.

Thanet turned back to Brent. "Bring him in. But first I want all these people back inside their rooms again. And make sure they stay there, this time."

Thanet and Mallard waited while these orders were carried out and within minutes the newcomer was half-led, half-carried into the house and propped against the wall, supported by a man on either side.

He was in his late forties, Thanet guessed, short, burly, and dressed in a good-quality dark gray worsted suit, blue and white striped shirt and blue silk tie. There were well-defined creases in his raincoat, as if he had been sitting in the same position for some hours. He looked like a successful businessman, but somewhere along the way something had gone badly wrong: the skin of his face was the color of dough, his eyes red-veined and puffy with recent tears. A sour reek of whisky hung in the air. He seemed unaware of his surroundings.

"Could you give me your name, sir?"

Somewhere at the back of the man's eyes awareness flickered briefly, and was extinguished.

"Sir?"

Still no response.

Thanet stepped forward and gently removed the man's wallet from his inside pocket. There was no reaction.

Thanet flicked through it and extracted a driving license: Harry Ronald Carpenter; address: Smallwood, Benenden Drive, Sturrenden. Benenden Drive was an exclusive residential area of large, relatively new detached houses on the far side of town.

Thanet frowned. Carpenter . . . The name rang a bell, but Thanet couldn't think why.

"You were talking about Mr. Long, sir . . ."

The man's body jerked, as if an electric current had been passed through it. His head lifted, his eyes narrowed, his mouth twisted. "Bastard," he said thickly. "Kill him . . ."

"Why?" said Thanet. "Why should you want to kill him, Mr. Carpenter?"

"Kill him," repeated Carpenter. "Kill him. Only thing to do." Suddenly he began to struggle, working his shoulders up and down to release himself from the restricting grip on his arms. "Where is he?"

"He's dead, Mr. Carpenter. Upstairs."

Carpenter stopped struggling as abruptly as he had begun and peered at Thanet as if he were trying to see clearly in dense fog.

"Dead?"

"Yes. Upstairs."

Carpenter's eyes rolled up in his head and he collapsed, his sudden dead weight causing the men to stagger. They lowered him gently to the floor and Mallard squatted to examine him.

"Passed out," he said, after a moment.

"Heart attack?"

Mallard shook his head. "I don't think it's anything serious. Just a shock, on top of too much to drink. But to be on the safe side I think we'd better put him into hospital for the night."

"Ambulance outside?" said Thanet to one of the men.

"Yes, sir. Waiting to remove the body. It arrived some time ago."

"Good. It can take Mr. Carpenter first, then come

back. Stay with him and let me know the moment he's fit for questioning."

When Carpenter had been removed and Mallard had left, Thanet glanced at his watch: twelve thirty. Was it too late to make that phone call about Lineham? Hines had probably gone home by now. But even if he hadn't it might be better not to arouse his antagonism unnecessarily by breaking the news of Lineham's imminent withdrawal at this hour of the night. The little patience Hines possessed would be at its lowest ebb. Reluctantly, Thanet decided to wait until morning.

So, what now?

As soon as the SOCOs were finished upstairs, Thanet wanted to take a really good look at Stephen Long's room, but meanwhile it might prove fruitful to have a chat with Mrs. Bence. According to Carson she had known the Longs quite well. And Thanet had been intrigued by that brief glimpse of her just now.

He walked along the short passage beside the staircase and raised his hand to knock on her door, but before his knuckles had made contact with wood it had opened. She must have been standing on the other side, listening. "Mrs. Bence?"

"Who wants to know?"

Her gray hair was short, unevenly hacked off just below the ears, and a cigarette still drooped from her lower lip. She was looking him up and down as if he were the prize turkey she wasn't sure whether to buy for Christmas. But there was no aggression in her gaze, only appraisal, and she must have approved of what she saw because she removed the cigarette and grinned to take the sting out of her words, revealing teeth the color of old piano keys.

Thanet introduced himself. "I understand you knew the Longs. I'd like to talk to you, if I may." Ordinary members of the public, he found, invariably responded well to courtesy.

18

Mrs. Bence was no exception. She stepped back.

"Come in, ducks. Welcome to my humble abode. And you can call me Dara."

"Dara," repeated Thanet. But he hadn't taken in the outlandish nature of Mrs. Bence's Christian name; he was too preoccupied with trying to absorb the extraordinary atmosphere of her sitting room.

Every available inch of wall space was taken up with posters, hand-bills and photographs large and small. The former all advertised the imminent arrival of BENJY'S, THE GREATEST LITTLE CIRCUS IN THE WORLD. Prominently billed was DARA, THE MOST SENSATIONAL HIGH-WIRE ACT THE WORLD HAS EVER SEEN. The photographs showed Dara, glamorously attired in spangles and tights, at some of the most sensational moments of her act: flying through space with the grace of a swallow, tightly curled up in the now-familiar ball of the triple somersault, suspended by the teeth from a gossamer wire high, high above the upturned faces of the awed spectators.

"Never believe it was the same woman, would you?"

Thanet turned. She was standing in the middle of the room watching him, enjoying his astonishment and absorption. What could he say? The truth was that no, he could scarcely believe it.

She waved her hand. "Oh, don't bother to deny it. I don't want to put you in a spot. 'Specially as I like the look of you." She lowered herself into a huge, sagging leather armchair and lit another cigarette from the stub of the old one. "Take a pew."

The "pew" was an ancient monster of tan moquette, bald and shiny with years of wear. Seen in a better light the scarlet kimono, too, was stained and faded, a mere reflection of its original splendor.

"Want a fag?"

Thanet shook his head, his hand unconsciously straying to his pocket.

"Smoke a pipe?"

He nodded. So she was observant. Good.

"Carry on, then. Light up, if you want to. My old man used to smoke a pipe. I miss it. Used to complain like hell at the time, but now . . . What d'you think of it all, then?" And she waved her hand at the display on the walls.

"Amazing," said Thanet with sincerity, feeding tobacco into his pipe. "Really amazing."

"Them was the days," said Mrs. Bence with a sigh. "I still miss it, you know. There's nothing like it in the world—the people, the animals, the atmosphere, the excitement, and above all, the smell . . ." She closed her eyes in ecstatic reminiscence. "Sweat, sawdust . . . If Benjy's hadn't folded, I'd probably be there still, helping out in some way . . . But you don't want to hear all this."

"On the contrary." Thanet paused to apply the first match. "It's fascinating," he said, waving his hand to dispel the clouds of smoke.

She peered at him through the haze. "You mean it, don't yer?"

Thanet nodded, smiled. "All the same, there's a lot to do. So if you don't mind . . ."

"Carry on."

"I'd like you to tell me about the Longs."

"What sort of things d'you want to hear?"

"Anything. Whatever comes into your head. Then, if there's anything else I specifically want to know, I'll ask you."

Mrs. Bence frowned, lit yet another cigarette. "They've been here about, let me see, oh it must be eighteen months, now. And I gather from Sharon—that's his wife—they'd been married about six months before that. If you ask me it's a miracle she stuck it as long as she did."

"They're separated, I gather."

"Yes. She's been gone about three weeks now. Found herself another boyfriend."

"How did Mr. Long take that?"

"Didn't like it one little bit, did he?" The thought obviously gave her satisfaction. "Didn't realize what he'd got until he'd lost it."

"You liked Mrs. Long, obviously."

"Yes. Nice little thing. Kind, sweet-natured—she must've been, or she'd never have put up with him."

"But you obviously weren't too keen on him."

"He was a real . . ." She paused, trying to find a word which would sum Long up to her satisfaction. "A real *bleeder*," she concluded triumphantly.

"In what way?"

"In every way. You should have seen how he treated that poor girl. Ordered her about as if she was a skivvy. 'Do this, fetch that . . .' And bad-tempered! I've had her down here more times than I care to tell, in tears . . ."

"He was violent?"

"Oh no, I'll grant him that," said Mrs. Bence grudgingly. "Far as I know he never laid a finger on her. But there's more ways than one of being cruel, as I'm sure you know full well. I don't know how she stood it. It wasn't even as if he brought home the bacon, either—not regular, anyhow. Poor kid didn't know where she was half the time, far as money was concerned."

"He was out of work?"

"Not at the moment, no. But he was in and out of jobs like a yo-yo. He was a mechanic—a good one, Sharon says, but unreliable, and people would get fed up with him being late for work or just not turning up, if he fancied a day off . . . Well, about three weeks ago he lost his job yet again, because he'd been late five days running. He'd been warned, but he just didn't pay attention . . . He got himself another one, since, but by then it was too late, she'd gone, and she didn't come back. She'd had enough, I reckon."

"What about the boyfriend?"

Mrs. Bence shook her head. "Don't know nothing about

him." She heaved herself out of her armchair, crossed to the sideboard and held up a bottle inquiringly.

"No, thanks." Thanet grinned. "Got to keep my head clear."

She poured herself a generous half-tumbler of gin, then returned to her chair.

Thanet relit his pipe, which wasn't drawing very well. "Did they have many visitors?"

"No. Not surprising, considering the way he went on. Sharon told me he come from quite a big family, but I never set eyes on any of them."

"On bad terms with them, was he?"

"Must've been."

"How many brothers and sisters did he have?"

"Not sure. One brother's a schoolteacher, I think. Don't know about the rest."

"What about his wife . . . er, Sharon?"

"Father's dead and she's got one sister. Does she . . . Anyone broke the news to her, yet?"

"I should think she's probably heard by now, yes."

"Poor kid. She'll be real upset, I expect."

"Even though they were separated?"

"I told you. She's a real sweet girl. She'll be upset, all right."

And even more so in the morning, after the unpleasant task of formal identification of the body, thought Thanet.

"Did you by any chance see Mr. Long this evening, Mrs. . . . Dara?"

"He was going out as I came in. About a quarter to seven."

That was a help. So he'd been alive until quite late. "You heard him come in again, later?"

She shook her head.

"But his room is directly above yours, isn't it?"

"Yes. I might've been cooking my bit of supper in the kitchen when he came in, I suppose. Anyway, I can't hear everything that goes on upstairs. If they're walking around a lot, or playing that awful pop stuff then yes, I can hear the thump, thump, thump, but otherwise this house is built pretty solid, not like the modern rubbish they put up these days. And I had the telly on most of the evening. Next time I saw him was flat out on the floor, when I let the policeman into his room. I has a spare key to all the rooms, in case of emergency. One thing I wanted to ask you . . ."

"Yes?"

"How did the police know there was anything wrong? I mean, there'd been no row, nothing to let on . . ."

No reason why he shouldn't tell her. "Someone rang in, to let us know."

"And I bet he didn't give his name and address, neither."

"You missed your vocation, Dara," said Thanet, smiling. "You should have been a detective."

She gave a snort of laughter and the long worm of ash on her cigarette dropped into her lap. She brushed it away, leaving a smear of gray on the scarlet silk. "That'd be the day!"

"So you have no idea what time Mr. Long returned home?"

"Not the faintest."

"Did you happen to see any strangers in the house this evening?"

"Once I shut the front door behind me, that was it, I didn't poke me nose out again until I heard that policeman hammering away at Sharon's door."

Pity. "Did either of them ever mention a man called Carpenter?"

Mrs. Bence looked at Thanet sharply and fumbled in the pocket of her kimono for her packet of cigarettes. "Oh," she said. "So that's the way the wind blows, is it?"

"What do you mean?"

She waited until she had lit her cigarette. "Soon after they came here, the Longs, he was involved in a car accident . . ."

The words "car accident" were enough, in this context, for Thanet immediately to realize why Carpenter's name had seemed familiar. About a year ago, in the neighboring town of Ashford, Carpenter's wife and daughter had been involved in a car crash. Mrs. Carpenter had been killed instantly, but the little girl had been taken from the wreckage unconscious and had remained in a coma ever since, kept alive by life support machines. Although the driver of the other car had been prosecuted for dangerous driving, his defense counsel had come up with a witness whose testimony had laid part of the blame for the accident on Mrs. Carpenter, and there had been a nasty scene in court when the young man had got off with a fine and a driving license suspension of nine months. Carpenter, Thanet had been told, had had to be forcibly restrained from attacking the accused there and then. So that other driver had been Steven Long . . .

But why should Carpenter wait a year to take his revenge? It just didn't make sense. And if he were the murderer, why should he be sitting outside, some time later, still uttering threats against his victim? Had he been too drunk to know that he had already killed him? Thanet made a mental note: get hold of the clothes Carpenter was wearing, and run tests on them.

Thanet waited until Mrs. Bence had finished talking, asked a few polite questions, then stood up. "Well, thank you, Dara, you've been a great help. I'll leave you now, to get your beauty sleep."

She grinned, stubbed out her cigarette and levered herself up out of her chair. "At my age what you need is the beauty, not the sleep."

"Look," said Thanet. "Would you mind if I came back some time, and you told me all about the circus?"

24

She frowned in disbelief. "You're having me on."

"I most certainly am not. I'd really like to."

She was suddenly radiant and Thanet caught a fleeting glimpse of the vivid creature she had once been. "I'll have to shake the moths out of the red carpet," she said.

three

"Hurry *up*, Ben!"

It was Joan's turn to take the children to school, and as usual Ben was late. She and Bridget were standing in the hall, muffled up in coats and scarves against the biting cold that awaited them outside. Thanet, still sluggish after only a few hours' sleep, was sitting at the kitchen table with a cup of black coffee.

Hurrying footsteps on the stairs told him that Ben was ready at last, and he got up and went into the hall to say goodbye. Hasty kisses from Joan and Bridget, a wave from Ben and they were gone. Thanet returned to the kitchen and sat down again, feeling for his pipe. He needn't leave for another five minutes yet. He made a conscious effort to think about the day's work, to force his brain to start ticking over at the necessary speed. At the beginning of a case there was always so much to do, it was essential to decide on priorities. And the first, of course, would be to get Lineham back.

The radio was on and although Thanet hadn't been listening properly a familiar name suddenly attracted his attention.

". . . Carpenter, in a coma for over a year, ever since the tragic road accident in which her mother was killed, has died. After many months of discussion the decision was finally taken yesterday to switch off Christine's life support machine. Her father, Mr. Harry Carpenter, was not available for comment."

So here was the explanation of Carpenter's behavior last night. Thanet could imagine the man's grief after the long months of hoping, his need to vent his anger against life for the cruel blow it had dealt him. What more natural than that that anger should have found its focus in the man who had been driving the other car? It seemed possible that Thanet would need to look no further for his murderer.

All the same, he couldn't afford to take Carpenter's guilt for granted. An interview with him was obviously a matter of urgency, but if Mrs. Bence was to be believed, Steven Long had been the kind of man to make enemies rather than friends. Who could tell, at this stage, what other, equally powerful motives might turn up?

It was time to go. Thanet adjusted the time-clock on the central heating so that the house would warm up before the children got home from school, then left.

The streets of Sturrenden, the small country town in Kent where Thanet lived and worked, were unusually deserted for this hour of the morning, and the few pedestrians were hurrying along with heads down, eyes watering in the persistent wind. Along the banks of the river the last remaining leaves had been stripped from the flowering cherry trees, and between banks slick with mud the water ran swift and treacherously, the color of molten pewter.

In the office a stack of reports awaited him, but he reached for the telephone, pushing them to one side.

Harry Carpenter, he learned, was not yet fit for questioning. He was conscious but still in shock, unresponsive and silent. Thanet arranged for a rota of men to await the moment when he could be interviewed, then rang Chief Inspector Hines.

"Hines here."

Hines's brusque bark was painful to the ear and Thanet winced, held the receiver further away.

"Good morning, sir. Thanet."

"Ah, morning, Luke. Had a spot of trouble over there, I gather."

"You've heard about it, then. That's why I'm ringing."

"Don't tell me you're stuck already." Hines's hearty guffaw sent shock vibrations through Thanet's eardrum.

Don't let him rile you. "Not exactly, sir. It's just that I need DS Lineham back."

"Ah. Well now, we have a slight problem there, I'm afraid."

"Oh?"

"Lineham's already been briefed this morning, and won't be back until lunch time."

Thanet silently ground his teeth. If Hines had heard about Long's murder, he must have known that Thanet would be requesting the sergeant's return. He was being deliberately obstructive. "That's a pity." *Pity!* "I really am very short-handed here. I don't suppose there's any chance of recalling him?" *Damn. Shouldn't have put it like that. Asking for the answer "No."*

"No," said Hines, trying but failing to keep the satisfaction out of his voice. "He's been given a job to do, he'll have to finish it."

"So he'll be reporting in around midday?" Knowing Hines of old, Thanet was determined not to let the conversation end without some definite arrangement being made.

"Somewhere around then, I should think." Hines wasn't enjoying being forced into a corner.

"So I can expect him back here by, say, two o'clock, at the latest?"

"Unless anything unexpected crops up."

Thanet was satisfied. Both men knew that Hines was now committed to returning Lineham and was just going through the motions of demonstrating that he still had the whip hand. "Thank you, sir."

Mission accomplished, Thanet could afford to be generous. Besides, he was genuinely interested. "How's the case going?"

"Well enough, Luke, well enough. We have an identification now, so it's just a matter of time, I expect. You know how it is."

"Quite. Good."

A few more pleasantries and Thanet rang off, relieved that the call had gone off relatively smoothly. It would be a nuisance having to manage without Lineham again this morning, but the inconvenience was a small price to pay for avoiding a head-on confrontation with Hines, whose overbearing, perverse nature had made him universally unpopular.

Thanet arranged for Carpenter's clothes to be brought in for examination, then settled down to read the reports. Carson had managed to trace both Long's mother (too drunk to take the news in properly) and his wife (very distressed, almost hysterical). He had arranged for someone to pick Sharon up this morning and bring her in to identify the body. There was a separate note from Carson informing Thanet that the post-mortem was scheduled to take place today.

A number of people who lived in Hamilton Road reported seeing Carpenter's car parked there last night. The earliest time mentioned was around six thirty, shortly before Mrs. Bence had seen Long go out.

Thanet tried to work it out.

If Carpenter had gone to Hamilton Road determined to revenge himself, he obviously hadn't killed Long when he first arrived because at a quarter to seven Long had been alive, kicking and apparently unscathed.

But Carpenter hadn't struck Thanet as being a naturally violent type. Perhaps he hadn't gone up to the flat immediately, but had sat in the car, drinking, to bolster up his courage. The police had found a large empty whisky bottle in his car. If so, then surely he would have seen Long go out.

But no, not necessarily. For one thing it was dark, and for another, Long might have left by car and Carpenter might not have been able to see who was driving.

Thanet made a note to find out about Long's car, and where he usually parked it.

In that case, Carpenter might eventually have gone up to the flat and found it empty, returned to the car and proceeded to drink himself senseless. On the other hand, Long might have been back by then, and this could have been when Carpenter finally attacked and killed him . . .

Thanet shook his head in self-admonition. It was pointless to waste time speculating like this. He really ought to know better. He didn't have nearly enough facts at his disposal, as yet.

Thanet read on.

Long's neighbors reported having heard more than one person knocking on his door last night, but wouldn't commit themselves to exact times, and with one exception hadn't actually seen any of the visitors. Nor did they know whether any of them had been admitted.

But someone had seen a man turning away from Long's door "getting on towards half past eight," as he himself was coming up the stairs. And there was a good description: early twenties, heavy build, around five feet ten, with longish, dark curly hair and a mustache. Wearing jeans, dark blue windbreaker, heavy brown leather trainer-style shoes.

Excellent. Full marks for observation, thought Thanet, noting that the description could not by any stretch of the imagination apply to Carpenter. One of Long's brothers, perhaps?

The obvious way to find out about Long's family would be to talk to his mother. Even if she had a job it would be most unlikely that she would be going in to work today. Thanet found Carson's report and scribbled down the address: Mrs. Lena May, 21 Orchard Road, Sturrenden. A different surname, Thanet noted. She must have married again.

Suddenly he was eager to be off, out of the confines of his office, away from the administration and paperwork which was for him the least interesting part of his job.

In a matter of minutes he was on his way.

four

Over the years Sturrenden had gradually expanded. Typical of many small Kentish towns, its architecture mirrored the centuries of change through which it had passed. In the center, black and white half-timbered buildings rubbed shoulders with elegant sash-windowed Georgian houses of mellow red brick which gradually gave way to larger, Victorian tradesmen's houses and rows of terraced cottages.

Around this older core the twentieth century had tacked on a hotch-potch of housing estates, both private and council-owned. The Orchard Estate was one of the latter and like most council estates demonstrated the varying attitudes of council tenants towards the accommodation provided for them, from pride to indifference. By the look of it, Mrs. May was well down in the spectrum: the windows of number 21 were grimy, its garden overgrown.

The woman who answered the door matched the exterior. Her pink satin dressing gown was grubby and stained, her slippers down at heel. She was, he guessed, in her fifties, with improbably bright blonde hair, deeply scored frown lines and a sour, discontented expression. Thanet could detect no signs of grief. She was heavily made up with startlingly blue eyeshadow and pillar-box red lipstick which emphasized the sallowness of her skin. As soon as she saw Thanet she gave him a coy smile, folded the pink satin more closely about her, emphasizing her bra-less breasts, and gave what she obviously imagined was a seductive little wriggle. "Yes?"

Thankful that he had had the foresight to bring Carson, who until now had been out of her line of vision, Thanet introduced himself, shuffling sideways so that his companion was visible.

When she saw the detective constable her smile didn't so much fade as switch off, like a light going out. "Oh, it's you again. So I didn't imagine it, last night."

"May we come in?" said Thanet.

She shrugged. "If you must."

Thanet and Carson exchanged glances behind her back as they followed the pink dressing gown along a narrow passage beside the stairs. She opened the door ahead of them and stopped so suddenly that Thanet cannoned into her.

"Sorry." Over her shoulder he glimpsed a squalor which made him shudder: a floor so dirty that it was impossible to tell what kind of floor-covering had been used, unwashed dishes piled on every available surface, and a rank, sour smell that was a combination of blocked drains, unwashed dishcloths and rancid fat.

"Haven't had time to clear up this morning yet," she muttered. "We'd better go in the other room." She shut the kitchen door and opened the one at right angles to it.

Chill air gushed out to meet them, laced with stale alcohol. The curtains were still drawn and she hurried across the room to open them. Some time in the distant past an attempt had been made to brighten the place up, but the swirling orange and black abstract design in the

33

wallpaper had faded, the pink and green cabbage roses in the carpet were stained and worn, the orange stretch slipcovers on the settee and armchairs were greasy along the arms and marked with dark, circular patches on the backs where countless unwashed heads had rested.

Mrs. May stooped to light the gas fire. "Bloody freezing this morning, in't it?" She stood rubbing her arms and watching the fire, as if willing it to warm the room up quickly. "I hope this won't take too long, I was just getting ready to go to work."

The morning after her son had been murdered?

Perhaps she had picked up Thanet's unspoken disapproval because she shot him a defensive glance and sat down. "Got to earn a living, haven't I? No one else is going to pay the rent, that's for sure."

Thanet perched on the edge of the settee and Carson sat down alongside him. "Your husband . . . ?"

She laughed, a harsh, ugly sound. "What husband?"

Thanet said nothing and she fished a packet of cigarettes out of her pocket and lit one, inhaling deeply and blowing the smoke out in a long stream. "Scarpered, didn't he? Like the last one."

"You've been married twice?"

She nodded. "Bastards, both of them. Just my luck. First time I was just sixteen. Fred was eighteen. We never had a chance. Only been married five minutes and along come twins. Twins, I ask you! And me hardly knowing which end of a baby was which. 'E wasn't very pleased, I can tell you. Really gave me gyp. As if it was my fault!"

"How did you cope?"

"I didn't. My sister took one of them. She'd been married several years and they'd given up hope. Hope! Some word, that. If you ask me, it's all one big con."

"What is?"

"The idea of babies being sweet and cuddly and all that. If they're not screaming they're puking or shitting, and as for having a good time, any hope of that is gone,

34

bang, out of the window . . . And of course, it was just my luck that I picked Steve . . ."

"Just a moment. Let me get this straight. You're saying that Steven Long, the man who was . . . died yesterday, was one of the twins?"

She nodded.

"Identical twins?"

"Yes. And he was trouble from the word go, believe me. Never stopped screaming, day or night. If it hadn't been for him Fred might never have left me. He just couldn't stand it no longer."

"What is the name of the other twin?"

"Geoff. Geoffrey."

Thanet remembered the bawdy birthday card on Long's mantelpiece. "And he's still living with your sister?"

"No. She died a couple of months ago." For the first time a shadow passed briefly across Mrs. May's face.

"I'm sorry."

"Who for? Her or me?" Mrs. May gave that harsh, cynical laugh again. "You certainly needn't be sorry for her. She may have had it short, but she did have it good."

"She married well, you mean?"

"Better'n I did, that's for sure, even first time round. Then, the second time, she hit the jackpot. Married her boss."

It took a little while to get Mrs. May's tangled family relationships sorted out.

Shortly after the departure of her first husband, Fred Long, Mrs. May had found herself another man, Stanley May, whom she eventually married. They had had two more boys, Christopher and Frank, both now married and living in Sturrenden. Carson took down their addresses.

"How did Steven get on with his half-brothers?" asked Thanet.

"He didn't. Full stop."

"They argued?"

"All the time. You got any children?"

"I'm not sure what that has got to do with it."

"You would if you had more than one boy. Squabble squabble all day long. Drives you round the bend." Mrs. May was getting restless, crossing her legs first one way, then the other, twiddling hair around her fingers, picking at a loose thread on the arm of her chair.

"Didn't they get on better as they grew up?"

"Not so's you'd notice. It was Steve's fault, really."

"What do you mean?"

"Well, Frank and Chris didn't go looking for trouble, if you see what I mean. Steve did, always . . . Fancy a little nip, Inspector?"

"It's a bit early for me, I'm afraid. But you go ahead, if you want to."

She jumped up with alacrity and crossed to the sideboard. "It's so bloody cold in here . . ."

By now the room was stifling. Thanet and Carson exchanged glances as she poured herself one glass of neat gin, tossed it off and poured another.

She returned to her chair with the second drink. "That's better . . . What were you saying?"

"You were saying that Steve always went looking for trouble."

She drank, nodded. "S'right. Always did, even as a little'un. Used to needle you. Go on and on until you . . ." She stopped.

"Exploded?"

"Sometimes." Her eyes were evasive.

"So you think that's what might have happened, last night? He provoked someone beyond endurance?"

She shrugged. "I haven't set eyes on him for months. How should I know?"

Or care. The unspoken words hung in the air, almost audible.

"What about his twin? Geoffrey? How did Steve get on with him?"

"A bit better than with the others, I suppose. Not much."

"I thought there was supposed to be a closeness between identical twins."

"You could have fooled me. Perhaps it was because they never saw each other till they were . . . oh, let me see . . . must've been when they were nine or ten."

"Why was that?"

When Mavis, Mrs. May's sister, had adopted Geoffrey, the other twin, she had been married to an insurance salesman called Hunt. Soon afterwards his work had taken him to another part of the country, where they had remained until his death, ten years later. Mrs. Hunt and the boy had then returned to Sturrenden, where she had found a secretarial job in a small but prosperous firm which manufactured engineering components. Her boss, the owner, was a widower and a year later they married.

"In clover, she was. He bought her a big house in Brompton Lane, then conveniently popped off, a couple of years later. Heart attack."

Thanet knew Brompton Lane well. He'd had a case there, once. The houses were Victorian, solidly built and spacious.

"He was jealous as hell, of course," she added.

It took Thanet a moment to realize who she was referring to. "Steve, you mean? Jealous of Geoffrey?"

"Can you blame him?" She waved her hand at their sleazy surroundings. "He wasn't the only one."

"How did Geoffrey react to that?"

"How should I know? They were hardly ever together and when they were I had better things to do than sit around staring at them."

"Were they much alike? In character, I mean?"

She frowned, as if she had never considered the question before. "No. Well . . . I dunno. A bit, in some ways, I suppose."

"What ways?"

"They both liked messing around with cars . . . Look, Inspector, I don't want to be rude, but is there any point in all this? I mean, I can see you've got to ask questions, but like I said, I got to get to work. I'm on at eleven thirty and it's ten past now."

She worked as a barmaid, apparently, in a pub on the housing estate.

"Just one more question, then, Mrs. May. Do you know anyone fitting this description?" And Thanet described the young man seen coming away from Long's flat the previous evening.

As soon as he began Mrs. May's face went blank. She waited until he had finished then said, "Dozens of 'em. Could fit half the customers I see every day."

"No one you know personally?"

"I know most of them personally. Why d'you want to know, anyway?"

"Just wondered," said Thanet, vaguely.

"Hard as nails, that one," said Carson as they walked back to the car.

"I know." Thanet turned up the collar of his coat. The sky was an unbroken, leaden gray and it was beginning to rain again.

"And she recognized that description all right, didn't she? She just wasn't letting on."

"I'm sure of it. I'm not too worried, though. We'll find out which of them he is, soon enough."

Once again Thanet was missing Lineham and the ritual discussion after interviewing a witness. He felt like a boxer trying to fight with one arm tied behind his back. *Hines had better keep his word, or there'll be fireworks.*

"Where now, sir?"

"When you talked to Mrs. Long last night, did she tell you when she last saw her husband?"

Carson grimaced. "I didn't have a chance to ask her

anything at all, sir. As soon as I broke the news to her she just fell apart. Of all the jobs we have to do, that's the one I hate the most."

"Me too. Well, I suppose we'd better try and have a word with her. Though I don't suppose she'll be in much of a state to talk, after doing the identification. What time was she being picked up?"

"Nine thirty."

So she should be back by now. It wouldn't be the ideal time to interview her but Thanet did at least want to introduce himself and establish some kind of initial contact with her.

The block of flats in which Sharon Long's boyfriend lived had been put up in record time a few years ago by a speculative builder, and had been the subject of a never-ending stream of complaints ever since. Chunks of ceiling fell down, the plumbing didn't work, and fixtures and fittings worked their way out of crumbling plaster. By now a number of the flats were empty and only the desperate moved in. Anything was better than being crammed in with in-laws, Thanet supposed, but looking around he sent up a silent prayer of thankfulness for his own comfortable, well-ordered home.

There was no answer to their knock and they were about to turn away when the door across the landing opened and a young woman came out, struggling with two toddlers and a stroller.

"You looking for Sharon?"

"Yes." Thanet held up his warrant card. "Detective Inspector Thanet, Sturrenden CID."

"That'll be about 'er 'usband, I suppose. Terrible wasn't it. Stop it, Darren."

Darren was jiggling the handle of the stroller.

"Sharon was that upset . . . Though I dunno, you'd think that, you know, her living with Ivor and all that . . . Will you stop that, Darren!" The baby's face was beginning to crease ominously. "She's out. Gone to 'er mum's for the day."

"Where does her mother live, do you know?"

"Nightingale Road. Don't know which number. Darren, if you don't stop that I'll give you to the policeman and he'll take you away."

Thanet winced inwardly. He hated being used as a bogeyman by ineffective parents. All the same, he sympathized with the girl. Three children under the age of five were enough for anyone to cope with and it couldn't be much fun struggling to do it here, with your home disintegrating around you and three flights of stairs to struggle up and down every time you went out because the lift was permanently out of order.

"Do you happen to know her mother's surname?"

"Sorry, no."

"Not to worry. I'm sure we'll find her. Do you know Mrs. Long well?"

"Not really. She's out at work all day. And they've only been here a coupla weeks. Darren, I told you . . ."

The baby had had enough. It began to cry and the girl gave her recalcitrant son a half-hearted slap on the bottom. His wails combined with the baby's to echo deafeningly off the bare walls of the landing and stairwell.

"Shall we give you a hand down with the stroller?" Thanet had to shout, to make himself heard.

"Oh, ta."

At the bottom of the stairs she smiled gratefully at them before setting off into the wind and rain, head down, one toddler clutching at the stroller handle on either side.

If there had ever been any of the fabled birds in Nightingale Road they had long since disappeared. Carson went off to knock on doors and track down Sharon's mother and Thanet stood looking about him. It was a short street of neat little early Victorian cottages, obviously owned by a conscientious landlord: the roofs were in uniformly good repair, identical replacement windows punctuated the well-pointed façades, and all the front doors were the same serviceable shade of milk chocolate.

Strange, thought Thanet, his imagination kindled by the poetry of the name, to think that this very spot where I am standing was once deep in the heart of the great forest.

This, he knew, had stretched a hundred and twenty miles from east to west, thirty miles wide, from behind Folkstone right across Kent into the neighboring county of Sussex, a wild, virtually uninhabited region of giant oaks, deer and wild boar.

"... sir."

He became aware that Carson was speaking to him. "Sorry, Tom. What did you say?"

"Her name's Mrs. Pinfold, sir. Lives at number 14."

The woman who opened the door reminded Thanet of a boxer dog: square jowls, pugnacious expression, solid build.

He introduced himself, but she was clearly reluctant to let them in.

She folded her arms belligerently. "My daughter's not well. She's very upset. She's only just got back from the mortuary."

"We are aware of that, Mrs. Pinfold," said Thanet gently. "And we do understand your concern for her." With a noncriminal aggressive witness he invariably retreated into mildness. He found it by far the most disconcerting way to react.

As now.

Mrs. Pinfold shifted uneasily and said, "Yes, well . . ."

"I assure you that I have no intention of interrogating her. But as I am in charge of the investigation into her husband's death, I thought it only proper to introduce

41

myself . . . I just wanted a word with her about the identification this morning . . . And to ask her, at this stage, just one question."

"What question?"

"Whether or not she saw him, yesterday. We are trying to build up a picture of his movements, you see, so far without much success. It really would be very helpful if we could . . ."

"All right, then," said Mrs. Pinfold ungraciously. "But only for a few minutes, mind."

She led them into a room of formidable cleanliness and neatness. Furniture gleamed, the window sparkled, even the aspidistra leaves looked polished, and everything was geometrically arranged: chairs at right angles to the fireplace, television exactly parallel to the wall.

"I'll fetch her," she said grudgingly.

The girl who came into the room a few moments later was a complete contrast to her mother; small and slim, she looked as though a strong wind would blow her right away. Her face was chalk-white, with dark hollows of grief and sleeplessness around the eyes. Her hair, though, was beautiful, an airy cloud of filigree-gold curls.

Mrs. Pinfold was close behind, steering her protectively with one hand.

They all sat down and Thanet chatted quietly for a few moments, to put Sharon at her ease. He would have liked to talk to her at length, but that would have to wait for another day. She was, he noticed, very fond of jewelry. She was wearing gold hoop earrings, three gold necklaces of varying lengths and thicknesses, and rings on most of her fingers.

"I expect your mother told you why I wanted to see you?"

She nodded. She had rolled her handkerchief up into a ball and was turning it over and over, tugging incessantly at one corner.

"I'm sorry to have to ask you to go back once more

42

over what must have been a very distressing experience for you, but I'm afraid circumstances make it necessary ... The identification this morning ... You're absolutely certain it was your husband?"

She nodded again, a single, jerky movement. She was having to exert all her self-control to contain her emotion.

"I have to ask you, you see, because we understand that he has a twin brother."

She immediately understood the implication. Her head snapped up. "You mean ... ?" Hope flared briefly in her eyes, followed by a gleam of calculation, then resignation. She shook her head, sadly. "No. It was Steve, I'm certain of it."

"I'm sorry ... You do understand why I had to ask?" Thanet waited for her nod before going on. "I won't trouble you much longer, but there is just one more point I'd like to raise with you. We're trying to get some idea of your husband's movements yesterday, and we haven't had much luck so far. We were wondering if you could help us. Did you by any chance see him, at any time yesterday?"

"Yes." She glanced apologetically at her mother. "Just for a few minutes."

Mrs. Pinfold's lips tightened.

"When was this?" asked Thanet.

"He came straight from work."

"And he finished work at what time?"

She shrugged. "I'm not sure, with this new job. But it must have been half past five, I think. He was there about twenty to six."

"And he stayed how long?"

"Five minutes, ten at the most. I ... He ..."

"Always pestering her, he was," burst out Mrs. Pinfold. "Just wouldn't leave her alone. You'd think he wouldn't have the nerve, after the way he treated her ..."

"Mum," said Sharon wearily. "Leave it out, will you?"

"What did he want?" said Thanet.

"What he usually wanted, of course," said Mrs. Pinfold, undeterred by Sharon's request. "He was always on at her to go back to him."

"It don't do no good, going on like that, Mum. Don't you understand? He'll never be coming round again." Sharon jumped to her feet, tears starting to her eyes, fists clenched as if to fight the onrush of pain. "He's dead. *Dead*, do you hear me?" Her voice had risen but now she broke off, sinking down on to her chair like a puppet whose strings have just been released. She buried her face in her hands and began rocking to and fro, shaking her head.

Mrs. Pinfold stood up and shot Thanet a furious glance. "Now look what you've done. Just when she was starting to pull herself together, too."

He opened his mouth to protest, then decided it wasn't worth it.

"I think we'd better go."

He and Carson rose. As they walked to the door Thanet laid a sympathetic hand on Sharon's shoulder.

At least one person, then, truly mourned Steven Long's passing.

five

It was twenty past two by the time Lineham walked into the office.

"Mike! I was just about to ring Mr. Hines, to find out where you'd got to."

Lineham grinned. "I'm afraid you're not too popular in that quarter, sir." He sat down and put his hands proprietorially on his desk. "It's good to be back."

"Any news yet?"

They both knew what he was referring to. After much heart-searching Lineham had finally decided to take the plunge and try for promotion to Inspector. He had taken the written examinations, had waited the usual interminable three or four months for the results to come through, and had passed. Unfortunately, promotion was not thereafter automatic, especially in Kent, where there is always a great press of applicants. Of the one hundred and fifty men who had passed the examinations, only a third would be called to the Selection Board, and Lineham was waiting to hear if he would be one of them. A further sifting would then take place and approximately twenty-five candidates would attempt the final hurdle, the Promotion Board. Only five or six of these would finally make the grade.

Thanet had very ambivalent feelings about the whole business. He didn't want to stand in Lineham's way, had even positively encouraged him to go ahead, once the sergeant had made up his mind to do so. But he suspected that it was Louise who had pushed Lineham into seeking promotion and that left to his own devices the sergeant would have been content to leave things as they were. Thanet himself very much doubted that Lineham would make it, and sincerely hoped that the sergeant's self-esteem, always somewhat precarious, would not be too badly damaged by the failure, if it came.

Lineham shook his head mournfully. "Not yet. It's really beginning to get me down."

And the sleepless nights inevitable with a newborn baby couldn't be helping either, thought Thanet. Lineham was very pale, with dark smudges beneath his eyes.

"Come on, cheer up. It'll be any day, now."

"Louise says if the suspense goes on much longer she'll run round the town screaming."

Thanet laughed. "That would make the headlines all right. Perhaps it would make the powers-that-be hurry things up a bit. Tell her I think she ought to try it."

Lineham grinned back. "I'll do that."

"How are things going over in Coddington?"

"Quite well. You heard we'd identified the body?"

"Yes. Mr. Hines told me. Who was she?"

"A woman by the name of Marjorie Jackson. Known as Marge. She lived in Barton. Around forty-five, divorced, with a local reputation as a prostitute."

"And Mr. Hines thinks one of her clients might have killed her?"

"Seems possible. We had a stroke of luck. She was seen leaving the Fox and Hounds in Coddington with some bloke. Unfortunately the pub was crowded—there was a local darts match on—and we didn't get much of

46

a description—average height, slight build, youngish. The one useful item of information was a description of the man's jacket. It was very unusual, apparently—gray leather, with the head of a dragon embossed on the back, in red."

"Sounds pretty distinctive. There shouldn't be too many problems in tracing it."

"No. Especially since TVS ran a photograph of it on *Coast to Coast* last night. We've been swamped this morning with calls from people who were in the Fox and Hounds on Sunday night and we've all been working flat out, interviewing them."

"Pity you couldn't have seen it through."

Lineham grinned. "Don't worry, I'd much rather be here, working with you. What's the story?"

Thanet told him, in detail.

"So what d'you think, sir?" said the sergeant when Thanet had finished. "Do you reckon it might have been Carpenter? Sounds more than likely, to me."

"I know, and I agree, it does sound probable. But as I said, the trouble is that Carpenter is incommunicado at the moment. I've got someone with him, and I'll be informed the minute he's fit for questioning, but meanwhile I don't feel we can just sit around doing nothing, in case he's innocent."

"Yes, I can see that. So presumably the next thing is to trace the bloke seen coming away from Long's flat . . . You think he might be one of the brothers?"

"Could be. Or it might be Mrs. Long's boyfriend, Ivor Howells. If Long kept on pestering his wife to go back to him, Howells might well have decided he'd had enough, gone around to tell him so, and lost his temper."

"Yes. Though from what you say about the position of the body, it sounds as though whoever did it struck in cold blood, deliberately, from behind."

"True. All the same, it did occur to me that for an estranged wife, Mrs. Long's behavior seems a little extreme. You can understand her being pretty upset, of course, but she's behaving as though she were still passionately in love with her husband. If that was so, and he kept on pestering her to go back to him, it's difficult to see why she didn't."

"Oh I don't know, sir. She might have been in love with him, but had finally decided that it simply wouldn't work and there was no point in trying again."

"Yes, possibly. But I was wondering if there's a little more to it than that. Now if she were feeling at all guilty, that could account for her somewhat hysterical attitude."

"Are you suggesting she might have killed him?"

"I shouldn't think so, for a moment. But if her boyfriend had got fed up with Long pestering her, she might either know or be afraid that it was Howells who killed him, and feel herself responsible. I certainly think we ought to take a good look at Howells, question the neighbors. If there'd been any quarrels they might well have heard something, the walls of those flats are paper-thin."

"I'll get someone on to it right away."

"Meanwhile, what I want to do is try and interview all of them today—the three brothers, including the twin, then Howells and, if he's up to it, Carpenter . . . You know what strikes me as odd, Mike?"

"What, sir?"

"Well, according to Mrs. Bence the Longs never had any visitors, but all of a sudden, on the very night Long was murdered, the place was crawling with them."

"True. I wonder what was going on."

Thanet had every intention of finding out.

six

Thanet and Lineham were just about to leave when Mallard arrived.

"Ah, *good* afternoon, Luke, *good* afternoon, Mike. Back from the wilds of Coddington, I see." He was beaming at them over his half-moons and rubbing his hands together as if in anticipation of some long-awaited treat.

He registered their raincoats. "Going out?"

"If it's about the PM, nothing that can't wait," said Thanet, hastily shedding his coat and wondering what on earth could be coming, to have put the little doctor in such a good mood. Usually any hint of cheerfulness on Mallard's part heralded the announcement of some especially significant medical evidence.

"Just a preliminary report," said Mallard. He crossed to the window and stood bouncing gently on the balls of his feet and gazing out benignly, as if he were contemplating the Elysian Fields rather than the deserted streets of Sturrenden swept by sheets of driving rain on a bleak November afternoon.

Behind his back Thanet and Lineham raised eyebrows at each other.

"Won't you sit down, Doc?" said Thanet.

"Don't want to delay you." But Mallard took a seat, all the same. "Nothing very interesting to say, anyway."

"Oh?" Thanet was puzzled. In that case, why all the bonhomie?

"Cause of death was that blow on the head, as we thought. Apart from that, nothing. He was in good health and in the normal way of things should have lasted another fifty years or so, poor devil. You'll get the written report, in due course, but I'm afraid you won't find it much help."

"I see. Ah well, pity, that."

There seemed little more to say, but Mallard was inclined to linger.

"How's it going?" he said.

Thanet shrugged. "So-so. There are one or two leads to follow up, but nothing very concrete as yet."

"What about the man who was picked up outside the house last night, Carpenter?"

"Still in a state of shock, apparently. Conscious but doesn't respond when talked to."

"You realize what's the matter with him?"

"Yes. Heard it on the local news this morning."

"So did I. Sad case, that. It's possible that you might not have to look much further for your murderer. The strain has obviously been too much for him. It might well be a day or two before he's fit to talk, though. The body has its own mechanisms for ensuring a proper period of recuperation, in circumstances like that."

"Yes."

Lineham shifted restlessly and Thanet knew that, like him, the sergeant was anxious to be off, now that Mallard had passed on the information about the PM. But Mallard, leaning back comfortably in his chair, fingers hooked into the armholes of his waistcoat, showed no sign of moving. What to do? Thanet didn't want to be

50

discourteous and bring the conversation to an abrupt end, especially with Mallard in this unusually amiable mood.

The silence stretched out and began to be uncomfortable. Thanet cast desperately around for a suitable topic of conversation.

"Long was an identical twin, we discovered."

"Really?" Mallard's face was alert with interest. "No chance you've got the wrong body, I suppose?"

"The possibility had occurred to me. But his wife seemed positive enough that the dead man was her husband, and she ought to know, if anyone does. We know very little about the twins yet, except that they were separated at birth."

"But the other man lives locally?"

"Yes. In Brompton Lane."

"Brompton Lane, eh? Well, well. A step up in the social ladder from Hamilton Road."

"Quite." Briefly, Thanet explained the circumstances which had led to the twins' separation, and their subsequent difference in life-style.

"Interesting, that. There's a fascinating book, you know, by a man called Shields, James Shields. It's a study of monozygotic twins, brought up together and brought up apart."

"It does sound interesting. Er . . . What did you call them?"

"Monozygotic. Identical."

"I've never quite understood the difference, myself," said Lineham. "Medically, that is. I mean, why is it that some twins are identical and some aren't?"

"Twins are conceived either as a single egg that splits into two within a few days of conception, which results in monozygotic or identical twins, or as two eggs that have been fertilized on the same occasion by two separate male sperms, which results in dizygotic or fraternal twins." Mallard was enjoying his lecture. "Fraternal twins are therefore no more alike than any other siblings—brothers and sisters—with the same parents."

"So what were the book's findings?" asked Thanet. "In terms of the identical twins who had been brought up apart?"

"You can read it for yourself, if you're really interested. I've got it at home, somewhere. I'll look it out for you."

"Thanks, I would be, very. But briefly . . . ?"

"It was astounding how little difference there was between them in terms of mental and behavioral similarities, mannerisms and gestures, interests, drinking and smoking habits, even in type of occupation."

"Really!"

"On the other hand, there were some intriguing findings. For example, it was found that the twin who stayed with the mother and was often brought up with brothers and sisters was frequently more neurotic than the one who was adopted and had been brought up as an only child, by older parents and probably in somewhat better social circumstances. And it was interesting that when they met, later on in life, they sometimes didn't get on at all."

"As in this case, to a certain degree, apparently. According to the mother, anyway."

"Fascinating." Mallard took out his pocket watch, flicked it open. "Good grief, is that the time? I must go." He jumped up out of his chair, said goodbye and was gone, in a matter of seconds.

Thanet and Lineham looked at each other, bemused.

"What on earth's got into him?" said Lineham.

"Search me. He was like this last night, too—well, perhaps it wasn't quite so obvious. But noticeable, all the same. D'you know, Mike, if it were any other man, I'd say . . ." Thanet paused. He had been going to say "he's in love," but somehow, with reference to Mallard, the words sounded slightly indecent, insulting, almost. Mallard had loved his wife with a loyalty and devotion that caused him to treat all other women with polite indifference. Was it possible that he had at last found someone to replace her? Thanet sincerely hoped so. But he wasn't going to voice his suspicions to Lineham, not yet, anyway.

"What?" But Lineham wasn't really interested. He was already buttoning up his coat, eager to be gone.

"Nothing." Thanet, too, hurried into his coat. There was a great deal to get through, today.

Just as they reached the door the telephone rang. A further delay? But it could be important and they couldn't afford to ignore it. Reluctantly, Lineham turned back.

"DS Lineham."

He listened intently for a few moments.

"Yes. Yes, I'm afraid it's true, sir, and I'm sorry you had to hear the news like that. Yes, very distressing for you . . . Just one moment, sir." He covered the receiver and said quickly, "It's the twin brother, sir, Geoffrey Hunt. Very upset. Just heard the news on Radio Kent. Do you want to speak to him?"

Thanet shook his head. "Tell him we were hoping to have a word with him some time today. Fix up an appointment, if you can."

Lineham spoke again, listened, covered the mouthpiece once more. "Says he's free now, if we'd like to go along."

"Tell him we're on our way."

seven

The last time Thanet had seen this face the eyes had been sightless, the features slack in death. Intellectually, of course, he had been prepared for the resemblance, but emotionally the impact was both unexpected and disconcerting; it was eerie, positively uncanny, to see the dead man standing before them in apparent good health.

"Inspector Thanet?"

"That's right." Thanet introduced Lineham, studying Hunt for ways to distinguish him from his brother. Here was the same thin face, beaky nose and very dark, almost navy-blue eyes. Geoffrey was a little thinner than Steven had been—or perhaps it was simply that he had been ill, and lost a little weight recently, for his jeans hung loosely on him. Thanet remembered the FOR SALE board by the gate and recalled that Geoffrey's adoptive mother had died only a couple of months ago. Perhaps grief— or perhaps simply a bachelor existence—had thinned him down.

"Ah yes. It was you I spoke to on the phone," Hunt said to Lineham. "Come in, won't you?"

Most of the houses in Brompton Road were Victorian,

but this one was of nineteen thirties vintage. Its rooms were spacious, its proportions generous, its one fault the stupefying dullness which seems to have hung like a pall over the domestic architecture of the period. Everywhere was evidence of material prosperity—thick fitted carpets, original paintings, antique furniture. Outside, in the double garage, was a new Scimitar SS1.

Lineham, always a car enthusiast, had come to an abrupt halt.

"Look at that, sir!"

"Very nice."

"Nice! 0–60 in 9.6 seconds, maximum speed 110 mph . . ."

"I can never see the point in being able to go that fast if it's illegal."

"It's just the knowledge that you've got the power, sir."

"Mike, come *on*. We've got a job to do."

"Costs around £7000, you know. And look, there's a hydraulic lift and a proper inspection pit . . ."

"A very fortunate young man," said Thanet drily. *Obviously overindulged by an adoring mum*. He put his forefinger firmly on the front door bell and concealed a grin at Lineham's undignified scamper to catch up with him. "But we knew that, already."

Hunt led them into a pleasant drawing room which ran the depth of the house, with windows on three sides. At the back, tall glass patio doors—obviously a recent innovation—opened on to a paved terrace and an extensive lawn which petered out in a little coppice of silver birch, their few remaining butter-yellow leaves valiantly clinging to the delicate, wiry branches.

The room was in a considerable state of disorder. A pile of bed-linen topped by two multi-colored Welsh blankets still in their polythene bags stood beside two packing cases, one full of books, the other half-filled with objects wrapped in newspaper. The bookshelves were almost empty and bundles of discarded books tied up with string were stacked near the door. A number of the smaller pieces of furniture had labels tied on to them.

"Sorry about the mess. I'm in the process of packing up, as you can see."

"Please, don't worry about it."

"Sit down, Inspector, Sergeant."

Hunt crossed to the low coffee table that stood in front of the settee, and piled on to a round silver tray the pair of coffee cups and two brandy glasses evidently left over from last night.

So Hunt had had company the previous evening, thought Thanet. Female? Probably. Two male companions would be more likely to have occupied separate armchairs and to have skipped the coffee.

Thanet took an armchair and Lineham chose a corner of the settee.

Hunt, after a moment's hesitation, deposited the tray clumsily on a small table near the door, knocking off a small china figure in the process. He grabbed for it, but missed it. It bounced harmlessly on the carpeted floor and he picked it up, restored it to its original position, then sat down in one of the other armchairs.

He shook his head. "I still can't believe it. It said on the radio he was found in his room . . . How did it happen?"

"He died from a blow to the head. I'm sorry. You must feel it especially, as a twin."

Hunt folded his arms across his chest and hunched forward, as if to try to contain his grief and pain. "It's difficult to describe . . . It's as if part of myself had died."

"Though you weren't especially close, I gather."

Hunt's head came up sharply. "Who told you that?"

"Your mother."

Briefly, Hunt looked disbelieving. "My . . . Oh, you mean my natural mother, of course. I'm afraid I never think of her as my mother. My own mother died, nine weeks ago." He glanced around. "That's one of the reasons why I decided to move. This place is much too big for one person. Well, it was too big for two, really, but she was very fond of it and wanted to stay on, after my stepfather died."

"Quite a big job, clearing out a house of this size."

"Oh, I'm not doing it all. I'm just packing up the things I want to take with me. I've bought a flat and most of the stuff here is much too big."

"Where are you going?"

"Tamworth, in Staffordshire. I had a job offer that was too good to turn down."

"A large company?"

"It's with Scimitar, actually. I've always had a love affair with Scimitars—you may have noticed that I've got one."

"Yes, I did. Beautiful cars, aren't they? So you're moving quite soon?"

"Tuesday of next week. At least, I was going to. But now . . . I shall have to stay on, for the funeral, of course. How soon do you think that's likely to be, in the . . . in the circumstances?"

"Not for some time, I should think. You'll be able to complete your move and then come back for it."

"Good. I was going to come back anyway. All the stuff I don't want is going to auction, and there are various other things to attend to . . . Oh God, what am I doing, talking about moving and auctions, when Steve . . ." Hunt raked his hair with hooked fingers. "I just can't believe it, that's why. It doesn't seem real. Who would want to do a thing like that?"

"That's one of the questions we wanted to ask you."

"Me?" Hunt stared at them. "How should I know?"

"You were his brother."

"Yes, but . . . We lived very different lives, Inspector.

Our paths did cross occasionally, yes, but we weren't close, I really have no idea who Steve's friends were—if 'friends' is the right word, in the circumstances."

"You know his family, though? His . . . your half-brothers?"

"I certainly never think of them as my half-brothers, I assure you! But yes, I know them, of course."

"Well?"

"Not especially, no."

"But enough to tell me a little about them?"

"Depends what you want to know."

Thanet waved his hand in an all-encompassing gesture. "Anything. Anything at all. I haven't met them yet."

Hunt frowned and shifted restlessly in his chair. "Well . . . er . . . There are two of them, as you probably know, Chris and Frank. Chris is the older."

"How old?"

"Twenty-three. Frank's twenty-two."

"And Steven was . . . ?"

"Twenty-seven."

"Sorry, go on."

"Chris is, well, of the three of them, I suppose you could say Chris is the odd man out."

"In what way?"

"He's the only one who's managed to make something of his life."

Thanet's attention sharpened. Had there been a hint of bitterness there? If so, why? Hunt himself had no reason to be envious. He was obviously in a very comfortable position.

"I can see you're wondering why I sounded rather bitter, Inspector," said Hunt, with disconcerting accuracy. "It was because I couldn't help resenting the fact that Steve never had the same chance."

"Why was that?"

"Chris was the favorite. So he was allowed to stay on at school when the other two were made to go out to work the minute it was legal for them to leave. Chris therefore went to university, got a good degree and is now teaching at the Grammar School, whereas Steve ended up as a mechanic and Frank as a delivery man."

"At least they all have jobs. That's not bad going, these days."

"That's not the point!" Hunt was getting angry. The navy-blue eyes were almost black and his hands were clenched into fists. "The point, Inspector, is that Steve was capable of so much more. And he never had a hope in hell of achieving it."

"You really cared about him, didn't you?"

"Yes, I did. And if you're wondering why I get so hot under the collar about it, believe me, I could tell you some stories about the way Steve was treated that would make your hair stand on end."

"What stories?"

Hunt shook his head. "I shouldn't have said that. Steve told me in confidence. Besides, of what possible interest could they be to you?"

"You'd have to let me be the judge of that."

Hunt shook his head again, vehemently this time, and it was obvious that he wasn't going to change his mind.

"You were telling me about Chris and Frank."

"There's not much more to say about Chris. As I say, he teaches at the Grammar School, he's married, to another teacher."

"What about Frank?"

"Frank's a very different kettle of fish. Not very bright, and he was on the dole for years, after leaving school. Then, just over a year ago, he got a job at last, at Passmore's, delivering furniture, and on the strength of it he got married. His wife's expecting their first baby soon."

Passmore's was Sturrenden's only department store.

"Does either of them fit this description?" And, once again, Thanet described the man seen coming away from Steven Long's door the previous evening.

"Why?" said Hunt, warily.

So the man had been one of the two half-brothers. "Because this man was seen outside Steve's flat last night."

"That doesn't necessarily mean he killed him."

"I'm aware of that, Mr. Hunt. Nevertheless, you must see that we have to trace him."

"You'll find out sooner or later, I suppose, whether I tell you or not . . . It sounds like Frank."

"I see . . . How did Steven get on with Chris and Frank?"

"Well enough, I think. He used to see them from time to time, but I wouldn't say they were exactly close."

"What about his wife?"

"Sharon?" Hunt shrugged. "You know they were separated?"

"Yes. How did Steve feel about that?"

"About the separation?" Hunt shrugged again. "He was put out at first, but I think he'd got used to the idea."

"He wasn't trying to persuade her to come back to him?"

"Not to my knowledge."

"That's not the impression we had from Sharon herself, or from her mother."

"Her mother!" Hunt gave a cynical laugh. "Well, that doesn't surprise me. Sharon's mother thinks that Sharon is God's gift to man, and if you ask me she was more responsible for the split between them than anything else. She never could stand Steve, and was against the marriage from the start."

Lineham, who had himself suffered much from an over-possessive mother, shifted uncomfortably.

"So you don't think he was too upset about his marriage breaking down?"

"I told you, no."

"He used to go and see Sharon, though. Yesterday, for example, he went straight round after work."

"I don't think he was too happy about the bloke she's living with."

"Ivor Howells, you mean. In what way?"

"Well, Sharon's very sweet, but she's not exactly a strong personality—not surprising, when you look at her mother—and I think Steve was a bit concerned that Howells would be too much for her."

"Too dominating, you mean?"

"Yes."

"So you think that the reason why Steve used to go and see her was because he was hoping to persuade her to leave Howells, rather than that he was trying to get Sharon back for himself?"

"Possibly. I don't really know. I told you, we never actually discussed it. This is just what I picked up, reading between the lines, so to speak."

"Tell me what he was like."

"Steve?" Hunt frowned. "It's always difficult to describe someone you know well. He was a brilliant mechanic, had a real feel for machines. I mean, I've got a degree in mechanical engineering, but I've never had his flair. You could have a really tricky problem, one that's really been bugging you, and Steve would come along, have a listen and say, 'Ah yes, that'll be the . . .' whatever it was. And he'd be right, every time. That's why he never had problems in finding a job."

"He seems to have changed jobs rather often."

"He got bored, easily. The truth is, he was never stretched, never had a chance to reach his full potential."

"Not like you?"

"I was lucky." For the first time Hunt smiled. "You know what Steve used to call me? 'The one who got away.' "

"Did he resent the difference in your circumstances?"

"A bit, I suppose. Understandable, of course." Hunt glanced complacently around. "Not that he ever *said* anything . . ."

"And it caused trouble between you?"

"Depends what you mean by trouble . . ." Hunt leant back in his chair and smiled. "If you mean, did we get on so badly that I went round last night and bashed his head in, then the answer's no."

"What did you do last night, Mr. Hunt?"

"Oh, so it's alibi time, is it?" Hunt stood up and strolled across to the french windows. "What time did you say Steve was killed, Inspector?"

"I didn't."

"Ah." Hunt swung around to face them. "And I don't suppose you're going to tell me, are you?"

Thanet said nothing, remained impassive.

Hunt shrugged. "Well, I've nothing to hide, so why should I worry?" He returned to his chair, sat down and folded his arms.

With a hint of defiance? Thanet wondered. What was coming?

"As a matter of fact I went to see Steve myself, last night." His eyes were watchful, assessing the effect of his words on the two policemen.

Thanet was deliberately noncommittal. "Really? What time was that?"

"I arrived at about, oh, a quarter to twenty past six. And left at about twenty to seven."

And Mrs. Bence claimed to have seen Steve leave at a quarter to. Was it possible that it was Geoff she had seen? If so, Steve might already have been dead . . .

"Why did you go to see your brother last night, Mr. Hunt?"

"I was a bit concerned about him."

"In what way?"

"Well, I'd last seen him on Sunday evening—it was our birthday, and I called round to wish him many happy returns. I thought he seemed a bit low, rather depressed." Hunt lifted his shoulders. "So last night I thought I'd just pop round to see how he was."

"And how was he?"

"All right, I suppose. I wouldn't say he was exactly full of the joys of spring, but then he hasn't been for some time."

"Why was that, do you think?"

Again the shrug. "I never actually asked him, outright. I just used to, you know, try to jolly him along . . . I suppose it was partly because of his marriage going wrong, partly because he could never really settle to a job for long, partly because . . . oh, I don't know, I suppose it was general, really, an overall feeling of disappointment in life, a sense of, well, failure, perhaps . . ."

"But he never actually discussed these things with you?"

"Not in so many words, no." Hunt hesitated. "He wasn't the sort of man to discuss his feelings. He'd be much more likely to try and cover them up."

"So what did you talk about, last night?"

"Nothing much. Cars—we always talked about cars . . . A job he'd been doing at work, how I was getting on with the packing . . . Nothing special, really."

"And how did he seem?"

"Rather more cheerful than he was on Sunday, I thought."

"That was why you stayed for only twenty minutes or so?"

"Partly. But also because I had a date."

"Oh?"

Geoffrey Hunt's date had been with a girl called Caroline Gilbert, who worked as a secretary in Sturrenden. After leaving Steve, Geoffrey had returned home for a quick shave and had then picked Caroline up at home, at half past seven. He had taken her out to dinner and later they had returned to Geoff's home for coffee and a final drink. Just before midnight he had taken her home.

"We shall have to check with Miss Gilbert, of course."

"Of course," echoed Hunt. "Do, by all means."

Thanet rose. "Well, I think that's about it, for the moment, Mr. Hunt. If you could come into the station to make a formal statement some time today . . . ?"

"Certainly."

"Good! In that case we'll leave you to get on with your packing. But . . ."

Hunt held up a hand. "Don't tell me! 'Don't leave town without informing us.' "

Thanet smiled. "You've been reading all the right detective stories, Mr. Hunt. Don't bother to come to the door. We'll see ourselves out."

Thanet and Lineham walked back to the car, got in and sat in silence for a few minutes, thinking back over the interview. Eventually Thanet stirred.

"Well, what d'you think, Mike?"

"I certainly think he ought to go down on our list. After all, he was there, last night. And I did wonder . . . D'you think it was him, not Steve, that that witness saw leaving at a quarter to seven?"

"I wondered too. Could well have been. We'll have to see how things shape up. So far we haven't come across anyone who's seen Steve alive after that time. In which case . . ."

"He might have been dead before Geoff left . . . If only that gas fire hadn't been left on full blast, we'd have a much better idea of the time of death. Do you think it might have been left on on purpose, sir?"

"To mislead us? Quite possibly. But it's equally possible that it was pure coincidence. It was very cold last night, if you remember. It would have been perfectly normal for Steve to have turned it on full when he got in, to warm the place up."

"Though I can't for the life of me see why Geoff should

have wanted to kill Steve. After all, he's got everything going for him—plenty of money, a new job he's really looking forward to . . . I'll check with Scimitar, shall I, sir?"

"Put Bentley on to it. We've got too much to get through today. Anyway, I can't think he'd lie about a thing like that, because it's so easily checked. This move of his has obviously been under way for some time. You might get Bentley to give the estate agents a ring too, though, just to be certain."

"What about Miss Gilbert, sir?"

"We'll send Carson. Hell, I suppose it would be simpler to nip back to the office and get all this organized, before our next call."

"Who are we seeing next, sir?"

"Frank, I think. He's the only one on whom we have something definite."

But when they got back to the office Thanet changed his mind. The house-to-house inquiries in the block of flats where Ivor Howells lived had produced an interesting piece of information: on Sunday evening, two days before the murder, Howells and Steven Long had had a blazing row, and Howells had been heard threatening to "chop" Steve if he ever came near Sharon again.

eight

Ivor Howells was employed by Sturrenden Council and a phone call ascertained that he was at present working on road repairs between Sturrenden and Nettleton, a couple of miles away.

It had stopped raining a little while ago but the landscape looked half-drowned, the branches of trees still drooping with the weight of unshed water, the bare earth of newly ploughed fields glistening like Christmas pudding. Sodden leaves lay in pulpy russet ribbons all along the edges of the road, their autumn glory prematurely extinguished, and the rolling curves of the North Downs were swathed in mist.

"Who'd be a cow, in this weather?" said Thanet as they passed a mournful-looking animal poking its nose through a five-barred gate.

"Light's beginning to go already." Lineham switched on dipped headlights. "Let's hope they haven't packed up and gone home. Shouldn't think they'd have been able to do much in these conditions anyway."

"There's the sign now." Thanet nodded at the familiar

ROAD WORKS AHEAD board propped at the side of the road.

Lineham was right, the men had obviously decided to give up for the day. Some of them were loading equipment into a lorry and one was walking along the side of an open trench half-full of water, checking that the warning lights were in position and functioning.

"Just in time, by the look of it." Lineham pulled up and they both got out.

"Hullo." One of the men, a tall, lanky individual with a drooping mustache, noticed their arrival and nudged the man next to him. "What have we here, then? Trouble?"

Four wary faces watched their approach.

"Is one of you Ivor Howells?" said Thanet.

Without taking his eyes off Thanet the lanky man turned his head to call over his shoulder. "Taff? Visitors."

The man who was adjusting the warning lights looked up, gave the last light a final nudge with his foot and started back towards them.

Thanet moved to meet him.

"What you been doing then, Taff? Robbing the bank?" shouted one of the men, and they all grinned.

Howells said nothing. He was of medium height and Thanet guessed that under his bulky waterproof clothes he would be slim, but he loped along with a controlled, muscled power that reminded Thanet of a tiger in the jungle. As he drew closer Thanet could see that beneath the windbreaker hood his hair was dark, his skin sallow and that on his right cheek he bore the bluish scar that is unique to the coal miner.

"Mr. Howells?" Thanet introduced himself. "I'm in charge of the investigation into the death of Mr. Steven Long."

"So?"

"I'd like to have a talk with you. There's a transport café back there . . . We could give you a lift back to town, afterwards."

Howells shrugged and began to walk towards the lorry. The men had finished loading up now and stood watching as he approached.

"No point in you all hanging on waiting for me," said Howells, and Thanet heard the strong Welsh lilt in his voice for the first time. "You go on back to the depot and I'll cadge a lift."

"You're sure? We can wait, if you like," said the tall man, and the others nodded and shuffled a little closer together, unconsciously demonstrating their solidarity.

"No, not to worry, boys. See you tomorrow, then?"

They nodded, packed themselves into the lorry and departed.

"Have you been working in Kent long?" said Thanet conversationally, as they drove the half a mile or so back to the café.

"Since '84." Howells could not conceal the bitterness in his voice.

Ah yes, the miners' strike. That long, disastrous struggle that had split the mining union right down the middle, turned miner against miner, father against son, and destroyed the unique community spirit of many mining villages, perhaps for ever. It had also left a strong residue of bitterness against the police. Thanet looked at Howells's profile and wondered: had he been amongst the pickets who had faced the riot shields? If so, Thanet had a tough task ahead of him.

At this time of day the café was empty. It was warm and spotlessly clean, the formica-topped tables gleaming, and the three men cupped their hands gratefully around the steaming mugs of tea.

"We heard about the row you had with Mr. Long, on Sunday night," said Thanet, coming straight to the point.

"So that's it." Howells had taken off his orange safety

waistcoat and his windbreaker and was hunched over his tea. He slurped at the hot liquid before continuing. "I might have guessed some nosy-parker'd open his big mouth."

"D'you mind telling us what the row was about?"

"Of course I bloody mind! But I suppose you'll find out anyway, if you don't know already . . . It was about Sharon, of course."

Thanet waited and Howells shot him a glance in which the embers of resentment against Long still smoldered. "Wouldn't leave her alone, would he?"

"He was pestering her?"

"Kept on coming round all the time, trying to get her to go back to him. I'd had it up to here, I can tell you."

"We heard that he wasn't particularly interested in patching things up between them."

"Huh! Don't know who's been feeding you that rubbish, but they were lying in their teeth. Not particularly interested . . . ! D'you call coming round most evenings after work not particularly interested? Or bringing her presents—rings, bangles, boxes of choc'lates, bunches of bloody flowers, bottles of scent, not particularly interested?"

Howells was working himself up into a fury at the memory.

"And Sharon? How did she react to all this?"

"What do you think? She was fed up to the bloody back teeth, I can tell you."

Remembering Sharon's distress, Thanet wondered if this were true. Perhaps Howells's anger was fueled by the fear that Sharon's reaction had been precisely the opposite, and that Long's persistence was showing returns.

"So what exactly happened, on Sunday?"

Howells drank off the rest of his tea, set the mug down on the table with a crash that brought a frown from the woman behind the counter and sat back, folding his arms as if to contain his rage at the memory. "It was around five in the afternoon. Sharon and me was just having a cup of tea when there's this knock on the door. I went to answer it and there he is, large as life, shoving past me. 'Hullo Sharon,' he says. 'Thanks for the card.' He's carrying this white cardboard box, see, and he plonks it down on the table and starts to open it. 'I thought you'd like a piece of my birthday cake,' he says, bold as brass. The nerve of it! I couldn't believe my eyes, that he'd just barge in like that . . . And I thought, I'll show him where to put his bloody birthday cake . . . I tell you, I'd just about had enough. I decided I'd really put the wind up him, this time . . ." Howells shrugged. "That's about all there was to it."

Thanet could visualize it: Sharon, in all her fragility, standing by helplessly while the two men, her husband and her lover, snarled at each other like two dogs over a bone . . . It seemed a miracle to him, now that he had met Howells, that it hadn't come to blows. From the neighbors' accounts it was, not surprisingly, Long who had gone off with his tail between his legs—and yet, he had gone back for more, two days later. The question was, had Howells known of this later visit? He should have been back from work by then but no one, as yet, had reported any kind of disturbance and surely, if he had been there when Long arrived, this time it would have ended in violence.

No, on balance Thanet thought it more likely that Howells had heard about yesterday's visit later, probably from some "friendly" neighbor. It was unlikely, in the circumstances, that Sharon herself would have told him. And there was also the possibility that he hadn't heard about it at all, was still unaware of it . . .

"What time do you usually get home from work, Mr. Howells?"

"About a quarter past five. Why?"

"And yesterday?"

"No, yesterday I was . . ." Howells leaned forward, eyes glittering like anthracite. "Here, what you getting at?"

"Nothing. As yet. Merely requesting information."

"Don't feed me that guff."

"It's true. At the moment. But I would remind you that this is a murder inquiry, and that so far you are the only person known to have been on bad terms with Mr. Long."

' "The only . . . !" Briefly, Howells was speechless. "You just have to be joking!"

Thanet was sure the man's astonishment was genuine. "You obviously know something we don't."

Howells was still shaking his head in disbelief. "The only person known to have been on bad terms . . . You haven't seen Frank, then. Or Chris."

"Not yet, no."

Howells jerked his head forward, thrusting his face to within a few inches of Thanet's. "Then may I suggest, Inspector, that before you start making any accusations here, you go and interview *Mr.* Long's beloved brothers?"

Thanet didn't flinch. "I think that perhaps you are jumping to conclusions, Mr. Howells. I am not making any accusations against you or against anyone else until I have satisfied myself that they are justified. I have every intention of going to see both Frank and Chris May as soon as possible, but meanwhile I would like to point out that there is only one way for anyone—anyone, Mr. Howells—to clear himself of suspicion, and that is for him to satisfy us that he could not have done the murder. To which end I shall be asking *everyone* involved for details of his—or her—movements between five o'clock and eleven o'clock last night. And the sooner I get that information from you, the sooner we'll all be able to leave."

Howells stared at Thanet for a moment, evidently trying to decide whether or not to believe him, then leaned back in his chair and shrugged. "OK. What d'you want to know?"

Thanet glanced at Lineham. *Take over.*

Now that Howells was disposed to be cooperative it didn't take long to get the information they wanted. He had left work at a quarter to five as usual, but instead of going home had, as previously arranged, gone to help a friend shift some furniture into a new house. This had taken well over three hours and it was getting on for half past eight when he had arrived home. He and Sharon had had supper and then they had gone out for a drink with some friends, returning home around eleven fifteen. Lineham took down names, addresses, times, routes, and then glanced interrogatively at Thanet. *Anything else you want to ask?*

There was.

"Did you know that Mr. Long went to see Mrs. Long after work, yesterday?"

"Yes, she told me. Sent him away with a flea in his ear."

"After the warning you gave him on Sunday, didn't you feel inclined to go and see him, carry out your threat?"

"What threat was that?"

"To 'chop' him."

"I don't know what you're talking about. I never said any such thing."

"You were heard to, by one of your neighbors."

"They don't know what they're talking about. 'Stop' him, more likely."

"Well, didn't you? Feel inclined to go and see him again?"

"No need to, was there?"

"What do you mean?"

"The show I put on, on Sunday night—it was as much for Sharon as for him, see. She was too soft with him, always has been. She can't help herself. So I thought, if I could put over the message that I'd really had enough

72

of him coming round, she might be a bit tougher with him, next time."

"You wanted to frighten her?"

"Not exactly, no. If she'd really wanted to go back to him, it would have been a different matter, but I knew she only put up with him coming because she felt sorry for him. And I thought it had gone on long enough. When she told me she'd refused to talk to him, last night, I knew I'd won. There was no need for me to go and see him."

So Sharon hadn't been completely frank with Howells. She had told Thanet herself that Long had stayed five or ten minutes. Whether or not Howells had intended to frighten her, it sounded as though he had certainly succeeded in doing so—if he was telling the truth, that is.

He could, of course, be lying. But there was no point in pursuing this line at present. Howells had his story and it was clear he was going to stick to it.

"You say that Mr. Long was on bad terms with most people. Why was that? Did he deliberately set out to rub them up the wrong way?"

"Search me. I'm biased, of course, I admit that, but I could never make up my mind if it was deliberate, or if he just didn't know he was doing it. Or even, if he did know he was doing it and didn't want to, but couldn't help himself, if you see what I mean. Anyway, the end result was the same. I mean, look at Sharon. She's a real sweet kid, very easy-going and that . . . It would take a lot to make her get up and leave anyone, but in the end even she couldn't stand it any longer. Believe me, he was bad news."

"He seems to have got on all right with his twin brother."

"Ah yes, Geoff. Well. I've never met him, so I wouldn't know. One of them was enough, two would be a nightmare."

Thanet rose. "Well, I think that's all for the moment, Mr. Howells. We'll give you that lift."

When they had dropped Howells opposite the block of flats, Lineham said, "Difficult to tell whether he was anti us, personally, or anti the police in general, wasn't it?"

"A bit of both, I imagine."

"In any case, he's a likely candidate, don't you think, sir? I can just see him bashing someone's head in."

"But from behind? When the man is seated? I'm not so sure. If it were a stand-up fight, then, yes, I'd agree with you. He's obviously capable of violence. On the other hand there could be circumstances . . . Just suppose, for instance, that he went round to Long's place last night determined to have a show-down. And say Long remained cool, refused to be drawn. I could imagine Howells getting more and more worked up . . . Long sitting there on the settee refusing to be intimidated . . . Howells is walking about in his agitation and suddenly his temper snaps, he grabs the nearest heavy object to hand and . . ."

"Wham. End of Long."

"Possible, don't you think?"

"Having met him, I certainly do. You could just feel the anger simmering away underneath all the time, waiting to boil over."

"I know. We'd better get that alibi of his checked."

"A lot of it depends on Sharon's corroboration, sir."

"Quite. Meanwhile, let's get a move on. I want to catch Frank May at work, rather than interview him at home with that pregnant wife of his around."

"We may be too late. It's ten past five now."

"Passmore's doesn't close till five thirty. We're only a few minutes away. We'll give it a try."

Lineham parked the car near the loading bays at the back of the store. A number of Passmore vans were neatly lined up, apparently abandoned for the night, and the place seemed deserted.

"Looks as though the drivers have all gone home," said Lineham, with an "I told you so" inflection.

"Mm," said Thanet. He got out of the car and strolled across to the end loading bay, where a faint light spilled out across the tarmac from a small door inset into the larger ones.

He pushed it open. The light was coming from a small, glassed-in office in a corner of the bay. Inside, bent over some papers, Thanet could see the top of a bald head. He walked across and tapped on the glass. "Excuse me . . ."

The head jerked up, the man's face a caricature of surprise and shock, eyes stretched wide, mouth a perfect O. He was in his seventies, small and bent, with arthritic hands.

"Sorry, I didn't mean to startle you."

The man's gaze switched to Lineham, who had just stepped through the door into the bay.

Thanet held his identity card up against the glass. "We'd like a word with Frank May. I understand he works here."

The man leaned across the counter top to peer at the card. His look of apprehension faded. He slid down off his stool and came to open the door. He was tiny, not much more than five feet, twisted and bent with arthritis. A blast of hot, paraffin-laden air gushed out.

"Come in, come in. It's warmer in here. Shut the door, that's right . . . About that business with his brother, is it?"

A strange way to refer to a murder, Thanet thought. "What business with his brother?" he said, warily.

"About the telly . . ." He was easing himself backwards up on to his stool as he spoke, his eyes bright with interest.

He looked, Thanet thought, rather like a gnome perched on a toadstool.

His eyes darted from Thanet to Lineham and back again. "No? What d'you want with Frank, then?"

"Look, Mr. . . . ?"

"Baines. Harry Baines."

"Well, Mr. Baines, it looks as though we might be at cross purposes here. Perhaps you'd better tell us what you meant. Which brother?"

"I didn't know he had more than one. That Steve, I was talking about."

"What about Steve?"

"Lost him his job, didn't he."

"Frank doesn't work here any more?" asked Lineham.

"Only till the end of the week."

"He's here now, then?"

"No, the drivers knock off at five. Most of the deliveries is finished by then."

Thanet remembered what Geoff had told him about Frank's years on the dole, the wedding arranged on the strength of this job, the imminent birth of the baby, and realized what a crushing blow this must have been. And a motive for murder? "So how did Steve lose Frank his job?"

"Tried to pull a fast one once too often. I warned Frank, told him that if he wasn't careful he'd be out on his ear. I know he spoke to him about it, but it didn't make any difference, seemingly." Baines thrust his chin forward. "Sixty years I've worked at Passmore's, in this very same department. Started straight from school, at fourteen, and I've seen an awful lot of blokes come and go. Frank's all right, a good lad. Not too much up top, but enough to make a sensible driver, and he was a hard worker, too. And there's that little wife of his, just going to have their first baby . . . Fair makes me sick, it does." The old man was getting so worked up that spittle was forming at the corners of his mouth.

"I'm sorry," said Thanet, "but I still don't understand . . ."

"First of all it were small things. Nicked straight off the vans, they were, while they were being loaded up. I couldn't understand it—like, I've had the odd rotten apple before now, but a number of the drivers seemed to be involved, good lads as I've had for years. So we kept our eyes open, and it soon dawned on us—it were always after that Steve came round looking for Frank that things went missing. I had a word with Frank, and it seemed for a while that that were that . . . Until yesterday, that is."

The old man paused dramatically.

Lineham fed him his cue. "What happened yesterday?"

"It was about a quarter past three in the afternoon. I was working here in my office, quiet-like, checking over the day's orders, when there's this disturbance in the yard, outside. I hurries out and I finds Frank and this chap I've never seen before, scrapping away like their lives depended on it. Some of the men were standing around watching. I were real mad, I can tell you. Scrapping, in my yard! So I picked up this bucket of water someone'd been using to wash his van and chucked it over the pair of them." He rubbed his back reflectively. "Didn't do my back much good, I can tell you, but it worked." He grinned at the memory. "They just stood there, dripping, for a few seconds, then they made as if to start again. But I wasn't having any more nonsense. 'Right,' I said, 'into my office and we'll get this sorted out.' It was just bad luck that Mr. Passmore himself chose that very moment to come down into the yard—he looks in, from time to time, just to keep an eye on things. 'What on earth is going on here, Baines?' he says. 'I'm not quite sure myself, Mr. Passmore,' I says. 'I was just about to find out.' 'Then I'll come with you,' he says. 'But I'd like to make it clear from the outset that I will not tolerate this sort of behavior on my premises.'

"So then, of course, it all come out. Apparently Frank's brother Steve had gone to this chap, the one Frank was fighting, and said, 'Look, I know you want a new color telly, right? Well, my brother Frank works for Passmore's and he can get a big discount, see. Just tell me what make you want, give me the money in cash, and I'll see you get it.' Well, of course, you can't blame the bloke for falling for it, can you?"

"Wait a minute," said Lineham. "Are you saying that the whole thing was a con trick? That Steven Long was just after the money and had no intention of asking Frank to get the TV set for this chap?"

"That's exactly what I am saying. Over three hundred quid this bloke gave to Steve, a week ago, and he's been expecting Frank to roll up with the telly every day since."

"And Frank knew nothing about it?"

"Not a whisper."

"So what happened, after you'd got all this sorted out?"

"Well, Frank finally managed to convince him that he didn't know a thing about it and hadn't seen a penny of his money and he went off breathing fire and brimstone. But the worst of it was, Frank got the push. Mr. Passmore said he simply couldn't risk this sort of thing happening again. Well, you can't blame him, I suppose, he's got the reputation of the store to think of . . . No, the one I blame is that danged brother of Frank's, that Steve."

"So how did Frank react, to losing his job?"

"How d'you think? Real mad, he was."

They thanked the old man and left.

"I'd have been mad too, in the circumstances," said Lineham as they walked back to the car.

"Ditto. Anyway, now we know why Frank went to see Long last night. The question is, just how angry was he?"

"And it's quite likely that one of Long's other visitors was this character he'd swindled. It shouldn't be too difficult to find out who he is. I must say our Steven seems to have had a real talent for stirring things up."

"Yes, he does, doesn't he?"

"I presume we're now going to see Frank."

Thanet grinned. "Full marks for deduction."

nine

Frank May lived on a small, relatively new council estate. The gardens were trim, the houses well-maintained, and it was obvious from the rash of sun porches that some of the tenants had taken advantage of the generous schemes available to those who wished to buy.

Thanet was surprised to find that number 6 was one of the larger houses. He wondered how the as-yet-childless Mays had managed to qualify. Perhaps the young couple was living with her parents.

It looked as though he was right. The door was opened by a comfortable little roly-poly of a woman in her late forties whose pleasant smile faded when Thanet introduced himself.

"You'd better come in. I'm Debbie's mum."

Debbie, Thanet presumed, was Frank's wife.

"That Steve," she said as she closed the door behind them. "I was sorry to hear what happened to him, of course, no one would wish that on anyone, but to be honest I'm not surprised, the way he used to carry on, and I can't pretend I'm sorry he's gone. As far as this family's concerned he was trouble when he was alive and it looks as though he's going to be more trouble now he's dead. Makes me mad. Frank's a good lad and deserves better."

She opened the door on the right. The smell of food drifted out and Thanet glimpsed a number of people—six? seven?—seated around a long table at the far end of the room, eating mechanically and watching a large television set enthroned on the sideboard.

"Frank? Someone to see you."

Thanet immediately recognized the man who rose. The description had been accurate: early twenties, heavy build, around five feet ten, with longish dark curly hair and a mustache.

The girl next to Frank swiveled her heavy body around to glance over her shoulder. "Who is it, Mum?"

Her mother answered the question with a shake of the head and Thanet could imagine the frown and the don't-ask-me-to-tell-you expression, the meaningful glance at the other children. There were, Thanet had worked out, four of them, two boys and two girls in their early to middle teens, all of them engrossed in food and television. Debbie didn't look much more than eighteen herself.

But Debbie refused to be put off. She frowned, heaved herself to her feet and followed her husband to the door. "What is it? What's the matter?"

Her mother was obviously determined to keep the news of the unwelcome visitors from her other children, if possible. "It's the police," she hissed. She tugged first Frank, then Debbie out into the hall and shut the door firmly behind them. "You'd better go in the kitchen," she said, beginning to shepherd Thanet and Lineham along the narrow passageway beside the staircase like a nervous sheep dog.

"Just a moment," said Thanet, stopping so abruptly that Lineham, who was behind, bumped into him. "There's no need for your daughter to come."

The woman hesitated, stepping back to consult Debbie with a glance, giving Thanet his first uninterrupted view of the girl.

He looked for the legendary bloom of pregnancy and failed to find it. Debbie's face and ankles were puffy, her skin sallow, her shoulder-length dark hair lusterless. She looked exhausted, anxious, but determined. She and Frank were holding hands, he noticed.

He gave her what he hoped was a reassuring smile. "I'd like a few words with your husband alone, first, if you don't mind."

She edged a little closer to Frank.

"We'd prefer to stay together."

Frank spoke for the first time. "I've got nothing to hide, Inspector."

Thanet looked from one to the other. United we stand, he thought. And divided? Well, if Debbie chose not to be protected he couldn't help but admire her for it . . . He could always see Frank alone later, if necessary.

He shrugged. "As you wish."

The kitchen was ridiculously tiny for a house of this size, no more than eight feet square, and by the time the two policemen, Frank and Debbie had all squeezed inside there was little more than a couple of feet between them. There was an overpowering smell of hamburgers and fried onions.

Lineham shot Thanet a resigned glance and wedged himself into a corner, between fridge and washing machine, clearing a space for his notebook on the latter with his elbow.

"If there's anything you want, then . . ." said Debbie's mother incongruously, and backed out, shutting the door behind her.

"Well now, Mr. May," said Thanet, "perhaps we'd better begin by introducing ourselves. I'm Inspector Thanet and this is Sergeant Lineham, both from Sturrenden

CID. And as you'll have guessed, we're investigating the death of your brother, Mr. Steven Long."

"Half-brother," said Debbie.

"Quite right, half-brother," conceded Thanet, with a smile. "And naturally we are having to talk to all those who were connected with him."

"Well you needn't think it had anything to do with Frank," said Debbie aggressively. "Frank wouldn't hurt a fly, ask anyone who knows him, they'll tell you." And she gave her husband a brilliant, adoring smile which imparted a fleeting radiance to her drabness.

"That may be true. Nevertheless, there are certain questions we have to put to him. It's a fixed and essential part of our routine in such matters."

He saw Debbie squeeze her husband's hand.

"What did you want to know?" she said.

"There's no point in beating about the bush," said Thanet. "I have to tell you that you, Mr. May, were seen coming away from Mr. Long's flat last night, and that this puts you in a very difficult situation."

He read dismay in their faces as they exchanged glances, and it was clear that they had been hoping no one had seen Frank in Hamilton Road the previous evening.

"We also know that yesterday afternoon you lost your job, because of your half-brother's deception over the television set . . ."

They stared at him numbly. They couldn't fail to realize where all this was leading.

"So you see, there's no point in pretending that you and Mr. Long were on the best of terms. And we can't escape the fact that not only did you have good reason to feel very angry with him, but you were also on the spot around the time of the murder . . ."

There was no mistaking the implication. The blow had fallen and for a moment they stood silent, struggling to recover from its impact. It was Debbie who found her tongue first. "You can't mean . . . Surely you don't mean . . ." Disbelief gave way to outrage. "It's not fair!" Her sallow skin was flushed with anger. "Why should this be happening to Frank? We've never done any harm to anyone. All we've ever wanted is to be left alone to get on with our lives, to work, and save up enough for a little home of our own, for the baby . . ." She clasped her hands protectively over her stomach. "And now . . . All through no fault of Frank's . . . That Steve, I could . . ."

Kill him? The words vibrated in the air, unspoken, as Frank cut her off. "Stop it, Deb," he said sharply. "It don't do no good carrying on like that. You know what the doctor said. Keep quiet, no excitement . . ."

"There's really no need for you to be here, Mrs. May," said Thanet gently.

She shook her head vehemently. "I'd rather, thanks."

"Shall I fetch a chair?" said Lineham solicitously. "I'm sure we could squeeze one in."

Louise, Lineham's wife, had had two very difficult pregnancies.

She shook her head. "No, it's all right, really . . ."

"So, Mr. May?" said Thanet.

Frank lifted his shoulders. "What is there to say? It's true. Yes, I have lost my job because of Steve, and yes, I did go to his flat, to try and see him last night . . ."

"*Try* and see him?" said Thanet.

Frank, it seemed, had made two attempts to see Steve the previous evening. On the first occasion he had gone straight from work, arriving in Hamilton Road at about twenty past five. He knew that Steve didn't usually get home from work until twenty to six so he hadn't gone into the house but had waited outside in the car, listening to the radio. By six o'clock there was still no sign of Steve and Frank decided that his half-brother had probably gone to see Sharon, and that there was no point in hanging around any longer. Also, Debbie would be wondering where he, Frank, had got to. He decided to go home, have his tea, and come back later.

By the time he had broken the bad news about the loss of his job to Debbie, had eaten and had been persuaded to watch their favorite quiz program, his temper had cooled and it no longer seemed quite so urgent to have it out with Steve. It was therefore not until around half past eight that he had found himself once more in Hamilton Road.

"Just a moment," said Thanet. "You said 'I.' Your wife didn't go with you?"

Frank shook his head. "She wanted to, but I said no. She's supposed to be resting a lot, she hasn't been too good lately. She went to bed, didn't you, Deb?"

Debbie nodded.

"Sorry. Go on, Mr. May."

"I could see there were lights on in Steve's flat . . ."

Frank had been puzzled, therefore, to get no reply to his knock. The door was locked and there had been no sound from within, so he assumed that Steve had been home and gone out again, forgetting to switch the light off. This was odd, because Frank had checked and Steve's car was still parked in the small car park at the back of the house. Frank had concluded that Steve must have gone out with a friend and he had decided to visit a few of Steve's favorite haunts, to see if he could track him down. En route he had run into one "mate" here and another one there and had ended up drowning his sorrows in drink, to the degree that he had had to be driven home by a friend.

"Right," said Thanet. "Let's go back a bit, then. Why did you assume that Steve had gone to see Sharon, when he didn't come straight home from work?"

"He often did," said Frank.

"He was always pestering her," said Debbie. "Couldn't leave her alone. A pity he wasn't a bit nicer to her when she was living with him, I say, then she mightn't have gone off. Couldn't recognize a good thing when he had it, if you ask me, but then, that was Steve all over."

"Odd, that," said Thanet. "Geoff, his twin, didn't seem to think Steve was all that bothered about the separation."

"Don't know where he got that idea," said Frank. "Steve used to go round there pretty often, after work. Ivor usually calls in to see his mum on the way home, see, she's got a bad heart and he does odd jobs for her . . . Steve knew he'd be pretty certain to find Sharon alone."

"Mind, he used to pretend to other people that he didn't care she'd left him," said Debbie. "Act cool, like. But I know Sharon pretty well, and she was always telling me he'd been round to see her."

"And you believed her?"

Debbie shrugged. "No reason not to. She used to show me the things he gave her—bits of jewelry, mostly, she's very fond of jewelry, is Sharon. He was forever giving her presents. He was trying to buy her back, if you ask me. As a matter of fact, Frank and me wondered . . ."

"What?"

"Well, we did wonder if that's what he might have wanted the money for—you know, the money he got from that man, for the telly."

"In order to buy Sharon an expensive present, you mean?"

"Yeah," said Frank. "Couldn't think why else he'd need that amount of money in a lump sum. I know he was out of work for a bit after Sharon went, but he soon found another job—he's a real genius with cars—and he only had himself to keep, so he couldn't have been too short of the ready."

"To tell you the truth," said Debbie, "it wouldn't surprise me if she had gone back to him in the end. But the point is, Geoff doesn't know Sharon at all well. I don't suppose he's seen her once since her and Steve split up. And he didn't see Steve all that often either, so it would've been easy for Steve to fool Geoff into thinking he didn't care about getting her back."

"Steve wouldn't have wanted to let on to Geoff that he was feeling down, see," said Frank. "He always used to have to act big with Geoff, on account of Geoff being so posh."

"He was jealous, really," said Debbie. "Couldn't stand the thought that if only he'd been the one who'd been adopted it would have been him up there in that posh house with that posh car. Whenever he'd been to see Geoff he'd come back that bad-tempered . . . You should have heard him taking Geoff off! Real good at it, he was. He could be a real laugh, Steve, when he wanted to."

"You saw quite a lot of him, then?"

"Well, like I said, Sharon and me've been friends for ages. It seemed natural, like, for us to make a foursome. Not that I've ever been what you might call keen on Steve. Got up my nose, most of the time. Always stirring people up. Like it was some sort of game . . ."

"You think it was deliberate?"

Debbie frowned. "I dunno, really. Seemed like he couldn't help himself."

"How did he get on with his other half-brother?"

"Chris?" Frank shrugged. "So-so."

"Oh, come off it, Frank. Driving Chris and Clare round the bend, he was, if you ask me," said Debbie. "Matter of fact, I bumped into Chris in town late Monday afternoon. He was still steaming about something that'd happened the night before. Him and Clare'd had some neighbors in for supper and Steve barged in, blind drunk, and was sick all over the carpet in front of the guests, while they were eating . . ."

Not a maneuver calculated to endear him to anybody, thought Thanet. Judging by the wooden expression on Lineham's face, he was thinking much the same thing.

"Well I think that's about it for the moment, Mr. May. What I'd like you to do now is this. I'd like you to sit down and write out a detailed timetable of your movements last night, from the moment you left here after the quiz program, to the time you got home, together with the names of the pubs you went to and any names you can remember of the people you met. Bring it down to the station, and we'll get you to make a formal statement at the same time."

"You're not going to arrest him, then?" Debbie's face was suddenly luminous with hope.

"I shan't be arresting anybody until I am satisfied that there is sufficient evidence of guilt. Oh, there is just one other point, Mr. May . . ."

"Yes?" Relief had made Frank eager to cooperate.

"The name of the man Steve defrauded over the television set . . . Do you know it?"

Frank scowled. "Cooper. Martin Cooper. Lives on the Orchard Estate. Plumtree Road, I think."

"Thank you."

"Inspector . . . ?" Debbie's face, like her husband's, had clouded at the mention of the incident which had had such disastrous consequences for them. "There's no chance Frank will have to find that three hundred pounds, pay it back, is there?"

"I shouldn't think so, for a moment—that is, assuming your husband really did know nothing about the deal."

Frank shook his head vigorously.

"In that case, I shouldn't worry about it. The arrangement was between Steve and Cooper. It's not your problem."

Outside there was a new crispness in the air and a timid moon was lurking behind high, ragged clouds.

"Looks as though it might be clearing up at last," said Thanet. Suddenly he felt exhausted. His brain, relieved of the immediate necessity to analyze, formulate, assess, seemed to have ground to a halt and his back, always inclined to play up when he was tired, was aching badly. The prospect of the evening's work ahead stretched endlessly before him—interview Chris May, return to the office, sift through all the house-to-house reports that would have come in, write up his own . . . He needed a break, he decided, if he was to face all this with equanimity.

"Yuk," said Lineham, as they settled themselves into the car. He sniffed at his coat sleeve. "I stink of hamburgers . . . D'you think Long was already dead by half past eight, when Frank got there?"

"Possible, by the sound of it. But there again, it might have been as he thought, and Long was out."

"But he was seen going out earlier, at six forty-five . . . I suppose he could have gone out, then come in again."

"Unless that was really Geoff."

Lineham was silent for a few moments and then said, "I don't know what you thought, but it seemed to me that it's Frank's wife who wears the trousers in that partnership . . . And she's very protective towards him, isn't she? I bet she was really furious when Frank came home with the news that he'd lost his job because of Steve. I'm reluctant to suggest it, sir, but it did occur to me . . ."

"Yes, it occurred to me, too . . . That was why I tried to find out what she was up to last night."

"Going to bed isn't much of an alibi, is it? D'you think she could have slipped out without anyone knowing?"

"Possible, I suppose. We'd better check. It's only a fifteen-minute walk to Hamilton Road, from here. And she's quite a determined person, I imagine. It's difficult not to let the fact that she's so pregnant and obviously not well get in the way."

"Toxemia, by the look of it," said Lineham. "Did you notice her face and her legs?"

"Exactly. There's some inner taboo which says no, no woman in her condition could possibly be suspected of murder."

"But you think she's capable of it?"

"Certainly not cold-blooded, calculated murder. But I could imagine her setting off determined to give Steve a piece of her mind, and being goaded into hitting out at him if his reaction was just to laugh it off. Or perhaps she could have decided to follow Frank because she thought that when it came down to it he'd be no match for Steve. If Frank's story is true and Steve really was out when he got there, Debbie would have arrived at Steve's place long after Frank had left, of course, and by then Steve might well have come back from wherever he'd gone."

"He seems to have done an awful lot of popping in and out last night," objected Lineham.

"I know . . . Look, Mike, I don't know about you, but I've got to the stage when I can't really think straight any more. I do want to see Chris May this evening, but I think it might be a good idea if we took a break, went home for supper, and interviewed him later."

"Suits me. Louise was going to make steak and kidney pie . . . I'll drop you at home, shall I, pick you up later?"

"Thanks. You might give Chris May a ring, to make sure he's there when we call. Let's see, it's a quarter to seven now . . . Make an appointment for eight thirty, if you can."

Lineham put the car into gear and it leapt forward. "Louise won't be able to believe her eyes," he said.

ten

As soon as he walked into the kitchen Thanet knew that something was wrong. Joan smiled a greeting, returned his kiss as usual, but after fourteen years of marriage he wasn't fooled. By now he could read every nuance of her moods. Something had seriously upset her.

"What's the matter?"

She pulled a face. She was mashing potatoes and she added margarine and a generous seasoning of freshly ground black pepper before putting the lid back on the saucepan and turning to face him.

"It's Ben. I got home a bit early and Bridget said he was around at Tom's, so I went over to fetch him. I thought it was time he got started on his homework. Marjorie wasn't there and the boys—about half a dozen of them—were watching a video." She paused. "*Driller Killer*."

"No!" Thanet had seen excerpts from this film and had been disgusted by them. In his work he came across much to sicken and appall, but the presentation of such sadistic and vicious material as entertainment was, he felt, one of the most pernicious evils of the modern age.

"Yes. I couldn't believe it. I was furious, as you can imagine. I really read the riot act, insisted they turn it off and give it to me." She reached up and took the cassette off a shelf, showed it to him.

"Fortunately they'd only watched about five minutes of it. I can't imagine what Marjorie will say."

"How did they get hold of it?"

"One of the older boys at school hired it to them, makes a profit, apparently, by sub-hiring . . . Oh Luke, what are we going to do? I can't believe that Ben would want to see this stuff."

"What does he say about it?"

Joan shrugged. "That he didn't know what it was going to be about . . . That everybody watches them . . ."

"Where is he?"

"In his room."

"Right. Give that to me." Thanet turned and marched upstairs, tiredness forgotten, his mind a cauldron of seething emotion: shock that Ben should wish to participate in such undesirable behavior, fear that his son's mind might already have been irrevocably corrupted, and the despair familiar to all parents trying to bring their children up decently in the face of the winds of evil which sweep across the face of contemporary society. Finally, there was anger, with Ben for letting him down, with the irresponsible senior who had provided the film and, above all, with himself. Where had he gone wrong? Somewhere along the line he had failed his children.

Ben's door was shut. Usually, Thanet knocked before entering, but tonight he flung it open and walked right in.

Ben was sitting at his desk, books spread about, apparently hard at work. He looked around apprehensively.

Thanet held up the cassette. "So this is what you get up to behind our backs."

Ben flinched.

"Well, what have you got to say for yourself?"

Silence.

"I'm waiting."

"I . . ."

"Well?"

Ben compressed his lips, struggled not to cry.

Oh God, what shall I do? Show me the right thing to do, the right thing to say . . . One thing was certain, anger would get him nowhere, could only be destructive. Thanet sank down on to the edge of the bed, and put his head in his hands. He shouldn't have come rushing upstairs like that. He should have taken time, first, to consider the best way to tackle the problem.

Silence.

Eventually Thanet looked up. Ben was sitting staring miserably down at the floor. The sight of his normally patient and tolerant father in a towering rage had evidently subdued him as nothing else could. Thanet couldn't ever remember being so angry with his son before. Perhaps, after all, it had been a good idea to let Ben see just how much the incident had upset him. The thought was encouraging. How best to capitalize on it, that was the problem.

"OK, Ben, the storm's over. Let's try and get this sorted out. Come here." Thanet patted the bed beside him.

Sullenly, Ben complied.

"Now then, let's begin by hearing your side of the story."

"What's the point? You've already made up your mind, haven't you?"

"No, I haven't. If I had, why would I be bothering to ask you to tell me?"

Ben shrugged. "To make it look as though you're trying to be fair? So I'll agree to whatever it is you decide to do."

Bang on target. Thanet was shaken, and experienced an uncomfortable mixture of pride and alarm. For his eleven-year-old son to show such perception was one thing; to have to take it into account in dealing with him was another. He'd always tried to be honest with the children, to enable them to understand his motivation, the reasons for his behavior. Now the chickens were coming home to roost with a vengeance.

"To a certain extent that's true. But it's not just that I want it to *look* as though I'm being fair. I want to *be* fair. Do you believe that?"

Ben looked directly at Thanet for the first time, studied his face. At last he nodded.

"Good. So come on, then, tell me how all this came about."

There wasn't much to tell. One of the senior boys had discovered the profitable sideline of hiring videos overnight and then renting them out to groups of boys in the school for more than one showing, before returning them to the shop next day. Business was thriving. If a number of boys clubbed together, it could cost only twenty-five to fifty pence to see a film. The trouble was, he was allowing the younger boys to hire from him videos which by law they were too young to rent. *Driller Killer* was a case in point.

"So how often have you joined in watching these things?"

"Three, no, four times. But," Ben added hastily, "they haven't been like this."

"What do you mean?"

"They've been the sort of thing you wouldn't mind me seeing. *Star Wars*, stuff like that."

Relief washed through Thanet's entire body, leaving a weakness in his legs, a slight dizziness which briefly blurred his vision. He was reminded of the time a year or two ago when one of Ben's friends had died of glue-sniffing, and Thanet had learnt that his son's involvement had been only peripheral.

"Good. In that case, things aren't quite as bad as we thought."

Thanet stood up and walked across to Ben's desk, seeing but not taking in the scatter of text and exercise books. He turned and looked at his son who was now watching him hopefully. "The question is, what do I do now? I'll be frank with you, I'm not certain of the best way to deal with this. There are several alternatives. I could put you across my knee and give you a good walloping. But that's not my way, as you well know. I never have thought force a constructive way of imposing discipline . . . I could punish you by saying right, no supper and early to bed, but in my mind this is too important an issue to deal with in such a short-term manner . . . Or I could say, right, if this is the way you use the pocket money we give you and the freedom we allow you, we'll take both away, get a baby-sitter in to stay with you after school until one or other of us gets home . . ."

Ben didn't like this prospect one little bit, he could tell.

"But to be honest, I'm not keen on that idea either, and I'll tell you why." Thanet returned to the bed and sat down again.

"You see, Ben, the only kind of result I'm interested in is a long-term one, the only kind of discipline the sort that comes from within. Within you, that is . . . What worries me most of all about this business is that we trusted you, your mother and I, and you have betrayed that trust . . . Oh, I know you may think I'm making an awful fuss about something pretty trivial—what's one film, after all—but it's the principle, you see . . . Yes? What were you going to say?"

Ben had looked up as if in protest.

"I'm not sure why you are—making such a fuss, I mean. I know, from the bit we did see, that that," and he nodded at the cassette which lay on the bed between them, "isn't the sort of thing you and mum'd approve of, but I can't see why it's that bad."

Thanet glanced at the cassette. "Can't you? The best way I can put it is to say that we, your mother and I, believe that this sort of thing," and he tapped the plastic casing with a fingernail, "is a sort of poison. It is slow and insidious and, what is worse, it is addictive, like heroin or cocaine, the difference being that it affects the mind." He sighed. "I know a lot of people don't agree with us, but parents can only bring their children up in what they feel is the right way, and your mother and I don't want you to have a mind like an open sewer, which is what you would have if you kept pouring this sort of stuff into it. And the process is irreversible, you see. Once these disgusting images are inside your head, they're there for good. And, however much you might laugh off the idea, they are bound to influence your behavior. Personally I really do believe that a great deal of the mindless violence we are seeing nowadays against the weaker members of our society, the old and the handicapped, is a result of children's minds being warped and twisted by watching this kind of thing. Now do you understand why I'm making such a fuss about it?"

Ben sat for a while, thinking. "I suppose so," he said at last, reluctantly.

Thanet stood up. "Well, I think we'll leave it there, for the moment. Supper's nearly ready, and afterwards I'd like you to have a quiet think about what I've said, and we'll talk about it again another time. OK?"

Downstairs Joan was waiting anxiously.

"Well?"

Thanet grimaced. "I don't think too much harm's been done. It's the first time he's seen anything like this, and I think I've managed to convince him that it's not a desirable activity . . ."

"Thank goodness . . . I suppose this sort of problem is going to get worse and worse, as they get older."

Thanet put his arms around her. "We can only lurch from crisis to crisis and hope for the best," he said, smiling.

She laid her head against his shoulder. "Oh, Luke, I feel so guilty."

He drew back a little, to study her face. "*You* do. Why?"

"If I hadn't gone back to work . . . I'd be here, every afternoon, to welcome them home from school. I sometimes wonder what on earth I think I'm doing. Most of my work is with people who've suffered in varying degrees from parental neglect, and here I am, subjecting my own children to the same thing."

A tiny voice inside Thanet said, *She's right, you know. You've thought this all along.* "Nonsense," he said, with as much conviction as he could muster. "You're getting things out of proportion. You know perfectly well that our children aren't in the least neglected, and anyway they are old enough, now, and should be responsible enough, to be left for an hour or so in the evening without getting into trouble."

But she knew him too well. "There's no point in pretending, Luke. Whatever you say, I know you agree with me, underneath. You never did want me to go back to work, did you?"

"Darling, please. Not that old chestnut again." He glanced at his watch. Five to eight, already. So much for his relaxing supper at home. "I hate to say it, but in twenty minutes Mike is picking me up, for an eight-thirty appointment . . ."

"Oh . . ." At once she was contrite, the dutiful wife, and in five minutes they were all seated in the dining room, the picture of a united, happy family. Thanet was relieved to see that tonight they were to be spared the doubtful pleasure of enjoying once again the pork chops with mint that was Sprig's choice of a main course for the competition. The first time he had thought it delicious, as he had on the second occasion, too. By the third his enthusiasm was waning and after that . . . well, after that it had become a matter of stoicism.

His enjoyment of tonight's steak and mushroom pie was marred, however, by the fact that Ben was only picking at his food. Joan glanced at Ben and made a face at Thanet, pulling down the corners of her mouth and raising her eyebrows.

Thanet shook his head. Ben was best left well alone at the moment, he felt.

"Are you all ready for Saturday, Sprig?"

"Oh Dad, I do wish you'd stop calling me that."

"Why? I always have."

"It's so *babyish*. I'm *thirteen* now, Dad."

"Quite an old lady," he said smiling.

"I'm serious. I do wish you'd stop."

"All right, if you really want me to." But he felt sad, as if he were finally waving goodbye to Sprig's childhood. "Anyway, are you? All ready?"

"Just about."

"She's checked her list and her equipment at least six times already," said Joan, smiling. "I must say it'll be a relief to have the kitchen clear again."

"I expect you'll be glad to get it over with, now," said Thanet.

"Sort of, I suppose." Bridget frowned. "In a way. It's exciting, though. Just think, three days from now it'll all be over." She looked anxiously at her father. "You are coming, aren't you, Dad?"

"You know I can't be absolutely certain, love. But I do promise that I'll do my very, very best to be there."

Bridget knew he meant it and nodded, satisfied.

Thanet tried to look pleased as the by-now-ritual lemon flummery was brought to the table. "That looks most attractive, Spr . . . Bridget."

"You think so?" She frowned anxiously at her latest attempt at decorating it, an exquisitely accurate reproduction of the emblem of Kent, the white horse, rampant.

"Oh, by the way," said Joan, "I meant to tell you . . . I ran into Louise today, in the town."

"Oh?" said Thanet, between mouthfuls. "How is she?"

"Very well, physically. And the baby's gorgeous."

"But?"

Joan pulled a face. "They're having problems with her mother-in-law again. The house next door but one to them has been put up for sale, and guess what?"

"Oh, no."

Thanet was appalled on Lineham's behalf. Mrs. Lineham senior had always been demanding, obtrusive, disruptive of her son's life. Just over a year ago the young couple had moved, taking themselves out of her immediate orbit, and Thanet remembered wondering at the time how long it would be before she followed them.

"I thought, as she hadn't shown any signs of moving till now, she was resigned to their being further away."

"Apparently not. She's just been waiting for something in Market Cut to come up. It's not certain yet, though, apparently. She may not get enough for her present house, to be able to afford the new one."

"Or someone might beat her to it."

"Let's hope so, for their sake."

The door bell rang.

Thanet scraped up his last spoonful of lemon flummery and wiped his mouth. "That'll be Mike, now."

eleven

In the car Thanet lit his pipe. There wouldn't be time for a proper smoke but it would help him to relax. Automatically, Lineham wound down his window. The sergeant seemed subdued, Thanet thought. Perhaps Louise had been going on at him about his mother. Thanet admired the way in which Lineham coped with the two women in his life, both of whom were pretty strong characters, but he didn't envy him the delicate juggling act he was perpetually called upon to perform to keep them both happy. Thanet sometimes wondered why Lineham hadn't chosen a wife with a meeker, more complaisant personality. Perhaps the sergeant needed that edge of conflict in his life. If so, he must get more than he bargained for at times like this, when the interests of wife and mother were diametrically opposed.

"You managed to make the appointment, I presume?"

"More or less. May was out when I rang at seven, but his wife was expecting him home at any minute. So he's sure to be there by now."

"Good steak and kidney pie?"

"Smashing," said Lineham, with an obvious effort at enthusiasm.

The sergeant obviously wasn't in the mood to talk and they drove in silence to Merridew Road.

The Christopher Mays lived on an enormous private housing estate, which had been under construction for several years now and was still uncompleted. There had been a tremendous outcry from conservationists when planning permission had first been sought, but it had been granted, nevertheless, and there had been mutterings about string-pulling, undue influence and back-scratching ever since. Even at night, however, it was obvious that a considerable effort had been made to make the place visually attractive. The houses and bungalows varied in size and design, and were set back at different distances from the road, and at varying angles to each other. This section must have been one of the first to be completed; the gardens here were already well-established, the young trees more than mere saplings.

Number 26 was one of the cheaper properties, a semi-detached house of modest size. There were lights in the hall and sitting room, and a wrought-iron lantern over the front door illuminated the path of crazy paving.

"Looks as though he might still be out, sir. There's no car in the garage."

The garage doors were open, in readiness for the return of their owner.

Thanet tapped his pipe out on the heel of his shoe. "Never mind. I'd like to talk to his wife anyway."

The girl who answered the door looked absurdly young, more like a child playing at being a housewife, an impression heightened by her Alice-in-Wonderland hair which streamed down her back and framed her small, pointed face.

"Mrs. May?"

She nodded.

"My sergeant rang you earlier to make an appointment to see your husband."

"I'm sorry, I'm afraid he's not home yet."

"You're expecting him shortly?"

"Yes, he should have got back some time ago."

"Could we wait for him?"

She hesitated. "May I see your identification?"

"Certainly." Thanet approved of her caution. He handed over his card.

She held it up to the light, actually looked at it properly before handing it back. So many people just gave it a cursory glance.

She opened the door wide. "Come in. He really shouldn't be too long. He's gone to see his mother."

They stepped into warmth, light and color. All along the blank, right-hand wall was a mural: the background was a stylized landscape of distant fields and hills, the foreground a road and on it, a procession. And what a procession! thought Thanet. There were people in wheelchairs, people on crutches, people with groping hands and white sticks, people wasted with illness supported on both sides by companions, mothers carrying deformed children and a small group of Down's syndrome children holding hands, their faces joyous with anticipation.

Thanet couldn't help stopping and staring and Lineham, too, was similarly fascinated.

Clare May smiled. "It's a pilgrimage to Lourdes," she said. "I went, last year—oh no, not for myself, but to accompany a group of handicapped children."

"You painted this yourself?"

She nodded. "I teach art."

"It's . . . amazing. I've never seen anything like it." He would have liked to linger. The longer he looked at the painting, the more there was to see. The detail was incredible—the doll trailing from a child's hand, the filigree cross on a gold chain around a woman's neck, an able-bodied man stooping to tie a shoelace . . . and everywhere, on every face, the same steadfast expression of hope.

She turned a knob and part of the painting became a door which led into the sitting room. Reluctantly, Thanet tore himself away and followed her.

The room was sparsely furnished with a cream carpet square, a black and white portable television set and a nineteen-thirties-style settee and armchair, with loose covers in rough-textured milk-chocolate linen. The curtains were beautiful, cream linen with a flowing hand-blocked design of birds and foliage in shades of brown and black. Mrs. May's work again? Thanet wondered.

She gestured to them to sit down. "It's about Steve's death, I suppose."

"Yes. Naturally, we are having to talk to all the members of his family."

"You have no idea yet, who did it?"

"No."

"It's horrible." She shook her head, her face somber. "Who could have done such a thing?"

"That, obviously, is what we're trying to find out. Did you know of anyone who wished him harm?"

"Not to that extent, no. Steve was . . ."

"Yes?"

"Well, he had this . . . unfortunate knack of getting people's backs up."

"So we understand. You don't think it was deliberate, then?"

"I don't know." She separated a strand of hair with her right hand and began to twist it around her forefinger. "I could never make up my mind. Sometimes I thought, yes, he did it on purpose, and then at other times I'd think he just couldn't help himself."

"Did you like him?"

She hesitated. "I suppose it would be more accurate to say that I felt sorry for him."

"Oh? Why was that?"

"Nothing ever seemed to work out for him. Sooner or later, things would go wrong."

"Like his marriage, for instance?"

"Yes. That's a typical example. He really loved Sharon, I'm sure of that, and yet, somehow, he couldn't help doing things to set her against him. In the end she couldn't stand it, and she walked out."

"He was hoping to get her back?"

"Oh yes, I'm sure of that. Whether she'd ever have given in and gone back to him is another matter. And yet, she did love him . . . I just don't know. Perhaps it would have depended on whether or not he could convince her that things were going to be different between them."

"And do you think they could have been? Do you think he was capable of changing, to that degree?"

"I don't know. I just don't know. Then, of course, there was Ivor, Sharon's boyfriend. He was being very possessive about her. Steve came round here on Sunday, in a terrible state. I felt so sorry for him. It was his birthday, and he'd been to see her, and Ivor threw him out."

"Yes, we heard about that. Made quite a scene here, I understand."

"Who told you . . . ?" She shrugged. "Why pretend? Yes, it's true."

"Your husband must have been pretty angry about it."

She looked down, veiling her eyes, and shrugged again. "He's used to it by now."

"You mean, Steve made a habit of embarrassing your husband?"

"I don't know that I'd put it quite like that . . . Anyway, my husband has always felt very sympathetic towards Steve."

"For any special reason?"

"There's no point in hiding it. You're bound to hear,

sooner or later, talking to everybody like this . . . And I must admit I don't feel any special loyalty towards my mother-in-law, even if my husband does . . . The truth is, Steve was ill-treated as a child."

"By?"

"By his stepfather, my husband's father. I don't know much about it, but I do know that the NSPCC were called in, and that the social services were pretty much in evidence."

"And the other two boys? Frank and your husband?"

"Oh no, they were fine. It was just Steve . . . So you see, my husband has always felt, well, protective towards Steve."

So this information had been given them in an attempt to put her husband in a good light. But Thanet wasn't convinced. Compassion was all very well, but it could wear thin if the demands made upon it were too high.

"So it was your husband Steve tended to come to, when he was in need of comfort."

"Yes."

What was she hiding? Thanet wondered. Most of the time he had felt that she was being completely frank with him, but for the last few minutes . . .

"And Sunday evening was the last time you saw him?"

She jumped out of her chair as though she had been scalded. "There's my husband now."

While she was out of the room Thanet and Lineham raised eyebrows at each other. Why that reaction to Thanet's last question? It could scarcely have come as a surprise to her. She must have realized that at some point she would be asked when she had last seen her brother-in-law.

He and Lineham rose as the Mays came in together. Clare May gave a nervous little smile. "My husband, Inspector. Chris, this is Inspector Thanet, and Sergeant . . . ?"

"Lineham." Lineham was used to people forgetting his name.

They all sat down and Thanet spent a few minutes on preliminaries, while he studied the elder of Steven Long's half-brothers.

Christopher May was as tall as his brother Frank, but thinner, almost to the point of emaciation. He had the stoop of tall men who are not proud of their physique, and he was all angles—beaky nose, high, bony forehead, sharp knees and elbows. If May's disposition matched his physical make-up, Thanet thought, he must be a very uncomfortable person to live with. His wife, Thanet noticed, was watching him covertly. What was she afraid of?

"Your wife was telling us that you always got on pretty well with Steve—I hope you won't object to my using Christian names, but your family relationships are a little complicated . . ."

"Not at all . . . We got on well enough, I suppose."

"She was saying—" now, this was tricky; according to Steve's twin it was Christopher who had always been his mother's favorite . . . "that Steve had rather a tough time as a child—for some reason your father took against him."

Christopher gave his wife a fleeting glance. *What have you been saying to them?* Almost imperceptibly she shrank back a little.

Did her husband bully her? Thanet wondered. Or was it simply that a man who has managed to haul himself up out of a deprived family into the respectability of a post at the local Grammar School does not like to be reminded of the more sordid aspects of his background. Perhaps both . . .

"Stepfathers often find it difficult to take to stepchildren."

A neat side-step. Well, if Christopher May didn't wish to discuss the matter, Thanet wasn't going to waste time

106

trying to pry it out of him. There were other sources available.

"Do you think that, for this reason, Steve was especially jealous of his twin?"

"What do you mean?"

"Well, I would have thought it might have been pretty galling to compare their relative positions—Geoff's adoptive parents seem to have been very fond of him, and since his adoptive mother's second marriage, he's also been pretty well off. That car of his, for instance . . ."

"Well it was only natural that Steve should have been a bit envious. Wouldn't you have been, in his position?"

"Quite. How did Geoff react to this?"

Christopher shrugged. "Tried to play it down, naturally. He always treated Steve as an equal, in every way. Though of course there's no point in trying to pretend that they were."

"Steve used to pretend to joke about it," said Clare. "But you could tell he didn't really think it was funny. I think you're right, he did find it pretty galling, understandably."

"They seem to have got on all right, though. I understand they used to see each other from time to time."

She nodded. "That was mostly Geoff's doing. I think he's always felt guilty about the difference in their situations."

"It was all talk, though," said her husband. "Since his mother died I haven't exactly noticed him being overgenerous with the goodies."

"I don't suppose he's even got any of the money yet," said Clare defensively. "Probate takes ages, always does."

"Well it's a bit late as far as Steve's concerned anyway, isn't it?" said her husband.

His spitefulness had wounded her. Thanet guessed that she didn't like her image of him tarnished, and that disillusionment lay ahead.

"Anyway," said Christopher, "I'm not sure of the relevance of all this."

"You never know which pieces of information might come in useful," said Thanet. "But to get back to the matter in hand . . . I understand Steve came here on Sunday night, and caused quite a scene."

"Who told you that?" said Christopher, with an accusing glance at his wife.

"Not Mrs. May, I assure you," said Thanet.

"Debbie, then," said May. "I suppose I shouldn't have mentioned it to her . . . My God, if you can't discuss family matters without having them bandied about all over the town . . ."

"For all we know," said Thanet icily, "this murder could be a family matter. Most murders are—sixty percent of them, to be precise."

"Are you implying . . . ?"

"I'm implying nothing. Merely attempting to obtain information, much of which, I am well aware, may turn out to be completely irrelevant, but some of which may not . . . I can't imagine you were very pleased about Steve's behavior on Sunday night."

"Would you have been?" May's nostrils were pinched and white with suppressed anger.

"Maybe not. But that's not the point. The point is that your brother—sorry, half-brother," Thanet corrected himself as May opened his mouth to interrupt, "has been killed, and I am trying to find out why."

"You're not seriously suggesting that I would have killed him just because of mere social embarrassment!"

"When did you last see Steve, Mr. May?"

There was an instant of shocked silence. Thanet had the impression that the young couple were preventing themselves from consulting each other with a glance only by exercising the most rigid self-control.

"Well?"

May exhaled slowly, then sat back with a resigned shrug. Now he did look at his wife and their faces said it all. *We'll have to tell them.*

"I suppose you'll find out sooner or later," said May. "We saw him last night."

twelve

So they were at last going to learn something about Steven Long's movements last night. Thanet was careful not to allow his satisfaction to show in his face. Instead he deliberately settled back into his chair and appeared to relax.

"What time was this?"

"About seven o'clock, wasn't it?" May glanced at his wife for confirmation, and she nodded.

"Tell me about it."

"There's not much to tell."

This was patently untrue. May clearly found the memory disturbing. His lips were compressed, his nostrils pinched white again, his eyes angry.

"All the same . . ."

May shrugged. "If you must know, he made a scene. Outside."

"Outside?"

So this was why May and his wife had shied away from admitting to seeing Steve last night. It was equally obvious that May had decided to get in first with his version, rather than allow Thanet to hear about the incident from neighbors.

"I'd made it quite clear, after that performance on Sunday night, that we didn't want him here again."

"So you refused to let him in?"

"Yes." May was sullen but defiant. "I was fed up with him making a laughingstock of us in front of our friends. Sunday was the last straw."

"It's got worse and worse since Sharon left him," said May's wife, determined as ever to present her husband in as good a light as possible. "Some of the things he's done have been pretty awful. He even went up to the school . . ."

"The inspector doesn't want to hear about that," cut in May.

"Oh, but I do. I'm interested in hearing anything which will help me to understand Steve better."

May gave his wife a quick glance. *Now look what you've done.* "My wife," he said tightly, with barely controlled irritation, "is referring to another occasion when Steve had had too much to drink. He rolled up to the school, insulted the secretary and humiliated me in front of a class of thirty fourth-formers."

"That must have been very unpleasant for you." Thanet was genuinely sympathetic. Any teacher would have found such a situation humiliating. And May, to whom respectability obviously mattered so much? Thanet was beginning to wonder if, in the case of this man, repeated doses of extreme humiliation could indeed have finally driven him to violence.

May gave a brief, cynical bark of laughter. "Unpleasant! Talk about understatement! Anyway, as I said, Sunday was the last straw, as far as I was concerned. Steve could look for moral support elsewhere."

Thanet couldn't make up his mind whether this moral support, of which both May and his wife had spoken, had been real or imaginary. It was difficult to tell. On the face of it, it would be difficult to conceive of a less comforting person to turn to than May. But even the prickliest of people are capable of compassion, especially towards those even more vulnerable than themselves, and perhaps, when Steve had been less extreme in his behavior, less desperate . . . Yes, that was it. Thanet felt as though he had groped his way towards a significant insight into the dead man. Steve had been desperate . . .

He became aware that the silence had become too protracted, that they were all looking at him expectantly. With difficulty he forced his mind back to what May had been saying.

"Was that what he came for, last night? Moral support?"

May shrugged. "Probably. Ostensibly, he came to apologize."

"For his behavior on Sunday?"

"Yes. Unfortunately, past experience has shown that his contrition would only last until the next time he needed to make a spectacle of himself in front of me. So I told him that this time I'd really meant what I said. He just wasn't welcome here any more."

"Needed," murmured Thanet. "You said, 'the next time he *needed* to make a spectacle of himself . . .' Was that true, do you think?"

May hesitated. His face softened and briefly Thanet glimpsed the young man May's wife had fallen in love with. "Yes," he said slowly. "If Steve was hurt, or upset, he'd usually try to make light of it by turning it into a joke. He'd start fooling around, making people laugh . . ."

"It was his way of dealing with pain."

"Yes . . . But lately, it always seemed to misfire. It just wasn't funny any more. The way he'd do it was all wrong. He'd have a few drinks to cheer himself up, try and get himself into a light-hearted mood, but it didn't seem to work and he'd end up drinking too much . . ."

"He was drinking steadily?"

"Oh no, don't get me wrong. He only ever used to drink if something had especially upset him. On Sunday, of course, it was that visit to Sharon. Ivor threw him out."

"And it was his birthday, too," said Clare May. "Steve's, I mean. It was so sad. You could see how miserable he was, but it was so difficult. He really was very drunk. We had some friends here to supper, and he . . ."

"No need to go over all that again," said May sharply. "The long and the short of it was, he'd gone too far this time, and I wasn't going to change my mind—not for a while, at least. Not that I told him that, mind. As far as he was concerned, that was it. But I thought it might teach him a lesson, pull him up short, show him you can't go around barging into other people's lives, embarrassing them right left and center, without paying for it in some way. Then, after a while, I'd have relented . . ."

Now it's too late. The words hung on the air as clearly as if they'd been spoken.

"So what did he do, last night, when you refused to let him in?"

"Wouldn't take me seriously at first. Then he began to argue. So I . . . I shut the door in his face . . . I should have known better, really."

"That was when he made a scene?"

"Yes." May was hunched in his chair, frowning as he brooded over the memory. "Banging on the door . . . shouting . . . kicking at it . . ."

"You opened it, eventually?"

"No," snapped May "What was the point? He'd roused the whole street by then, things couldn't have got any worse . . . He went on and on, for a good ten minutes, then he left."

"Had he been drinking?"

"No, I don't think so. If he had, it certainly didn't show."

"What was he wearing?"

May frowned. "Jeans and a navy windbreaker, the one he usually wore."

"Shoes?"

"I didn't notice. Probably those scruffy old sneakers of his."

"And he came by car, presumably."

"I assume so."

"It wasn't parked outside?"

"I didn't notice. I was merely concerned with getting rid of him as quickly as possible."

"So he would have left about, what, ten or a quarter past seven?"

"Around that, yes."

"So what did you do, after he left?"

"What do you mean?"

There was tension in the air again and Thanet sensed that both May and his wife were being careful not to look at each other. Had they quarreled after Steve left? Thanet could well imagine that they might have. May would have been tense, angry over the commotion which Steve had caused, and his wife might well have disagreed with her husband over his treatment of Steve. It would have taken only a hint of reproach from her for May to have exploded, perhaps even have flung out of the house in anger . . .

"Did you stay in, for the rest of the evening?"

"No. As a matter of fact, I went to see my mother."

"What time did you leave?"

"What are you getting at?"

"Mr. May, I don't have to remind you that this is a murder investigation. It is a matter of routine that we should find out the movements of everyone connected with your half-brother. Everyone."

May shrugged. "Well, I've nothing to hide. I left around eight thirty."

Well over an hour later. So, if there had been a row after Steve's departure, it had probably been patched up.

"And what time did you get back?"

"About a quarter to ten."

So May had been out for an hour and a quarter. Plenty of time to have called in at Steve's flat, either on the way to or from his mother's house.

"You visit your mother often?"

According to Geoff, Chris had been his mother's favorite. All the same, from the little Thanet had seen of either Chris or Mrs. May, it was difficult to imagine them having much in common.

"From time to time. I wouldn't normally go around two evenings running, but tonight, of course, I thought she might be upset about Steve."

Thanet wasn't sure whether he believed this, but he was prepared to let it pass. "Last night . . . Did you call in at Steve's flat, on the way?"

"No! Nor on the way back, either."

Thanet suspected that May was lying, but he decided to leave it at that, for the moment.

Before returning to the car he and Lineham separated to question the neighbors on either side. In both cases May's story was confirmed, Steve having made enough noise to bring most of the people in the street to front doors or windows. But although there was plenty of parking space, neither remembered seeing Steve's car outside, and one of them was certain that after abandoning his assault on the Mays' front door, Steve had walked off down the street and around the corner.

"Odd," commented Thanet, when Lineham told him this. "If that was Steve, not Geoff, who was seen leaving Steve's flat at a quarter to seven, he must have come by car to have arrived here by seven. Unless he got a lift, of course. And why should he have done that, with a car of his own sitting outside?"

"It could have been temporarily out of action."

"It was working all right earlier, when he went to see Sharon. At least, we've assumed it was. Perhaps we'd better check with her."

"Well, at least we're a little bit further on with finding out what he did last night. I wonder where he went next."

"Back home, perhaps? I shouldn't have thought he'd have left the lights and the television on in the flat while he came to see Chris May. In which case, he must have gone back afterwards, because they were both on when Frank got there at half past eight. Though I suppose we can't assume anything. We'd better check, with the neighbors. And another thing . . . I can't recall seeing a navy windbreaker in the flat."

"Perhaps he left it wherever he went to later. If he did go out, later."

"Possibly." It was another small discrepancy.

"Where now then, sir?"

It was ten o'clock, and there were still reports to be done. Remembering all the interviews they'd conducted today, Thanet quailed at the thought. The impetus which had carried him through the session with the Mays had suddenly ebbed and he wanted nothing so much as to go home, have a hot drink, go to bed and sink into oblivion. His back was crying out for the luxury of a horizontal position. He sighed. "Better have another word with May's mother, I suppose, see if she confirms his story. It would be nice if we could go to bed tonight knowing that the alibi of at least one suspect has checked out."

"Shouldn't think there's much hope of that at this time of night," said Lineham as he started the engine.

"I should think she'd be pretty well sloshed by now, on past performance."

Thanet groaned. "You're right. I'd forgotten. Still, we'd better go through the motions, I suppose."

There was a light on in the hall of Mrs. May's house, but no answer to their knock.

"Perhaps she's working at the pub tonight," suggested Lineham.

"Possibly. Let's take a look around the back."

The light was on in the squalid kitchen but they could see through the uncurtained window that the room was empty and once again there was no response to their knock.

"She's probably in the living room." Lineham nodded at the slash of yellow light which fell across the back yard.

They both moved to peer through the gap in the curtains.

Mrs. May, wearing a tight black skirt, frilly red blouse and black tights, was lying in one of the orange armchairs, head thrown back, eyes closed, mouth open. Even from here they could hear her snoring. Her right hand still limply clutched the glass in her lap and beside her on the floor was an almost empty gin bottle.

"Dead to the world by the look of it," said Lineham.

"It's pointless to try and talk to her now. We'll have to come back in the morning."

thirteen

During the night the last of the rainclouds had finally moved away and when Thanet drew the curtains next morning he saw that it was a clear, crisp, frosty day. Impulsively he opened the window, leaned out, and took several deep breaths of the icy air. Over to the right the orange globe of the winter sun was just beginning to peep over the horizon and the sky was suffused with an apricot glow which became more and more spectacular by the second.

"What are you doing, Dad?" Bridget had paused by the open door.

"Admiring the sunrise," he said, with a grin.

She smiled back. "I hate to say it, but it is ten to eight, and it's your turn to take us to school."

"Time you started taking yourselves," he grumbled, closing the window.

"When you have to pass the school gates on the way to work? You know your conscience would never allow it." She skipped out of the door and down the stairs as Thanet advanced on her in mock anger.

As always the prospect of a sunny day had raised

Thanet's spirits, and despite the fact that for the second night running he had had very little sleep, by the time he had done his back exercises, shaved, showered and dressed, he was eager to get back to work.

Sturrenden was looking its best this morning and people were walking briskly, shoulders back, faces turned to the sun. Just inside the school gates a winter-flowering cherry was coming into bloom, its delicate clusters of blossom sugar-almond pink against the clear blue of the sky. Thanet dropped the children off and arrived at the office in good time. Even so, Lineham was before him.

"Morning, Mike. What's new?" Thanet sat down and began to fill his pipe.

"Morning, sir. Not a lot. Bentley's been checking up on Geoffrey Long and Scimitar confirms that he'll be starting work with them a fortnight on Monday. Also, the estate agents say that the house was put on the market six weeks ago—presumably just after he knew he'd got the job in Staffordshire. The PM report's in, but there's nothing there that we didn't know already. I put it on your desk, in case you want to look at it. Oh, and there's good news from the hospital. Harry Carpenter is showing signs of getting back to normal and if the doctor who's been looking after him gives the go-ahead, we'll be able to talk to him today."

"When will the doctor be seeing him?"

"Later on this morning."

"Good." Thanet was skimming through the PM report, but as Lineham had said, there was nothing new in it. He tossed it on to the table and sat back in his chair. "Well, Mike, I think we'd better try and sum up where we've got to."

Lineham put down the report he was reading. "Not very far if you ask me." He yawned and rubbed his eyes wearily.

"Bad night?" asked Thanet sympathetically. The sergeant was, he thought, looking distinctly the worse for wear. Lineham's eyes were bloodshot, sunk into dark hollows of strain and sleeplessness. He couldn't have been in bed before three, and the baby would have woken to be fed at six . . . Then there was the anxiety over the question of whether his mother would soon be moving in nearby and the strain of waiting to hear about the selection board . . . Thanet deliberately hadn't inquired about that this morning. Lineham would be sure to tell him, the moment the news arrived.

Lineham grimaced. "The baby woke us at five, and I couldn't get back to sleep again. I started thinking about the case . . . In the end I got up and came in to work early."

"Did you reach any conclusions?"

"Not really. As I said, I don't really feel we've got very far, yet."

"Oh, I don't know. We're beginning to get some idea of what Steve was like, and of the various people involved."

"Yes . . . Sounds to me as though he was a pretty miserable sort of bloke, one way and the other. Seems as though he had everything going for him—he was a first-rate mechanic, which meant he'd always be able to find a job, he had a nice wife who by all accounts was pretty fond of him . . . but he just couldn't seem to make it work. It's almost as though . . ." Lineham trailed off, sat frowning into space.

"As though what?"

"I'm not sure. As though . . . Well, as though he had to *make* it go wrong, somehow."

"Yes, I'd come to pretty much the same conclusion myself."

"And he seems to have had a real talent for putting people's backs up . . . Look at what he did to Frank, for example. I mean, he wasn't stupid, he must have known he'd be putting Frank's job at risk, with that business of the television set . . . And Chris, too. I can't say I liked the man, but some of the tricks Steve pulled on him must have made him feel pretty sick. You couldn't blame him, really, for washing his hands of him . . . Then there's Howells. Oh, I know Steve had every reason to be jealous of him, but to walk in on Sharon with that birthday cake as if Howells didn't exist . . . I just can't make up my mind whether he was simply unaware of his effect on people, or if he did it on purpose to needle them, or if he knew what he was doing but simply couldn't help it."

"I know. But the interesting point is, that whatever the reason for his behavior, the effect was the same. The question is, was that effect sufficiently drastic for any of them to have killed him?"

Lineham frowned. "If so, I would have thought it probably happened in the heat of the moment. I can't really see any of those three deliberately setting out from home with the intention of killing him—with the exception, possibly, of Howells. But what I can imagine is that if either Frank or Chris went to have it out with him, his attitude might have goaded them into violence. I can just see him sitting there refusing to take them seriously, trying to laugh it off, and them getting more and more angry . . ."

"I agree."

"And I don't know what you think, sir, but it sounds to me as though the situation had steadily been getting worse ever since his wife left him. I think the separation hit him pretty hard. His behavior became more and more extreme . . ."

"Except with Geoff."

"Yes, that's true. Though by all accounts they didn't get on all that well."

"Maybe. But Geoff himself seemed quite sympathetic towards him, I thought."

"Perhaps it's something to do with the fact that they're

twins. Anyway, it was easy enough for Geoff to feel sorry for Steve. He was the one who got the best of the bargain, by far."

"And Steve resented it, by the sound of it."

"Can you blame him, sir? After all, it must have been pretty galling to compare their circumstances, and to know that it was pure chance that their positions weren't reversed."

"All the same, there seems to be general agreement that there weren't any major rows between them, and we've heard nothing about Steve playing Geoff up in the same way as the others."

"True. Anyway, now we know that Steve didn't leave Chris May's house until around seven fifteen, it looks as though Geoff's in the clear."

Lineham got up and began to leaf through the reports stacked on the corner of Thanet's desk. "I forgot to tell you. Carson interviewed the girl, and Geoff's alibi checked out. Here we are."

Thanet glanced through the report. As Geoff had claimed, he had picked up Caroline Gilbert from her home at half past seven. He had taken her out to dinner at the String of Beads, a new restaurant out on the Canterbury Road. They had returned to Geoff's home for coffee and brandy, and had listened to records until just before midnight, when he had driven her home. She was most emphatic that they had been together all evening. There was no question that she was lying to protect him through long-standing loyalty, as they had only met the previous week and had gone out together for the first time on Sunday. Carson was as sure as he could be that the girl was telling the truth.

"You're right," said Thanet. "Steve couldn't have got home from the Mays' house, even by car, until twenty-five to half past seven. So if Geoff collected this girl from—where was it? Hillside Road—at half past seven, and stayed with her all evening, there's no way that he could have committed the murder. All the same, I think we'd better interview the girl again. This timing is pretty crucial, if we're to eliminate Geoff as a suspect, motive or no motive."

Lineham made a note. "Right, sir. Will we go and see her ourselves?"

"Possibly. It depends on what else we have lined up today. Which brings us back to Carpenter. All this," and Thanet waved his hand at the stack of reports, "may prove to have been unnecessary. Of all the possibilities, the likeliest, on the face of it, is that Carpenter, distraught after his daughter's death, went round to Steve's flat and killed him. Then he went out, sat in his car and drank himself into a stupor."

"Maybe. But it could still be tricky proving it. So far forensic haven't come up with any sign of Carpenter's prints in the flat. And where's the murder weapon? The ashtray or whatever it was the murderer grabbed to hit Steve with? It hasn't turned up in the garden or along the road, and it wasn't in Carpenter's car."

"True. Make a note, Mike. When we send someone to check with Sharon whether or not Steve took his car when he went to see her after work that night, we must also find out exactly what it was that fitted that clear patch in the dust. It would be useful to know if we're right about it being the murder weapon, and if so, exactly what we're looking for."

"Right, sir."

"Meanwhile, we've got a lot of checking to do. I want someone to check timings with the friend Howells claims to have helped move furniture, and I also want Sharon asked about the time he arrived home. I want the names of the friends they had a drink with and details of the evening. I want details of his car, Frank's car, Chris's car, and I want further house-to-house visits to ask more questions about that anonymous phone call, about all the cars seen in Hamilton Road that night, and whether or not anyone noticed lights and noise coming from Steve's flat and when. I want someone to check on the movements of Cooper, the man Steve swindled over the television set . . ." On and on it went, the endless list of queries, a boring but essential part of any murder inquiry. Every good policeman is aware of the fact that many a difficult case has been solved by just such meticulous attention to detail, and it is the constant hope of alighting upon such a crucially important but apparently insignificant piece of information that keeps many a policeman on his toes, especially since the cases of the Yorkshire Ripper and the Railway Rapist.

Thanet came to the end at last and Lineham laid down his pen and massaged his aching hand.

"We need three times as many men as we've got," he said gloomily.

"Well, there's no prospect of getting them," said Thanet. "So we might as well resign ourselves to doing the best we can. I'd like to see the mother myself, and I want you to come with me, but after that we can split up, if necessary. Apart from that, well, let's see how we can best get this covered."

Both men were pouring over Lineham's list when there was a knock at the door and Mallard poked his head in.

"Busy?" he said, with a beaming smile. He didn't wait for an answer but advanced into the room. Once again, this morning, he was looking distinctly pleased with himself. "Brought you a present," he said to Thanet. "Well, a temporary one, as I'll want it back." He held up a book. "The one you said you'd like to read. On twins." He handed it over.

"Thanks, Doc. It's very kind of you to remember." Thanet opened it at random. "Looks fascinating."

Mallard gave a gratified smile. "Oh, it is, it is. Er . . . how's it going?"

"So-so. Nothing very startling at the moment. We're just plodding on with all the routine stuff . . ."

Mallard nodded. "Good, good . . . Well, I'll leave you to it, then. Hope you enjoy the book."

If I ever get time to read it, thought Thanet gloomily.

"I must say I never thought the day would come," said Lineham, when Mallard had gone.

"Which day?"

"When Doc Mallard would go around spreading sweetness and light."

"Mmm." Thanet grinned. "He didn't even complain about the fug in here."

"That's what I mean! Mark my words, sir, something's up."

"Such as? No, don't bother to answer that. We've better things to do than sit around gossiping. Come on, let's get all this organized."

Half an hour later they were parking in front of Mrs. May's neglected council house.

"Let's hope she's up," said Lineham.

"You haven't met her yet, have you?"

Lineham shook his head.

"You're in for a treat."

Mrs. May answered the door wearing the sleazy pink satin dressing gown. Once again she was heavily made up, with green eyeshadow this time, and orange lipstick. Thanet was startled to see that today her hair was a bright, glossy brown and much longer, falling in elaborate curls about her shoulders. A wig, then. He wondered what her own hair was like.

"Oh, it's you again."

She led them into the sitting room. The gas fire was on and the room was stiflingly hot. A plate covered with toast crumbs and a half-empty cup of coffee showed that she had been having her breakfast.

"Want a cup?"

Thanet shook his head. "This won't take long."

"Take a pew." She drained the cup, fished a packet of cigarettes out of her pocket and lit one. "What is it this time?"

"The night before last . . . Could you tell us where you were?"

Her eyes narrowed and she blew out a long, thin stream of smoke before answering. "The night Steve was killed, you mean? What are you getting at?"

"Nothing. Just checking something, that's all."

She shrugged. "What's the odds? I got nothing to hide. I was here, of course. Where else would I have been?"

Thanet smiled. "Bingo? Darts match? Having a drink with friends?"

Her mouth twisted. "What friends?"

She glanced at the new bottle of gin on the sideboard and Thanet heard the words as clearly as if they had been spoken. *That's the only friend I've got.*

"So you stay in most evenings?"

"Yeah. Anything wrong in that?"

"Oh no, not at all. And you're sure you were here on Tuesday?"

"I told you." She stubbed out her cigarette, glanced at the sideboard again and laced her fingers together so tightly that the knuckles gleamed white.

Thanet recognized the signs. She wanted a drink. Badly.

"Did you have any visitors that night?"

She stared at him. "Visitors?"

He nodded, waited.

She frowned and her eyes glazed as she thought back, trying to penetrate the alcoholic haze in which her evenings were spent. "No," she said at last.

"You're sure?"

"I was tired," she said defensively. "I fell asleep, in my chair. If anyone came, I didn't hear them."

"And last night?"

"My son came to see me." Her expression softened. "Chris. Thought I might be upset, you know, about Steve."

126

So there were still vestiges of maternal feeling beneath that unlikely exterior. Thanet was glad that he had not asked her outright if Chris had been here the night Steve died. It looked as though she would be prepared to lie, to protect him.

Outside, at the gate, Thanet paused. "Well, Mike, either he didn't come at all, or he came and she didn't hear him, or he came, spent some time with her and she was so drunk she doesn't remember. Take your pick."

"She remembered him coming last night, all right."

"I agree, the third possibility is the least likely."

Lineham shrugged. "If he did come, and she didn't hear him knocking, he obviously didn't mention it when he saw her last night."

"That could be significant. It might well mean he's innocent and it simply didn't occur to him that he'd need an alibi. If he were our man and knew he would need one, I'd have thought it would have been easy enough to persuade her into thinking either that he did come and spend some time with her the previous evening but she simply didn't remember, or to lie outright to protect him. Anyway, we might as well try and check, while we're here. You take the next couple of houses on that side, I'll take this."

As Thanet approached the front door of the house next to Mrs. May's he saw the curtains twitch at the downstairs window. Good, a nosy neighbor, he thought. Just what I need.

He had to wait several minutes before the door opened on the chain. A segment of wrinkled cheek and a wisp of gray hair appeared in the crack, and a bright eye peered up at him.

"Yes?"

Thanet introduced himself and produced his warrant card, cursing a society which forces its frail and elderly to bar themselves into even greater isolation than old age already brings, through fear of violence.

A little claw of a hand plucked it from him and he saw the dull yellow glow as the hall light went on. He waited, beginning to wonder if there was any point, if he was simply wasting time. But he remembered the twitching curtain and that bright, knowing eye and schooled himself to patience. By now Lineham had visited three houses on the far side of Mrs. May's and was approaching this one.

"Anything?" asked Thanet.

Lineham shook his head. "No answer at two of them, the other saw nothing, heard nothing." He nodded at the door. "What gives?" he added, lowering his voice.

"Old lady being cautious."

The eye reappeared at the crack. "What are you whispering about, on my doorstep?"

There was a rattle as the chain was released, and the door swung open.

Mrs. May's neighbor was small and thin to the point of emaciation. She was supporting herself on an aluminum walking frame. She held out Thanet's card. "What do you want?"

He took it from her. "Thank you. We were wondering if by any chance you might have noticed any visitors at Mrs. May's house, next door, the night before last."

"The night before last . . ." She thought for a moment, then said, "Chris came round, knocked on her door. But he couldn't get an answer, went away again." The sharp old eyes said, *And we both know why, don't we?* "Came round last night, too, but that time she let him in. Two nights running, miracles will never cease. Sometimes he don't come near her for months."

"He hasn't got a key?"

"Why should he? Got a house of his own now, I hear."

"What time was this?"

"Look, it's all right for you, with coats on, but I'll freeze to death if I stand here much longer. You better come in."

128

They followed her painfully slow progress along the hall into the sitting room, where she shuffled to an upright armchair in front of the gas fire and subsided into it with a sigh of relief. "That's better." The large marmalade cat on the hearth glanced sleepily up at her as she spread a blanket knitted in brightly colored patchwork squares over her knees. She looked at Thanet expectantly. "What were you saying?"

"I was wondering if you could remember what time it was that you heard Chris knocking on his mother's door, the night before last."

"Just before the nine o'clock news," she said promptly.

"You're sure of that?"

"My joints might be a bit creaky, but I've still got all me marbles, you know." And she tapped her head, as if to demonstrate the soundness of her brain. "I've got arthritis, see, and once an hour I makes meself get up and walk around a bit. Otherwise I'd seize up altogether. And I always takes my little stroll around the room just before nine o'clock because I likes to sit down after, and watch the news. And one of the things I always does is take a look out of the window. That's when I saw Chris."

"You're sure it was him?"

"Dead sure. I've lived in this house for forty years, haven't I? Known him since the day he was born. Known the lot of them."

"Have you indeed?"

Thanet's tone had betrayed his interest and she gave a high-pitched cackle of laughter and rocked a little, hugging herself with glee. "I have. If you want to know all about them next door you've come to the right place."

fourteen

Thanet glanced at Lineham, who unobtrusively took out his notebook.

"So, Mrs. . . ."

"Sparrow," she said, with so broad a smile that her false teeth slipped. She pushed them back in impatiently, in a gesture that was clearly habitual.

Thanet looked at the small, bent figure with its little beak of a nose, twig-like limbs and tiny claws of hands and wondered if the name had always suited her as well as it did now. He smiled back.

"So, Mrs. Sparrow, you're saying that you've lived next door to Mrs. May ever since her first marriage?"

The cat stood up, stretched and looked at its mistress, and she patted her lap. It jumped up, turning round and round several times before finally settling down with its front paws neatly tucked under. She began to stroke it and it started to purr.

She nodded. "Seen her husbands come and go, haven't I? And a rotten picker she was, too. Bad apples, both of them, not like my Bert. Mind, I'm not saying they had much of a bargain, either. Though to be fair, her and Fred, her first, didn't have much of a chance, really. Not much more than kids, either of them, and to be lumbered with twins before they'd been married five minutes . . ."

"She didn't keep both babies, though, did she?"

"No. That sister of hers, that Mavis, adopted one of them. Insisted on taking her pick, though, so Lena was left with the sickly one, Steve. I tell you, the first time I laid eyes on him I never thought he'd make it. Puny little thing he was, never stopped crying. He used to go on and on and on, you could hear it right through the wall. Really got on our nerves it did. We had to change our bedroom in the end, sleep at the back. Wasn't surprising Fred up and went. Well, I mean, youngsters like that haven't got the patience, have they? I mean, they want to be out having a good time, and a baby soon puts a stop to all that, don't it? And, like I said, Steve was enough to get on anyone's nerves . . ."

"How old was he when his father left?"

"Three or four months. Something like that. But Lena wasn't on her own for long. Fred had only been gone a couple of months when Stan moved in."

"How did she meet him?"

"At the pub, I s'pose. A couple of weeks after Fred went she came to me and said she was desperate to earn a bit of money and she'd heard there was this job at the pub, lunchtimes. Would I look after Steve for her, for a couple of hours each day? I had a cleaning job at the time, but I was home by half past eleven and I was always here midday because Bert used to come home for a bit of dinner, so I said yes. Well, I felt sorry for her . . . Anyway, it wasn't long before Stan was coming home with her and before we knew where we were he'd moved in. Never took to him meself."

"Why was that?"

Mrs. Sparrow shifted uncomfortably in her chair. "Great

big bear of a man, he was. Couldn't understand what Lena saw in him. Still, there's no accounting for taste . . ."

"He made you nervous?"

"You could say that . . . Well, to tell you the truth, I didn't like the way he treated the baby . . . He couldn't stand the sight of it, if you ask me. They was always asking me if I would babysit for them, and some of the things I saw . . . Well, I mean, I know Steve was enough to get anyone down, with that never-ending crying and that, but . . ."

"He used to ill-treat the child?"

Mrs. Sparrow nodded, lips compressed. "You ought to have seen the bruises that baby had on him, sometimes."

"What was his mother's attitude to all this?"

Mrs. Sparrow shrugged. "I don't think she cared, really. I don't think she ever really took to him. Blamed him, I shouldn't wonder, for Fred leaving her."

"Did you report this ill-treatment to the NSPCC?"

The old lady frowned, looked guilty. "Not to begin with. I kept hoping Stan would move out, or things would improve, as Steve got older and didn't cry so much."

"But you did later?"

"Well, Stan and Lena got married, and first Chris then Frank came along, and I kept on hoping that with other kids . . . But things didn't get better, they got worse."

"In what way?"

"Well, Steve was the one they always picked on, both Lena and Stan. He just couldn't do anything right. For instance, the number of times I've seen that kid walking round with his left hand tied behind his back . . ."

"Why? Because he was naturally left-handed, you mean?"

"Yes. I used to say to Lena, what does it matter whether he does things with his right hand or his left, but she wouldn't listen. 'It's all wrong,' she'd say. Or, 'Stan says we've got to get him out of the habit somehow.' But to tell you the truth, I think it was just that they had to have something to pick on, as far as Steve was concerned. I mean, I didn't particularly like him, always whining he was, but then that wasn't surprising, was it, in the circumstances?"

"So what happened, in the end, to make you report them?"

"Well, like I said, Steve used to aggravate Stan that bad . . . One day, when Steve was about four, it was summer, I remember, and I was hanging the washing out in the back garden. There's a high fence that separates us, and I could hear the kids playing next door. Then suddenly I hears Stan's voice. 'Steve!' he shouts, in that great roaring voice of his, 'what the hell do you think you're doing?'

"Well, I was curious to know what Steve had been up to, so I put down the clothes basket and went over to the fence. There was an old box beside it and I stood on that and looked over. I got there just in time to see Stan give Steve a great clout on the side of the head, and then pick him up off the floor and throw him, yes, throw him away from him, towards the back of the house. Steve's head went crack against the kitchen windowsill, and as he fell his foot got caught in one of them little concrete squares they put around drains . . . The ambulance came, that time, and carted him off to hospital. He had a broken leg and concussion, and when I heard Stan and Lena was putting it about that Steve had had an accident by falling off a swing I decided that enough was enough. I put on my hat and coat and went straight off to the hospital. Told them what I'd seen. After that they had the social worker in keeping an eye on Steve. There was talk about putting him into care, but that didn't come off. Stan knew he had to toe the line, or there'd be trouble."

"Did they know who'd given them away?"

Mrs. Sparrow grimaced. "Stan saw me looking over

the garden fence, didn't he, so he didn't take long to put two and two together. Came round here breathing threats, but my Bert soon told him where to get off. 'You lay a finger on her and I'll get the police round,' he said. 'And you're in enough trouble over Steve, already.' "

"So that was that? When Steve came home there were no more problems?"

"I wouldn't say that. Six months later Stan upped and went, and Lena always blamed me for that. Said Stan couldn't stand having the social services breathing down his neck all the time, and it was all my fault he'd gone. I was an interfering busybody and if I'd kept my mouth shut everything would have been all right. 'Yes,' I said, 'for everyone but Steve. What about him? You can't just stand by and see a kid being knocked about like that.' "

"What did she say?"

"Nothing. Just gave me a look as if to say, 'Why not? It didn't worry me.' "

"So what happened after her husband left? How did she treat Steve then?"

"Well, at least she didn't knock him about, I'll grant her that. Stan was the one who did that. But she still used to pick on him something terrible. Not that we was ever on what you might call visiting terms, after that bust-up over reporting them to the hospital. But living next door you can't help hearing sometimes, can you? I mean, in the summer the windows are open, and sometimes you're in the garden . . . Nothing he ever did was right. It's not surprising he turned out like he did."

"What do you mean?"

"Well, he got into this way of needling people, if you see what I mean. Like as if he'd said to himself, nothing I can say or do is going to make people like me, so I might as well give them a good reason."

"He used to behave like that with his brothers?"

"Oh yes. Especially with Chris. Chris was his mum's

favorite, see, and it was as plain as the nose on your face that Steve was jealous. Not surprising, really. Used to make me sick to see the difference in the way those kids were treated."

"What about Frank?"

"He was sort of pig in the middle. He wasn't favored in the same way as Chris, but he wasn't picked on, like Steve."

"And Geoff?"

"Who? Oh, that twin of Steve's . . . Haven't set eyes on him for years. Mavis went up in the world like a skyrocket, by all accounts, and he's much too posh for the likes of the Orchard Estate." The twisted hands were still rhythmically stroking the cat and for a few moments there was silence while they all thought over what she had been saying. Then she sighed. "And now look what's happened. Poor Steve. Went a bit too far, this time, I daresay."

"So it doesn't surprise you, that it came to this in the end?"

"Not really. Can't help feeling sorry for him, though. He never really had a chance to make the best of himself."

The cat raised its head sharply, there was a knock at the door, and Mrs. Sparrow looked at the clock. "That'll be Janet, my home help. D'you think you could let her in?"

Lineham stood up. "Sure."

The girl who followed Lineham into the sitting room was a surprise to Thanet. She couldn't have been more than eighteen and was wearing jeans and a boxy nineteen-forties-style fur jacket. Her hair was brilliantly streaked in fluorescent colors, orange, green and yellow.

"Hullo Janet, love," said Mrs. Sparrow, her face lighting up with pleasure.

"Got visitors today, have we?" said Janet teasingly.

"We're just going," said Thanet.

"Would you like a cuppa, before you go?" said Mrs. Sparrow. "Janet's just going to make me one."

"Sure, no trouble," said Janet. "Won't take a tick."

Thanet declined, politely, and they left.

"Life is full of surprises, isn't it?" said Thanet as they got into the car.

"Janet, you mean? Seemed a nice girl."

Thanet shook his head in self-disgust. "You'd think we'd have learned by now that you can't judge by appearances. If I'd seen her in the street . . ."

Lineham grinned. "Wait till Bridget starts dyeing her hair orange."

The radio crackled. There was a message for Thanet. Someone had come into the police station asking to see the officer-in charge of the murder investigation. He was refusing to talk to anyone else.

"We'll be there in ten minutes," said Thanet.

fifteen

Back at the station Thanet went straight to the inquiry desk.

"This man who's asking to see me. Do we know what it's all about?"

"Not really, sir. He wouldn't say. Just said he had some information about the murder and asked for the officer in charge. I told you you were out and I wasn't sure when you'd be back, but he said he'd wait. I gave him a cup of tea and put him in interview room four."

"What's his name?"

"Bennet, sir." The station officer glanced at the Occurrence book. "Lives in Pearson Road, number 15."

"A crank, d'you think?"

"I wouldn't say so, sir. Very sensible sort of chap. Well, you'll see for yourself."

Mr. Bennet was in his early seventies, tall, thin and mournful. Everything about him seemed to droop—hair, mustache, the pouches under his eyes, the corners of his mouth. He was neatly but shabbily dressed in an old fawn raincoat and a brown suit which, judging by the frayed cuffs, had seen better days. The collar of his white shirt was creased and slightly grubby. A widower finding it difficult to cope on his own?

Introductions over, Thanet sat down. "I understand you have some information for us?"

Bennet nodded. "I hope I'm not wasting your time . . ."

Thanet gave a reassuring smile. "I can't tell until I've heard what you've got to say, can I? But in any case, we much prefer members of the public to come to us if anything is bothering them . . ."

"On the television the other night . . . It said you were trying to trace a jacket . . ."

So whatever the information was, it concerned Hines's case, not his. Thanet was disappointed. He glanced at Lineham who, as he expected, was looking interested. Although the sergeant had been taken off the Coddington murder, he had worked on it long enough to want to know the outcome.

"That's right."

"It was very unusual, it said. Gray leather, with a red dragon on the back."

"Yes. You've seen someone wearing it?"

Bennet nodded. "Boy across the street. Well, a youth, really."

"He lives across the street from you, you mean?"

"Yes."

"So you know his name."

"Kevin Quarry."

"You noticed him wearing the jacket before the television appeal?"

"Oh no. No. I saw him wearing it this morning, for the first time."

"I see . . . Well, we're really most grateful to you for coming in . . ."

After getting all the relevant details Thanet thanked Mr. Bennet for the information then rang Hines, who listened in silence, grunted and then rang off without a word of thanks.

"What did he say?" said Lineham.

"Not a lot," said Thanet, noncommittally.

"Probably furious that the information came to us, first."

The telephone rang. It was one of the men who had been checking up on cars seen in the vicinity of Steve's flat, the night of the murder. One of them, apparently, had belonged to Ivor Howells.

"What time was this?"

"Between eight forty-five and nine in the evening, sir."

"Good. Well done," said Thanet. He put the phone down and told Lineham.

"So," said the sergeant. "I bet what happened was that when he got home he managed to get out of Sharon that Steve had been round to see her, and he decided he'd teach Steve a lesson once and for all."

"Maybe. But the question is, what happened when he got there? Did he manage to see Steve? If Frank's story is true, at half past eight Steve wasn't answering his door, and we have no idea as yet whether he was already dead or had simply slipped out for a while."

"Perhaps we'll know more after talking to Carpenter, sir."

"Quite." Thanet sighed. "Though I have a sneaky feeling we're not going to come away from the hospital with a nice cut and dried solution. Have they rung yet, by the way?"

"No, sir. Any minute now, I should think. It's twenty past eleven, surely the doctor should have finished his rounds by now."

Thanet shrugged. "Anyway, I think Howells has got some explaining to do, in view of the fact that we now have proof that he lied to us. But I think we'll wait to see him again until after we've talked to Carpenter."

Just before twelve the hospital rang through to say that Carpenter was now fit for a brief interview.

He was in a small side-ward, up and dressed and sitting in an armchair beside the bed. Head bowed, hands clasped loosely in his lap, he seemed to have shrunk since Thanet last saw him. When Thanet entered the room he slowly raised his head and gazed at him without recognition. Thanet experienced a painful shaft of empathy. If it had been Joan who had been killed in that accident, Sprig who had just died after being kept alive for a year or more on life support machines . . . Mentally, he shook himself. He couldn't allow himself to think that way.

"Good morning, Mr. Carpenter."

Formalities over, Thanet and Lineham drew up two of the stools provided for visitors and sat down.

"Now then, Mr. Carpenter, I suppose you can guess why we're here."

Carpenter gazed at him blankly, without response.

"We'd like to talk to you about the night before last. Tuesday night."

Carpenter frowned, blinked.

"Do you remember anything about that night?"

"No. I . . ." Carpenter's voice trailed away. It was hoarse with disuse, and he cleared his throat, shook his head. "No," he said again.

Thanet sighed inwardly. This was going to be difficult. It was his duty to try to activate those memories, but he was well aware that by doing so he would also have to tear down the barrier with which Carpenter had anesthetized himself against the pain of remembering. Nevertheless, a man had been killed, and the loss of one human life does not justify the unlawful taking of another.

"We found you sitting in your car, just before midnight, in Hamilton Road. You had been drinking heavily."

Carpenter frowned again, trying to relate this information to himself. "Hamilton Road . . ." he murmured.

Thanet saw his expression change, his features slacken in shock then begin to harden, settle into grim lines of mingled anger and despair.

"I see you have recalled what Hamilton Road means to you. It was where Steven Long lived."

Carpenter's lips tightened at the mention of Long's name. For a moment he was silent, then he said slowly, "Did you say 'lived'?"

"Yes. He was killed, in his flat, on Tuesday night."

For several moments Carpenter stared blankly at Thanet, and then gradually, painfully, his features began to change. A spark of animation appeared first in his eyes and then a slow tide of color began to creep up his neck and suffuse his face. He licked his lips, as if his mouth had suddenly gone dry.

It was almost like watching a dead man come back to life, thought Thanet.

"So," Carpenter murmured at last, in a tone of wonder, "I did it after all." His voice strengthened, and he made no attempt to hide the triumph in it. "I actually did it!"

"Did what?" Thanet knew what the man was going to say, of course, but he felt none of the usual rush of relief at a confession.

"Killed him, of course." Carpenter had straightened up and his whole demeanor had changed. He was no longer vanquished but a conqueror.

"Perhaps you'd better tell us about it."

Something in Thanet's tone must have betrayed his skepticism because Carpenter looked at him sharply and said, "Well, aren't you going to caution me?"

Thanet doubted if there was any point, at this stage, but he decided to play it by the book. He nodded at Lineham, who duly delivered the familiar words.

Carpenter was watching Thanet's face. "You don't believe me, do you?"

"I'm not sure what to believe at present, Mr. Carpenter. One moment you're saying you don't remember a thing about Tuesday night, the next you're saying you killed a man."

"I didn't remember at first, no," said Carpenter. He leant forward in his chair, eager to convince Thanet of the validity of what he was saying. "But that was because I've been ill. Then, when you mentioned Hamilton Road, I suddenly remembered . . . It all came back to me . . ."

"What, exactly, did you remember?"

"Driving to Hamilton Road. Sitting in the car in front of that Gothic monstrosity where Long lives—*lived*—having a drink to bolster my courage . . . I am not by nature a violent man, Inspector."

And with any luck, thought Thanet, that nature might have saved you. "What time was this?"

Carpenter frowned. "I'm not sure . . . Late afternoon, I think."

"You can't be a little more precise?"

Carpenter hesitated. "Somewhere between six and half past?"

Thanet noted the question in his voice. "But you can't be certain?"

Carpenter shook his head.

He was beginning to sweat, Thanet noticed. Was he really fit for questioning, after all? Perhaps it would be best to leave it for the moment, come back later, tomorrow, perhaps. In the circumstances it seemed positively inhuman to press the man like this. But if Carpenter really had killed Long, it was grossly unfair to all the other people involved, to have to go on feeling themselves under suspicion, if by a further few minutes' conversation the truth might emerge.

"Never mind," said Thanet gently. "Tell us what you did when you got there."

"I . . . I sat in the car for a minute or two." Carpenter took a handkerchief from his pocket and passed it over his forehead, then gave a wry smile. "I was trying to pluck up the courage to go up and tackle Long, I think."

"And then?"

"I went up to his flat, knocked at the door."

"And?"

"He opened it." Carpenter suddenly began to talk very fast, the sweat beginning to trickle down his forehead and drip into his eyes. He brushed it away impatiently with the back of one hand. "I was wearing a hat that I'd pulled well down to shadow my face. He'd seen me at the inquest and I didn't want him to recognize me. I thought he might not let me in. I said I'd heard he was a very good mechanic, specialized in solving difficult problems, and I wondered if he'd be prepared to take a look at my car . . ." The words were tumbling out now, becoming almost incoherent, Carpenter's breath coming in irregular, panting gasps.

Thanet rose and pressed the buzzer, and almost at once a nurse came into the room. She took one look at the patient and reached for Carpenter's pulse.

"We'll go," said Thanet. And he hustled Lineham out of the room.

"Just when we were on the point of getting a full confession!" said Lineham in disgust, when they were in the corridor.

"Yes, well there are certain limits beyond which I'm not prepared to go," said Thanet.

"Oh I'm not saying we should have gone on, sir. Just that it was so frustrating to have to stop just there."

"Couldn't be helped."

Lineham glanced sharply at Thanet. "You don't believe he did it, do you, sir?"

"I honestly don't know. Do you?"

They walked in silence for a moment, oblivious of the busy life of the hospital teeming around them.

"I'm not sure either," said Lineham at last. "He did admit to it, and on the face of it he does seem the obvious choice . . ."

"But?"

"Well, at the end when he was speaking so fast . . . In a way you felt you had to believe him, he was giving us so much detail, but I don't know . . ."

"You didn't feel he was telling the truth?"

Lineham hesitated. "I think he was telling us what he *believed* to be the truth, and at the time yes, I did believe him, but thinking about it now, I'm not convinced it was what really happened."

"That's what I thought. I'm not sure if, in fact, what he was doing was describing a scene that he had enacted so often in fantasy that, when he heard Long really had been murdered, it became for him the reality. That's why yes, it was frustrating to have to stop at that point. If he'd been able to go on for just a few more minutes and describe the actual murder, we'd have known if it really was the truth or not."

"So you still think it could be?"

"Well, as you say, he is the obvious choice, the man with the most powerful motive of all . . . And we have to face the fact that it often is the obvious suspect who turns out to be the murderer."

Lineham paused in the act of opening the car door. "Well, I hope that in this case it doesn't." He got into the car and slammed the door, hard.

Thanet got in beside him. "Mike, don't tell me that that heart of stone is softening at last, and you're actually sorry for the man?"

"Knock it off, sir. Don't try and tell me you don't feel exactly the same, because I wouldn't believe you."

"You're quite right, Mike, and I apologize. I do feel

exactly the same. Nevertheless, we have to face the fact that he might well turn out to be our man, in the end."

"I know. In that case the only consolation would be that he wouldn't get much of a sentence, in the circumstances. Might even get a suspended."

"Possibly."

"So, what now, sir? Are we going to see Howells?"

"Yes, but I think we'll take a breather first, get a bite to eat."

"How about the Cow and Mistletoe, sir?"

"Down on the river, isn't it? I've passed it but I've never actually been in."

"I go there quite a bit. The food's good and it's very quiet at lunchtimes. Gets a bit crowded in the evenings, though."

Thanet buckled his seat belt. "Lead me to it," he said.

sixteen

The Cow and Mistletoe was everything Lineham had promised, quiet and unpretentious. While they waited for the food to arrive, the sergeant went off to check Howells's whereabouts.

"He rang in this morning to say he was sick," Lineham reported when he came back, "so he's probably at home. D'you want him brought in for questioning?"

"No, we'll go to the flat. With any luck we might find Sharon there, too. Kill two birds with one stone. This looks good."

The food had arrived and Thanet tucked in to a generous slice of succulent cold beef and a baked potato, garnished with a salad which was more adventurous than usual, while Lineham enjoyed a homemade leek and potato soup and a ploughman's lunch of hot, crusty French bread and well-matured cheddar. The beer was good, too, and the two men left feeling well-fortified against the cold.

"Shouldn't think the temperature's risen above freezing all day," said Thanet, turning up his collar and pausing to admire the inn sign, which depicted a rather endearing cross-eyed cow standing under a huge branch of mistletoe growing from the fork of an apple tree.

"I rather like this weather," said Lineham, gazing at the river sparkling in the sunlight. "Just the day for a good, brisk walk along the towpath. That's how I discovered this place."

"Not much chance of that today, Mike. Come on, let's see if Howells is at home."

Sharon answered the door.

"Good afternoon, Mrs. Long. Is Mr. Howells in?"

"Who is it, Shar?" Howells loomed up behind her. "Oh, it's you again."

"I'm afraid so. Could we have a word?"

Howells stepped reluctantly back and putting an arm around Sharon's shoulders led the way into a depressing sitting room. All along the outer wall the ceiling was blotched and stained with damp, and in one corner it sagged dangerously. In many places the peeling wallpaper had been torn away, revealing irregular areas of crumbling gray plaster, and the battered furniture looked as though it had passed through countless salerooms.

In all this drabness Sharon looked as out of place as a fairy in a pigsty. She was wearing a spotless long-sleeved white blouse with frills at neck and wrist and a bright red corduroy skirt gathered in to a wide belt which emphasized her tiny waist. Her spun-gold hair seemed to halo her head with light. It was easy to see why Steve had been so reluctant to let her go, why Howells had been determined to hang on to his prize.

He was still standing with his arm possessively around her shoulders.

"What do you want?"

"Perhaps we could sit down . . ."

Howells gave a grudging nod.

"I'm glad to see you're feeling better, Mr. Howells," said Thanet pleasantly, when they were all seated.

Howells frowned. "Feeling . . . ?"

"We understood you'd reported sick, this morning."

"Ah, yeah . . . I was feeling a bit off, wasn't I, Shar? Had a bit of a temperature, so I thought it would be stupid, like, to go and work outside all day in this cold."

Thanet's guess was that Howells had simply wished to spend the day with Sharon, fearing, perhaps, that if he left her too long under her mother's influence she might not want to come back to him. Thanet couldn't really see Mrs. Pinfold approving of her daughter's latest boyfriend, and who could blame her?

"And I hope you're feeling a little better today too, Mrs. Long."

Once again Thanet noticed her fondness for jewelry. Presents from Steve? he wondered.

Sharon bit her lip, nodded. "It was going to . . . to identify him, that . . ."

"I do understand," said Thanet, gently. Anticipating that Howells's reaction to being confronted with a lie might be somewhat disruptive to the interview, he had already decided to tackle Sharon first.

"My sergeant has a few points to raise with you. Do you feel up to answering some questions?"

Sharon glanced at Howells, who shrugged. "Yes," she said softly. Then, "Yes," she repeated, more emphatically. "Of course. If it'll help."

Thanet glanced at Lineham. *Take over, then.*

"The first question we have to ask you, of course, Mrs. Long, is whether your husband had any enemies."

"Enemies." She gave an uncomfortable little laugh and her eyes flickered in Howells's direction. *His biggest enemy is sitting right beside me.* "No," she said. "Not what you'd call enemies."

"What do you mean, exactly?" said Lineham.

"Well . . . Steve wasn't very easy to get along with. He . . . he tended to put people's backs up. But not to that extent. Not so they'd want to *kill* him."

"There was that bloke who . . ." Howells snapped his fingers. "Hey, that could be it!" he said excitedly. "You know, Shar, the bloke whose wife was killed in that accident."

"Mr. Carpenter, you mean?"

"That's it, Carpenter. I heard on the radio his daughter died, on Tuesday . . . And on Tuesday night Steve was killed . . . Yeah, that's *it*, it must be." He turned back to Thanet. "There's your answer."

He leaned back in his chair with the air of a man who has satisfactorily disposed of a knotty problem and gave Thanet a smug grin. *It's easy when you know how.*

"One of many possible answers, Mr. Howells."

"Oh come on, Inspector." Howells leaned forward in his eagerness to make his point. "It's obvious, isn't it? I remember now, Carpenter actually threatened to kill Steve, didn't he, Shar, after the court case when Steve got off with a suspended sentence . . ."

"We are aware of all this, Mr. Howells," said Thanet. "And believe me, we're bearing it in mind. But we can't afford to neglect other possibilities." He ignored Howells's derisive snort and turned to Sharon, his voice softening. "So you can't make any other suggestions as to who might have wanted to kill your husband?"

She shook her head. "Not want to *kill* him," she repeated.

Thanet nodded and sat back.

Lineham took over again. "Right. Well, the next thing we want to ask you is whether or not you know if your husband came by car, when he visited you after work on Tuesday."

"Well, I didn't actually see the car, of course, but I should think so, because he was here by about twenty to six and he'd have been much later if he'd had to walk or catch a bus."

"But you've no idea if it was his own or if he got a lift."

"No. But it would be unusual for him to beg a lift. If there was anything wrong with his car, he could usually put it right pretty quick. And it's only a few months since he was allowed to start driving again, after that disqualification. He loves . . . used to love driving. He'd never let anyone else drive him if there was any chance of doing it himself."

"But you don't actually *know* how he got here on Tuesday?"

She shook her head.

Lineham reached into his pocket. "Perhaps you could now take a look at this photograph."

He handed it over and she took it by the corner, gingerly, looking apprehensive.

"Oh, you needn't worry," said Lineham. "It's nothing distressing. Just a picture of the top of the sideboard, in your husband's flat." He leaned forward, pointed. "What we're interested in is this clean, circular patch in the dust. Could you tell us what usually stood there?"

"That's easy enough. A big round ashtray Geoff gave Steve. He brought it back from a holiday in . . . Italy, I think it was."

"What was it made of?"

"A pinkish marble."

"Heavy?"

"Oh yes, ver—" She broke off abruptly and her eyes dilated. "Are you saying . . . D'you mean . . ." She gave the photograph a dazed look, her face crumpled and she began to cry, turning her head into Howells's chest.

He folded his arms around her protectively and murmured into her ear, glowering at Lineham across the candyfloss curls. *Now look what you've done.*

Lineham raised his eyebrows at Thanet and gave a helpless shrug.

Thanet shook his head. *Not your fault. The question had to be asked.*

"I didn't mean to distress you, Mrs. Long," said Lineham.

"Rubbish," snarled Howells. "You couldn't care less, as long as you get what you want."

"We have a job to do, Mr. Howells," said Thanet. "And, believe it or not, we don't like upsetting innocent people unnecessarily."

"Then you shouldn't choose the bloody job in the first place!"

"Someone has to do it. Just as someone has to repair the roads ... Anyway, we're getting off the point. The point is, that we have only one or two more questions to ask Mrs. Long, then she could go and lie down, if she wishes. Perhaps you could make her a cup of tea ..."

Howells was not deceived, and Thanet had not expected him to be. The message was clear. *We want you out of the room for a few minutes.* He hesitated then eased away from Sharon, put his forefinger under her chin and tilted up her head so that he could see her face. Taking out a grubby handkerchief he gently wiped the tears from beneath her eyes. "Would you prefer me to stay, Shar? I will if you want me to." He pressed the handkerchief into her hand.

She blew her nose, sniffed, shook her head. "I'm OK."

"You'd like a cuppa?"

She essayed a smile. "Yeah, I would. Ta."

He went out, leaving the door ajar, and without a word Lineham got up and closed it.

Thanet leaned forward, lowering his voice. "Now then, Mrs. Long, I'll make this as quick as possible. First, can you remember exactly what time Mr. Howells got back here on Tuesday night, after helping his friend to move the furniture?"

She hesitated and a faint color crept into her pale cheeks. "About half past eight, I think."

She was a bad liar, thought Thanet. No doubt Howells had put her up to this.

"But I couldn't be sure," she added quickly. "I was washing my hair, you see . . ."

Thanet nodded. He had no intention of putting any pressure on her at this stage. She was in too fragile a state. Later on, if the point became crucial, yes. "There's just one other matter, then. When your husband came here on Tuesday, did he by any chance bring you a present?"

She stared at him. "How did you . . . ?"

"A rather expensive present, perhaps?"

She bit her lip, glanced uneasily towards the door and nodded. "A gold bracelet. Steve was ever so upset, because I didn't want to take it, in fact I refused. I knew Ivor would be mad, if I accepted it . . ."

"So what happened to it?"

"Steve wouldn't take it back. Said he'd bought it for me and I was going to keep it. He tried to persuade me to put it on, but when I wouldn't he just put it down on the table and left it there, when he went."

"So where is it?"

"I'll get it." She hurried from the room.

It was a heavy gold link bracelet, with a tiny gold padlock and safety chain.

"What shall I do with it?" she said despairingly. "I don't want to keep it, it would always remind me of what happened to Steve that night."

"May I make a suggestion?"

She nodded, eagerly, and he explained the trick that Steve had pulled on Frank over the television set. She was clearly upset at the news that Frank had lost his job as a result.

"It was his wife's idea that your husband might have

done it in order to have some spare cash with which to buy you a present. What I would suggest is that you give the bracelet to Frank, so that he can sell it and give the money back to the man your husband defrauded."

"I will." She shook her head in despair. "Oh Steve . . ."

"Shar?" called Howells.

Quickly she snatched up the bracelet.

Howells came in. "I've put your tea on the table by the bed."

"I'll go and fetch it," she said, rising. "I'm all right, now."

"I think it would be best if you did lie down for a while, Mrs. Long. I want to talk to Mr. Howells for a few minutes."

She hesitated, nodded. "All right." She left, the clenched fist holding the bracelet concealed in the folds of her skirt.

"My turn for a grilling, eh, Inspector?" said Howells, sitting down and folding his arms belligerently across his chest. Now that Sharon had left the room he was allowing his animosity free rein.

"Your word, not mine," said Thanet. "But the matter is fairly simple. We just want to know why you lied about your movements on Tuesday night."

Howells tensed, and Thanet was reminded of his first impression of the man. He looked feral, dangerous.

"What do you mean?"

"Well, according to what you told us yesterday, on Tuesday evening you went straight from work to help a friend who was moving house. You then came directly home, arriving here at about eight thirty. You had supper and then you and Mrs. Long went out for a drink with some friends, returning here at around eleven fifteen."

"So?"

"If all this is true, perhaps you would explain how

your car came to be parked in Hamilton Road—*Hamilton Road*, Mr. Howells, where Steven Long lived—between eight forty-five and nine o'clock that evening?"

Howells's eyes glittered like cut jet. "You have to be joking."

"Far from it, Mr. Howells. On the contrary, I'm very serious."

Howells lifted his hands in apparent incomprehension. "It's obvious. Someone has made a mistake."

Thanet shook his head. "No mistake."

"But it must be. Or they're lying."

"To what purpose?"

"Well, to land me in it, obviously."

"And who do you suggest 'they' are?"

"Search me."

"So you absolutely deny being anywhere near Hamilton Road on Tuesday night."

Howells folded his arms. "Absolutely."

As they walked down the interminable flights of stairs Lineham said, "You're not going to let him get away with it?"

Thanet shrugged. "Depends on whether we eventually decide it's important or not. I certainly don't intend pulling him in at this stage. We'll leave him to stew for a while."

"I must say I wouldn't like to have him for my enemy on a dark night."

"Dangerous, I agree."

"But did he do it? That's the question."

"Patience, Mike. One thing's certain, if he did, we'll get him, in the end." Thanet wished that he felt as positive as he sounded.

In the car a message came over the radio: Chief Inspector Hines was at the station, waiting to see Thanet.

"Did he say why?"

"No, sir. But they've picked up the boy with the jacket. He's in one of our interview rooms."

154

"And Mr. Hines?"

"In the canteen, with the rest of his team. Said they might as well grab some food while they could."

"Tell him I'll be with him shortly."

Thanet glanced at Lineham. "Hear that? Better put your foot down, Mike. We've a treat in store."

"That," said Lineham, "is a matter of opinion."

seventeen

At this hour in the afternoon the canteen was deserted except for Hines and his team, DS Draycott and DCs Roper and Flint. An aura of celebration surrounded them.

"Good grief, sir, he's actually smiling," whispered Lineham as he and Thanet approached the table.

It was true. With a broad grin on his face Hines looked positively unfamiliar. He was a mountain of a man, tall and grossly overweight, with a thick neck, balding head and small, piggy eyes sunk in folds of flesh.

"Ah, Thanet," he said. "Our TV appeal paid off, then."

"He's confessed?"

"Not yet," said Hines. He glanced around at his men and winked. "But he will. Any minute now. We're just leaving him to sweat it out for a while."

"Good . . . You wanted to see me, sir?"

"Just wondered how your own case is going."

"Slowly."

"Ah." Hines leaned back, tucking his thumbs into the armholes of his waistcoat, which strained across his huge belly in a series of horizontal creases. "You know your trouble, don't you, Thanet?" He glanced around at his men, to make sure he had their attention. "You're too soft."

He curled his meaty hand into a fist and thumped the table. "Punch, that's what you need, punch—metaphorically speaking, of course." He waited for the dutiful little ripple of laughter from his team. "Go in there and let them have it, I say. It's the only way."

That is a matter of opinion, you great fat insensitive oaf. But Thanet had no intention of allowing himself to be drawn into an undignified argument in front of junior officers. "We can't all work in the same way."

Hines sat forward. "Tell you what, Thanet, chummy's just about ready to cough now, by my reckoning. Why don't you come down and see how it's done, eh?"

Thanet sensed rather than saw Lineham tense beside him and flashed him a warning glance. He knew that Hines was deliberately trying to needle him and had no intention of giving him the satisfaction of seeing that he had succeeded. It was obvious that the chief inspector was still smarting from having to return Lineham before he was ready to do so.

"I've got rather a lot on my plate at the moment, sir. Some other time, perhaps."

He turned away and was startled when Hines, moving surprisingly fast for such a heavy man, was at his side in a flash, grasping him by the arm and hustling him towards the door. "Oh come on, Thanet. This shouldn't take too long."

Unthinkable that he should allow himself to become involved in a brawl with a superior. Short of tearing his arm out of Hines's pincer-like grip or shoving him away with his left hand, Thanet had no option but to comply. He clamped down on the anger surging through him, took a deep breath and glanced over his shoulder at Lineham. "Mr. Hines seems rather keen to have my company, Sergeant," he said with an attempt at lightness. "Looks as though you'll have to carry on without me for a while."

"Right, sir," said Lineham in a strangled voice, his face wooden. The two DCs studiously avoided looking at Thanet, embarrassed no doubt by their chief's boorish behavior, but Hines's sergeant was watching with something approaching satisfaction. Perhaps he was enjoying the spectacle of someone other than himself suffering humiliation at the hands of his superior.

Hines snapped, "You too, Draycott."

Halfway down the stairs, satisfied that Thanet had resigned himself to accompanying him, Hines released Thanet's arm. "This character fits to a tee the description of the chap seen in the pub on Sunday with Marge Jackson—medium height, slight build, brown hair . . ."

A description which could fit a large proportion of the adult male population of the British Isles, thought Thanet.

"But he's denying the whole thing, of course. Claims he found the jacket in a rubbish heap, yesterday. Some story, eh? Who'd chuck an expensive jacket like that away?"

A murderer trying to get rid of a piece of highly incriminating evidence? thought Thanet. Was Hines really so stupid as not to have thought of this, or had he simply fallen into the all-too-common trap of refusing to consider any explanation which did not fit in with his current theory?

"What's his name?"

"Quarry." Hines gave a great bark of laughter. "Rather appropriate in the circumstances, don't you think?"

"How old?"

"Nineteen. Here we are." Hines flung open the door of the interview room so hard that it crashed against the wall behind and rebounded.

The boy slumped at the table leapt up as if at a signal. "I didn't do it!" he shouted. "I don't know nothing about it!"

He had a bad case of acne, Thanet noticed.

"Oh dear, oh dear, oh dear," said Hines, advancing towards the table. "We are getting upset, aren't we? Now I wonder why that is. Could it be guilt, I ask myself?" He thrust his face to within inches of the boy's and bellowed, "Could it?"

"No! No! I told you, I don't know nothing about it!"

"Sit down," snarled Hines. And when the boy didn't respond, "Sit!" as if he were talking to a disobedient dog. Putting his hand on the boy's shoulder he shoved him down into a sitting position with such force that the chair almost overturned.

"Now listen to me, *Mr.* Quarry, let's get one thing clear. You're not leaving this police station until we've got the truth out of you. If it takes all day and all night, we'll do it, d'you hear me?"

"But . . ."

"Do you?" bawled Hines.

"Yes, but . . ."

Hines turned on his heel and stalked out, nodding to Draycott. *Take over.*

It was obvious to Thanet that they were playing the bad-cop-good-cop routine. Theoretically Quarry, having been frightened out of his wits by Hines, would now respond all the more quickly to an apparently sympathetic Draycott. This had never been Thanet's favorite *modus operandi* and it had little appeal for him even though he knew that it was often highly effective. He followed Hines out of the room.

"He'll crack soon now," said Hines, nodding with satisfaction. "Getting really twitchy, isn't he?"

But for the wrong reason? wondered Thanet. Was it anger, not panic, which had caused Quarry's outburst?

If so, the boy might well be innocent and Hines doomed to disappointment. Thanet felt no shame at the glow of satisfaction that this prospect afforded him.

"What, exactly, did he say about the jacket?"

"Like I said, he claims to have found it in a skip in Masters Road yesterday morning, along with a number of other saleable items."

"What, for example?"

Hines shrugged. "Kid's tricycle, some seat cushions, some old saucepans, a shoebox of cutlery, an old gas cooker, and an assortment of old clothes—a couple of suits, half a dozen dresses, a windbreaker, a few jumpers . . . I've got the complete list somewhere. Someone was moving, I reckon, and had been having a good clear out."

"He's still got all these items at home?"

Hines gave a sarcastic smile. "Of course, Thanet. All lined up for my inspection, just to back up his story."

"What does he claim he did with them, then?"

"Borrowed a van, took them round to a pal of his who runs a junk stall and travels all over the south-east. Different market each day, you know the sort of thing. Quarry claims it's a regular arrangement and they split the proceeds."

"And what does the pal say?"

"Sold the lot, of course, what did you expect him to say? Always back each other up, don't they, these scavengers . . ."

"But Quarry kept the jacket because, presumably, he fancied it?"

"That's the story."

"So, assuming that forensic come up with evidence which proves the jacket to be the one worn by the murderer of Marjorie Jackson . . ."

"They'd better!" said Hines. "Because, get this, Quarry says he didn't wear the jacket until this morning because he wanted to clean it up."

"Ah. So you could have a problem there. But assuming

they do manage to link it with the murder, you have two possibilities. One, that Quarry has owned the jacket all along, and is telling a pack of lies, or two, the real owner saw the television appeal on Tuesday evening, decided it would be wise to get rid of it, and dumped it in the skip later on that same day, or during the night."

Hines gave Thanet a basilisk stare. "The trouble with you, Thanet, is you've got such a convoluted mind you can't see the truth when it's staring you in the face." And swinging around he barged back into the interview room again, slamming the door in Thanet's face.

Thanet stood staring after him for a moment or two. How, he wondered, did anyone like Hines ever manage to reach his present rank? It was enough to destroy one's belief in the efficacy of the promotion system. Fortunately, Hines was the exception rather than the rule. The answer, he supposed, was that no filtering system is completely foolproof.

Lineham looked up and grinned as Thanet entered the office. "Have a good time, sir?"

Thanet gave a noncommittal grunt, determined not to encourage Lineham in criticism of Hines, who was, after all, their superior officer. "Enlightening, perhaps . . . Anything come in?"

"Nothing much. We've had several phone calls from people who saw the lad wearing that jacket this morning. What's his story?"

Thanet told him.

"Makes sense to me," said Lineham. "It's a very striking design, that, with the red dragon on the gray background. Surely, if he'd owned it for some time, someone would have seen him wearing it before today."

"Unless he'd just bought it, say on Saturday, the day before Mrs. Jackson was killed."

"Then surely someone in the shop that sold it to him would have recognized it and come forward."

"You're assuming it was a local shop, Mike, and it

might not have been. The TV appeal didn't go out nationwide, only on TVS."

"Anyway, there'd still have been several days since for him to have been seen wearing it—it's two days, now, since the appeal went out. He obviously didn't see that himself, or he wouldn't have dared wear the jacket today. And it's interesting that it's only this morning, when he claims to have worn it for the first time, that Mr. Bennet spotted him wearing it. Sounds to me as though his story could be true."

"I'm afraid Mr. Hines wouldn't agree with you. Anyway, Mike, intriguing though the problem might be, I think we're letting ourselves get too bogged down in all this. It's not our case, after all . . . What else has come in today?"

Lineham riffled through the pile of reports on his desk. "Let me see . . . It's mostly negative stuff, I'm afraid. We can't find anyone willing to swear either that they did or did not see lights in Steve's flat during the early part of the evening of the murder. So we don't know yet if Steve left these on while he went to see Chris May and still wasn't back by the time Frank arrived at half past eight, or if he switched them off while he was out and put them on again when he got back, which would have meant that he was in when Frank arrived. Though even if he was, he could still have been dead by then, of course."

"Hmm. Have they finished checking over Steve's car yet?"

"Yes. And I asked. There was nothing mechanically wrong with it. So there wouldn't seem to be any reason why he couldn't have used it to go and see Chris."

"But if he did, why didn't he park it outside the house?"

"Quite. Anyway, Frank was pretty positive that it was in the car park at the back of the house in Hamilton Road, at eight thirty."

"So we have to assume either that Steve got a lift to

Chris May's house, which seems unlikely, or that for some reason of his own he parked around the corner, which seems improbable." Thanet sighed. "Ah well, perhaps we'll see daylight in time." He took out his pipe, peered into it, blew through it and began to fill it with tobacco. "Anything else?"

"The chap Steve cheated over the TV seems to be in the clear. He and his wife spent the evening in Tunbridge Wells, and they were over there by six thirty. It was his son-in-law's birthday and they all went out for a meal —confirmed by the restaurant owner. Oh, and you'll be pleased to hear there's no whisper of a pregnant woman being seen in the vicinity of Hamilton Road that evening, so Frank's wife seems to be out of the running."

"Good."

"Apart from that it's just a lot of vague stuff about cars, nothing of any use."

Thanet glanced at his watch. "Then we might as well go and see Chris May again. He should be getting home from school soon."

"If what Mrs. Sparrow said is true, then he'd have had plenty of time to stop off at Steve's flat, either on the way to his mother's house or on the way back."

"I know. And he certainly gave us the impression that he spent some time with his mother, wouldn't you agree?"

"Definitely."

Dusk was falling by the time they drew up in front of the Mays' house in Merridew Road and lights had been switched on in many of the houses, but number 26 was in darkness, the garage doors closed.

"No one home yet, by the look of it," said Lineham. "Shall I go and knock?"

"Might as well."

But as they had expected, there was no reply.

"I suppose we should have made sure he was going to be here," said Thanet. "For all we know he could have stayed at school for some extra-mural activity, or even gone out for the evening. We'll give him half an hour or so, then go."

But ten minutes later a red Metro came up behind them and turned into the Mays' drive. The Mays got out, and Clare May walked around to stand beside her husband as the two policemen approached. The top of her head barely reached his shoulder. She was wearing a red knitted scarf and bobble hat and with her hair in a long plait she looked more like a schoolgirl than a married woman.

"Sorry to trouble you again, Mr. May, but could we have another word?"

"Yes, of course."

He turned and led the way in, switching lights on as he went.

In the hall, his wife unwound her scarf and pulled off the hat. "Did you want to talk to me, Inspector?"

"No."

"It's just that there's always such a lot to do, when I get home from work."

"Do, please, carry on."

She gave him a quick, nervous smile, shrugged out of her coat and hung it in the cupboard under the stairs. Then she disappeared into the kitchen, closing the door behind her.

May, meanwhile, had shed coat and briefcase and gone ahead of them into the sitting room. Thanet gave the mural a lingering glance before following. May was drawing the handsome cream linen curtains.

"Please, sit down," he said, taking up a stance in front of the empty fireplace.

Thanet shook his head. He had no desire to have May towering over him while they talked. "Why did you give us the impression that you spent some time with your mother on Tuesday night, Mr. May?"

"Oh, did I? I'm sorry, I didn't mean to mislead you . . . What I actually said, if you remember, was that I went to see my mother."

"But you did not, in fact, see her."

"No." May stepped sideways and sank into an armchair, hands loosely clasped across his stomach, the epitome of a reasonable man whose behavior has been misinterpreted. "I knocked at her door, but couldn't get an answer."

"And that was at what time?"

"Around nine, I should think. It usually takes about half an hour."

"To get to your mother's house, from here?"

"Yes . . ." May glanced from Thanet's face to Lineham's, then back again, giving a little laugh of comprehension. "I walked, Inspector. And that's how long it takes. About half an hour."

"You didn't tell us this last night. We assumed you'd gone by car."

May gave an eloquent shrug. *I'm not responsible for your assumptions.*

"Your wife can confirm this?"

"Certainly." May waved his hand in the direction of the kitchen. "Ask her, by all means. And I can give you the names of one or two people I met between Merridew Road and the main road."

"You went and returned by the same route?"

"No. I prefer never to do that. I don't like covering the same ground twice."

"Perhaps, then, you could tell us briefly the route you took, both ways."

May reeled off a list of street names.

Thanet listened carefully and when May had finished said, "Your route back would take you to within a few minutes' walk of Steve's flat."

"True. And to be frank with you, Inspector, that

is why I didn't tell you last night that I had walked, not gone by car, and why, admittedly, I deliberately misled you into thinking I'd spent some time with my mother. It was stupid of me, I can see that now. It's just that I thought it would . . . stir things up, unnecessarily. I had nothing whatsoever to do with Steve's death and I didn't want to get involved, if I could possibly avoid it."

"But you already were involved, to a degree."

"What do you mean?"

The relaxed pose had gradually disappeared and by now May was sitting upright, bony knees clamped together, fingers hooked over the arms of the chair.

As May's attitude had slid to one end of the scale, Thanet's had tipped over towards the other. Now he sat down on the settee and relaxed into it.

"Well, the night Steve was killed, you saw him."

"Not by choice," said May, tightly.

"Maybe. But you saw him, nevertheless. What is more, it might interest you to know that you are, so far as we know, the last person in the family to see him alive."

May ran his tongue around his lips, a darting little snake that would no doubt have liked to shoot venom into Thanet if it could. But he was managing to keep his wits about him.

"In the family, you say . . . So someone else saw him after me?"

"Your neighbors saw him leave."

May relaxed a little, closing his eyes in relief.

"Not that that really makes much difference, of course," said Thanet. "The fact remains that on the night he was killed you had every reason to be furiously angry with Steve—when you refused to let him in he made yet another embarrassing scene, causing you further humiliation in front of your neighbors . . . It wouldn't surprise me at all if you decided to follow him home, have it out with him on his own ground, away from here, where there would be no possibility of still more embarrassment."

"No! My wife will tell you. I didn't. We . . . I stayed here, and we had supper together."

"And after supper you walked over to the Orchard Estate, to see your mother."

"That's right."

May was sweating now, and Thanet was becoming more and more convinced that the man was hiding something.

"You were still feeling pretty upset, I imagine."

May made a pretense at nonchalance. "A bit, I suppose."

"You thought the fresh air might clear your head, calm you down, I daresay?"

"Yes, I did."

"And you had absolutely no intention of going to see Steve."

"None." May was beginning to relax.

It was the right moment to attack. "So what made you change your mind?" said Thanet softly.

May stared at him blankly for a moment before fear began to tighten the flesh over the prominent cheekbones, curl the long, bony fingers.

Thanet could almost hear him thinking. *How much does he know?*

"I—I don't know what you mean," he said at last, hoarsely. He cleared his throat.

"Look, Mr. May. You tell us that after leaving here at eight thirty, you walked to the Orchard Estate, which takes about half an hour. We have, in fact, an independent witness who confirms that you arrived there just before nine, and that after finding your mother apparently out, you left. But you didn't arrive home until a quarter to ten. Perhaps you wouldn't mind explaining why a walk which took you half an hour one way, took you three-quarters of an hour the other."

"I explained to you. I came back by a different route. It takes longer."

"I'm a native of Sturrenden, Mr. May, and I really cannot believe that it would have taken you a whole fifteen minutes more to walk home by the route you gave us. But no matter. We can easily check. We'll get someone to walk it, in the morning."

May stared at Thanet, his gaze fixed and unseeing. Clearly, he was thinking furiously, trying to reach some kind of a decision. Then he lifted his hands in a little gesture of surrender and said wearily, "Oh, what's the point? I can see you'll only go on and on till you find out, in the end . . . Yes, I did go to Steve's flat, on the way back. As you say, I decided it couldn't go on . . . All those hideous scenes . . . I decided to have it out with him, once and for all . . . But when I got there, he was out." May leaned forward in his chair, desperate, now, to convince Thanet that he was telling the truth. "I knocked on the door, but there was no reply . . . I knew the lights were on, I'd noticed as I came up the drive . . . But *there was no reply*, I swear it. If Steve was in there, he wasn't answering the door."

"What time was this?"

"About twenty, twenty-five past nine. Something like that, it must have been."

"So what did you do?"

"Knocked again, waited, hung about for a few minutes, in case he'd just slipped out to a neighbor's . . . After a while I decided he must either be out or wasn't going to answer for some reason of his own. But since . . . Well, I've been wondering . . . Do you think he was already dead?"

Thanet did not answer the question. "Did you see anyone, while you were there?"

May shook his head. "No. And I swear, that really is the truth."

"You've already lied to us not once, but twice. Give me one good reason why I should believe you this time."

Outside, Lineham said, "Do you think he was telling the truth, sir?"

Thanet shrugged. "Your guess is as good as mine."

eighteen

It was after midnight when Thanet got home. As he turned into the driveway he could see that the sitting room was in darkness. Not surprisingly, Joan must have gone to bed. This would be the third night running that he had returned to the sleeping silence of his home, and he experienced an uprush of resentment against the work that was keeping him from his wife and children.

After leaving Chris May, he and Lineham had gone back to the office and spent the rest of the day catching up on paperwork and, when that was finished, going right through the entire accumulation of reports on the Steven Long case. This was an exercise that, though tedious, frequently proved invaluable. It was so easy to get so bogged down in detail that you lost an overall view of the case, ignored crucial areas of investigation and, occasionally, became so obsessed by one particular aspect of a case that objectivity was lost. But today the task had proved relatively fruitless. Apart from giving Thanet a clearer picture of the overall shape of Steve's life, they had found no glaring omissions, no unexpected revelations, no coalescing of hitherto apparently unrelated facts to produce a new vision of the truth.

So Thanet was feeling tired, tired and dispirited, and what he needed above all was the company of his wife.

He had thought he was past hunger and thirst, but as usual the light and the electric fire had been left on in the kitchen and there was a note propped against a thermos flask on the table:

> Darling,
> Tea in flask, lager in fridge, lasagne in
> oven. If u can't face latter, please remove
> plate and turn off oven.
> XXXXXXXX
> J.

He stared at the note for a moment, his mind almost incapable of choice. Tea in flask, lager in fridge . . . No, not lager. What he needed was something hot. Tea, then. He unscrewed the flask, poured himself a cup and sipped. The hot liquid slipped down to his empty stomach and gave him a comforting glow. He began to feel that perhaps he could eat something after all. *Lasagne in oven.* Lasagne. He hadn't had lasagne for ages and it certainly sounded more interesting than bangers and chips or even roast meat and two veg. He picked up the oven cloth, opened the oven door, removed the plate and uncovered it. A savory aroma ascended to his nostrils. Ah, yes . . .

He was about halfway through the meal when he heard someone on the stairs. His heart lifted.

"Joan?"

A moment later she came into the kitchen, blinking a little in the bright light and tying the sash of her cornflower-blue dressing gown.

"I hope I didn't wake you."

She shook her head. "I'd only just switched out the

light, when you got home. I took some work to bed with me, and that's always fatal. My mind starts going round and round . . . After I heard you come in, I lay there for a few minutes telling myself I really ought to go to sleep, I'd be tired in the morning, and then I thought oh, what's the point? I'll go and talk to Luke . . . I wasn't sure if you'd feel like eating that or not."

"When I got home, I didn't, but when I took it out of the oven . . ."

Joan laughed. "Sprig'll be pleased."

"She made it?"

"I had to give her something to do, she was driving me mad . . . She's all tensed up about Saturday and there was absolutely nothing else she could do, as far as the competition was concerned. After she finished her homework she was wandering around like a lost sheep. So I said, why not try something new for a change, something completely fresh?"

"Delicious," said Thanet, finishing the last forkful.

"Good. I wasn't sure if you'd like it."

"Why?" he said suspiciously. Then he grinned. "What was in it? Hemlock?"

Joan smiled back. "Deadly Nightshade, as a matter of fact . . . Actually, it was a vegetarian dish . . ."

"Veget . . ." Thanet looked at his empty plate in pretended horror.

Joan rested her chin on her folded hands and gave him a cat-like grin. "It was delicious, wasn't it? I told Sprig I didn't think you'd be too pleased, but she just said you were an old stick-in-the-mud and it would do your taste buds good to be shaken up . . . Oh, by the way, talking of taste buds . . . I have a bit of news for you."

"Oh?" With relief Thanet abandoned his pose of dismay. The lasagne really had been very good, meat or no meat. "What?"

"You remember you were saying how much more cheerful Doc Mallard has been lately?"

"Yes . . . Don't tell me! You've seen him with a woman!"

Joan nodded, eyes dancing.

"Well?" said Thanet impatiently.

"I had lunch in town today and on the way back to the office I was just passing the Black Swan when the door opened and out he came, with this woman."

"What was she like?"

"Gorgeous! Oh, not in the glamorous sense, but sweet and gentle, just what he needs."

"How old?"

"Early fifties, I should say. A little roly-poly type with a lovely smile and the bluest eyes you ever saw. Her name's Helen Fields."

"He introduced you?"

"Why not? We practically bumped into each other. He was so sweet—went all pink and bashful . . . Anyway, you might meet her yourself soon. He was asking after the children, and I told him about the competition on Saturday. He asked her if she'd like to go along, and she seemed quite keen."

"Good." Thanet leaned back, smiling. "That's terrific. I suspected that might be it . . ." His hand had strayed to his pocket and came out holding his pipe. He looked at it regretfully. "I don't suppose I've got time for this. We really ought to go to bed."

"You go ahead and smoke. I feel quite wide awake, I told you. Anyway, it's nice to be able to sit and talk in peace. We hardly ever seem to get the chance these days . . . I think I'll make a fresh pot of tea. Want some?"

Thanet was already filling his pipe. "Please."

Joan's company, the food, this late-night intimacy, had generated a warm glow deep within him and he felt that he would be prepared to sit up all night basking in this pleasant, undemanding domesticity. He watched his wife fondly as she moved about the routine task of making a pot of tea, and thought that it was moments such as this that cemented their marriage. The physical side was important, of course, and he knew how fortunate they were that their lovemaking had become more and more satisfying over the years, but it was the pleasure they found in each other's company that was the bedrock of their relationship. He couldn't understand people who were happily married jeopardizing something so precious for a few cheap thrills. What fleeting excitement, what temporary massaging of one's ego could possibly replace the knowledge that one is known through and through and loved despite all one's faults and foibles?

As for Joan . . . They'd had their ups and downs, of course, and there had been times when he had felt perilously close to losing her, but he was a lucky man, and he knew it.

She dropped a kiss on the top of his head as she put a fresh cup of tea in front of him. Then she sat down opposite him.

"Luke, I was thinking."

"Mmm?"

"About this video business, with Ben. All right, maybe he did get involved thoughtlessly, because he didn't realize the seriousness of what he was doing, but the fact remains that we can't possibly keep him under supervision all the time. Even if we managed to arrange something for the interval between school ending and our coming home, there are still weekends . . . Of course, I'd like to think that now we've talked to him we could trust him not to do it again, and leave it at that. In fact, I think we probably could. I honestly don't believe he would get hooked on such stuff. But we have to accept that at that age it's very important to be one of the crowd and the temptation to join in just because everyone else is doing so is very strong."

"So? What are you suggesting?"

"Well, I know we've always held out against getting a video, for various reasons, but now they've become a fact of life for so many people . . . To be honest, I've been wondering if it wouldn't be sensible to get one of our own."

Thanet grimaced. "I feel as though we're almost being blackmailed into this."

"Oh darling, I don't think that's true. I honestly don't believe Ben is that devious."

"No, I know . . . But all the same, that's how I feel. . . . But I agree, the one advantage of having one of our own would be that we'd have control over what he watches—but even so, it wouldn't be total control. There'd still be nothing to stop him seeing all sorts of pernicious rubbish in other people's houses."

"I think we could get around that by laying down conditions from the start."

"You mean, by saying we'll get one so long as it's on the clear understanding that under no circumstances, unless he has our express permission, would he watch videos hired by anyone else?"

"Something like that, yes. I think it would work. I think he's basically trustworthy, and I think also that he'd be so delighted we've given in, he'd agree to anything."

"What about when the novelty wears off?"

"I think we'd have to make it clear that if we find he's broken the agreement, the machine would go straight back to the shop. We'd hire it, not buy it, of course, for that reason."

"And what then? What if we get it, he goes back on his word, and we get rid of the thing? We'd be back where we started—worse off, really, because Ben would then feel he's got nothing to lose and the reins would be well and truly off."

"One step at a time, darling. I think we'd have to deal

with that situation if it arose. But I honestly don't think it would. Besides, we have to trust him, and I think he'd appreciate being shown that we do."

Thanet lifted his hands in surrender. "All right, we'll give it a try. I agree, it might work."

Joan smiled. "I'll tell them tomorrow." She sat back, satisfied. "Now, tell me how the case is going."

She listened intently as he talked, chin on hand, gray eyes solemn. He had always shared his work with her, right from the beginning. He had seen so many policemen's marriages break up because of irregular hours and broken promises that he had been determined to ensure that exclusion from his work did not erect yet one more, unnecessary barrier between them. When Joan had finally taken the decision to train as a probation officer his resolve had faltered, for the probation service and the police frequently find themselves diametrically opposed. But he had decided to continue and Joan, he knew, had appreciated this demonstration of trust. He himself had certainly never had cause to regret it.

Now and again she interrupted to ask for clarification or amplification, and when he had finished she sat back, looking thoughtful.

"Sounds to me as though Steve was hell-bent on disaster."

"I know."

"It's as if he were impelled to behave so badly that even the people he was closest to would turn against him—Frank, Chris, even his wife, who according to that funny little woman, Mrs. . . . ."

"Mrs. Bence. Dara." Just the memory of her was enough to make him smile.

"That's right, Dara."

"You'd have enjoyed her, love. In fact, you must meet her. I'm sure she'd be pleased. I told her I'd like to go back, some time, and hear all about her days in the circus, and she was tickled pink. You could come with me."

"I'd love to . . . But, as I was saying, according to her, he even treated his wife so badly that in the end she left him, and it really does sound, from his behavior since, that he was still very much in love with her . . . It's the classic rejection syndrome, I suppose. He grew up thinking he was unlovable and had to keep on behaving in such a way as to make people reject him, just to see if they would. Then, when they did, he'd say to himself, 'There you are, I knew they would, in the end.' "

"There speaks the probation officer," said Thanet with a grin. "All the same, I agree with you. But I have the impression that since Sharon left, this process was accelerated. His behavior became more and more outrageous, impossible, almost as though . . ."

"What?"

"I'm not sure. Almost as though he was trying to precipitate some kind of crisis, I suppose."

"And look where it got him," said Joan sadly. "He didn't have much of a life, did he? His mother sounds awful."

"She is."

"And I suppose the fact that his twin did so much better than he . . . It does sound so unfair, doesn't it? What's the twin like?"

"All right. Can't say I really took to him. But he seems to be the only person Steve didn't manage to alienate. I suspect that's because Geoff, the twin, felt distinctly guilty that Steve was so much worse off than he, and was prepared to make considerable allowances for him. And I think he appreciated the misery Steve had suffered as a child, at the hands of his mother and stepfather. He got quite hot under the collar at one point, when he touched on this, in passing."

"Were they close, d'you think?"

"I don't think so, no."

"Strange, isn't it? I thought twins were supposed to have this tremendous empathy."

"Not necessarily, apparently. Doc Mallard gave me a book about it." Thanet reached for his briefcase, delved inside.

"*Monozygotic twins, brought up together and brought up apart*," read Joan. "Hmm. Sounds fascinating. I'd like to read it, after you, if you don't mind."

"Sure . . ." said Thanet abstractedly. His eyes were glazed and he was frowning.

Joan, recognizing the signs, said nothing, continued to leaf through the book, and for a few minutes there was silence in the room but for the faint hum of the refrigerator and the soft flutter of pages turning.

At last Thanet stirred, as if coming out of a long sleep. "You know . . ." he said slowly.

Joan laid the book gently on the table. "What?"

"It's only just occurred to me . . . thinking of Steve and the way he's behaving to the people around him . . . What he's been doing, really, consciously or unconsciously, is systematically destroying what matters most to them."

Joan stared at Thanet, assessing what he had just said. "Yes," she said, finally. "I see what you mean. The most important thing for Frank was security for his wife and the baby, in other words the job he had taken so long to find. And Steve went out of his way to make sure Frank lost it."

"Yes. And as far as Chris is concerned, well, I suppose that what really matters to him is reputation, respectability. He's managed to get himself a decent education, escape from his background, and then along comes Steve and proceeds not only to humiliate him at school, in front of his pupils, but at home, in front of neighbors . . . Then, going outside the family, the same principle applies to our other two suspects, Carpenter and How-ells."

"He was obviously determined to take Sharon away from Ivor Howells. But Mr. Carpenter is different, surely, in that you couldn't say the car accident was intentional, could you? That isn't what you're suggesting, is it?"

"Oh no. But the end result is the same. Carpenter lost what he obviously valued most in the world, his wife and his daughter."

Joan shivered. "It's almost as though he—Steve—had some sort of destructive power, which reached out to the people around him . . . I don't know whether to feel sorry for him or appalled by him."

"Does one necessarily preclude the other?"

"I suppose not." Joan glanced at the clock. "Look at the time! Come on, darling, we'd better go to bed, or neither of us'll be fit for work in the morning."

Reluctantly, Thanet allowed himself to be persuaded up the stairs. He took Mallard's book with him. After such a long day he should be only too eager to get a decent night's rest, but after the discussion with Joan his mind was fully alert and he knew that there was no point in trying to get to sleep just yet. He would only lie there in the darkness, tossing and turning. He would try to read himself into oblivion.

For an hour or more he attempted to do just that, but he had chosen the wrong bedside reading. The book was, as Joan had predicted, fascinating, and confirmed what Mallard had told him. Steve and Geoff were typical in that the most common reason for the separation of twins was the mother's inadequacy, and it was usually the mother's sister or the grandmother who took one of them, a temporary arrangement often becoming a permanent one. The mother often kept the weaker, lighter-born twin, and the home was often poorer, both economically and psychologically. As a result, this twin would often be more neurotic than the one brought up probably as an only child in better circumstances. The first-born twin tended to be heavier and often one of the twins would be left-handed. Thanet found himself constantly relating what he was reading to Steve and Geoff and eventually he decided that the only way he was going to get to sleep was by switching off the light and hoping that he would eventually wind down.

Joan was fast asleep and for a while he tried to empty his mind completely and match the rhythm of his breathing to hers. But it was no good, he simply couldn't do it. In the end he gave up, eased his aching back into a more comfortable position and allowed his thoughts to roam at random.

With his late-night reading fresh in his mind he continued to think for a while about the twins. It was interesting that Geoff was the one person in the family who didn't seem to have washed his hands of Steve—quite the contrary, in fact. Thanet thought of the two birthday cards on Steve's mantelpiece, one from Sharon and one from Geoff, and wondered if Geoff's tender conscience as far as Steve was concerned might even have prompted him to take his twin a present when he visited him on Sunday evening. Steve had seemed depressed, he said, and this wasn't surprising, Thanet thought, in view of what they now knew. The unpleasant scene at Howells's flat, followed by the disastrous incident at the Mays' house, would be enough to depress anyone, let alone someone in such a vulnerable state as Steve. The former, no doubt, had sparked off the drinking which had led to the latter, a chain reaction which had finally culminated in Chris May refusing even to let Steve into the house, when he later came around to apologize on Tuesday. Over the last few days of his life doors were constantly being slammed in Steve's face, it seemed, and apart from Sharon, who was dominated by Howells, Geoff was the one person who had remained sympathetic to him. Guilt, perhaps, as Thanet had suggested to Joan, at having had by far the best of the bargain? Or perhaps because Geoff had not been as close to Steve as the others, nor had his life been disrupted by him.

Thanet lay for a while thinking of those others. Frank, Chris, and Carpenter all admitted going to Steve's flat the night he was killed. Howells had been there too, Thanet was certain of it, despite his having denied it. And always the same story—lights on, no answer to their knock. If only forensic could have come up with some nice, clear, prints, some shred of useful evidence. If only they could have found that ashtray . . .

Thanet turned over, restlessly, and Joan stirred in her sleep, murmuring. He lay quite still until her breathing had resumed its steady rhythm.

Where could that ashtray be? At the bottom of the river, probably, or dumped somewhere, like that jacket young Quarry had picked up. Hines had all the luck. Although Thanet was convinced the youth was innocent of Marjorie Jackson's murder, that jacket would, sooner or later, get Hines his man.

Thanet's eyes snapped open in shock as a truly incredible idea winged its way into his restless mind. What if . . . ?

Suddenly, it was impossible to lie still a moment longer. Mind racing, he slid quietly out of bed, reached for his dressing gown and slipped out of the room.

In the kitchen he went to lean against the sink, gazing out of the darkened window. Was it possible?

He sat down and, elbows on table, head in hands, began to think.

nineteen

Thanet often found that an idea that in the middle of the night had appeared to be a stroke of genius proved in the cold light of morning to be as full of holes as a colander. Not so this time. The moment he opened his eyes his new-found solution to the Steven Long case blossomed in his consciousness, flawless as a rose in high summer.

He couldn't wait to put it to the test. Despite his relatively sleepless night he felt fresh and alert, buoyed up by elation, and he threw back the bedclothes and hurried to the bathroom.

When he went down to breakfast Joan was alone in the kitchen, drinking coffee. She raised her eyebrows as he came in, whistling. "You sound cheerful this morning."

Thanet gave her a beaming smile. "I think I just might have solved the case."

"Really?" She leant across, put a congratulatory hand on his arm. "Darling, that's terrific!"

"Well, don't let's get too excited, just in case I'm wrong.

There are various things I'll need to confirm, before I'm sure.''

"So who . . . ?''

"Sorry, love. I daren't give hostages to fortune. Ask me again tonight.''

"Daddy! You're up early!'' Usually Bridget was down before him in the morning.

He smiled up at her as she came to kiss his cheek. "Some of us have work to do.''

"You won't have to work tomorrow, Dad, will you?''

He put on a blank expression. "Tomorrow? What's happening tomorrow?''

"Daddy! It's the comp . . .'' She saw his face and stopped. "Oh, really!''

He got up. "Don't worry, poppet. Wild horses wouldn't keep me away from the Black Swan tomorrow morning. Your mother and I will be sitting there beaming rays of encouragement and moral support in your direction. None of the other parents will be able to compete, will they, darling?''

Joan laughed. "Of course not.''

At the office Lineham was sitting hunched at his desk, staring dejectedly at a single sheet of paper. Thanet's stomach clenched as he realized what must have happened. The sergeant had failed to get through to the Selection Board.

There was no point in avoiding the issue. "It's come, then.''

Lineham nodded speechlessly.

"And no luck?''

A shake of the head.

Thanet crossed and put his hand on Lineham's shoulder. "I'm sorry, Mike, I really am. But you mustn't be too disheartened. Only a third of those who passed the exams would have got through, you know that.''

"Some consolation! That still leaves me in the two-thirds who'll never make it. I suppose I was a fool to think I could."

"Oh, come on, Mike. Cheer up. Maybe next time . . ."

Lineham shook his head. "Oh no, there won't be a next time, I can assure you of that."

"Why not? The trouble is, Mike, that this has come at a bad time for you, just after Louise has had the baby and you're both tired and on edge from lack of sleep." *Not to mention worried sick that your mother is going to come and live practically next door and start causing trouble right, left and center.* "Just look at you! Bags under the eyes, pasty as an uncooked doughnut . . . In another month or two you'll feel quite differently about it, you'll see."

Lineham shook his head again, vehemently. "No, I've learned my lesson, believe me."

It was, Thanet knew, the right decision. If Lineham hadn't even managed to get as far as the Selection Board, there was little chance that he would ever get through the even more rigorous Promotion Board. He felt desperately sorry for the sergeant and angry with Louise who was, he was sure, responsible for this fiasco. He wondered how she would react, when she heard.

"Have you told Louise yet?"

A despondent shake of the head. "No."

Thanet gestured towards the phone. "I should get it over with."

Tactfully, he withdrew while his sergeant made the call.

"Meanwhile," he said when he went back into the office, deliberately ignoring Lineham's set face, "I've got to admit that from a purely selfish point of view it's a relief that I'm not going to lose the best sergeant I've ever had. I didn't say this before, Mike, for obvious reasons, but I was really dreading having to get used to working with someone else. At the beginning of this case, when you were over at Coddington, I felt as though I was working with my hands tied behind my back."

Thanet was not normally given to making sentimental speeches, but it was the best he could do, to restore just a little the sergeant's battered ego. And it had, in fact, helped, by the look of it. Lineham was looking marginally less gloomy.

"And talking of the case . . ." Thanet went on.

"What?" For the first time this morning Lineham looked at him properly, took in Thanet's air of suppressed excitement. "Don't tell me you've cracked it?"

Thanet held up crossed fingers. "With any luck."

Thanet had anticipated a look of eager inquiry, but instead Lineham merely looked depressed again.

"What's the matter, Mike?"

"I suppose that that alone should have told me I was aiming too high."

"What?"

"The fact that I've never yet got there before you."

"You almost have, on several occasions."

"Precisely. Almost, but not quite. The story of my life."

Thanet could see that if he didn't do something fairly drastic the sergeant would allow himself to sink into a slough of self-pity which would help no one, least of all himself.

"Mike," he said sharply. "No one could be sorrier than I am that you've had this disappointment, but I would remind you that we have got work to do."

Briefly, Lineham compressed his lips and looked hurt, then he shook his head as if to clear it of the preoccupations of the last half an hour and muttered, "Sorry, sir . . . You were saying you think you might have cracked it."

"I was."

"Well?"

"Well what?"

"Aren't you going to enlighten me?"

The sergeant was beginning to look more his usual self, Thanet was pleased to see.

"Not yet, I'm afraid. No, don't groan, Mike. You'll hear soon enough. In fact, I can't wait to hear what you think . . ."

"But sir . . ."

Thanet shook his head. "No, Mike. I want your opinion, but I'm not saying another word until I've confirmed one or two points. So come on, the quicker we get through them the sooner you'll hear what I've come up with."

Lineham gave a resigned shrug.

"Now, first of all, can you tell me what happened about the lad CI Hines brought in for questioning? Did he get a confession?"

"No. He had to let him go. Wasn't too pleased, I gather." Lineham grinned at the understatement. "But the word is he's still swearing he'll get him, sooner or later. He's taken away a whole lot of his clothes, for analysis."

"And the jacket? Did forensic come up with anything to link it definitely with the murder of Mrs. Jackson?"

"I don't know, sir. But what's this got to do with Steven Long?"

Thanet waved a hand. "Patience, Mike. All in good time. Find out for me, will you?"

While Lineham made the phone call Thanet reread the PM report, nodding with satisfaction. Yes, it was as he thought . . .

Lineham put the phone down. "Yes, sir. A couple of hairs, caught around the left-hand cuff button, and traces of her face powder in the crease of the cuff opening."

"Good. Excellent. Right, now I'd like you to go and have a word with Mrs. Bence. This is important, which is why I want you to go yourself. If you remember, she saw Steve going out as she came in, around a quarter to seven on the night he was killed. Ask her if Steve was carrying anything."

"What, for example?"

Thanet shook his head. "I don't want ideas put into her head. Just say 'anything.' "

"Right." Lineham hesitated. "What are you going to be doing, sir?"

"Don't worry, Mike, I'm not going to get up to anything dramatic, like making an arrest, while you're out of the way. I told you, there are various things I've got to check. With any luck, by the time you get back, I'll be finished. What's more, I wouldn't mind betting that by then you'll have worked it out for yourself."

"Fat chance of that," grumbled Lineham, as he left.

As soon as he had gone Thanet consulted his list of queries, then reached for the telephone. First, he rang Sturrenden General Hospital. This piece of information was really crucial to the case he had built up and his stomach churned with anxiety while he was passed from one department to another. At last he found the right person and put his question. Again, there was a long wait, and he found he was gripping the receiver so tightly his fingers were aching. Deliberately, consciously, he relaxed. *Please let them come up with the right answer.*

"Hullo?"

"Yes?" Thanet's voice was hoarse with tension.

"Sorry I took so long. The records took a bit of finding."

"But you've got them?"

"Yes. Shall I read what they say?"

"Please."

He listened, holding his breath. Then relief flooded through him. "Could you repeat that?"

Again, he listened. No, there had been no mistake. "Thank you," he said. "Thank you very much indeed."

"Not at all," said the voice, bewildered. "Only too pleased to help."

Thanet replaced the receiver and sat staring into space. He would have liked to get up and dance for joy. Instead, he looked up the number of the hairdressing salon where Caroline Gilbert worked, the girl Geoff had taken out on the night of the murder.

"Miss Gilbert?"

"Yes." The voice was fresh and young.

"We've not actually met, but my name is Thanet, Detective Inspector Thanet of Sturrenden CID. I'm in charge of the inquiry into the death of Mr. Steven Long. There are one or two questions I'd like to put to you, if I may."

"I told the other policeman, there was no way Geoff could have been involved. He . . ."

"No, you misunderstand me. I wanted to ask you about Sunday."

"Sunday?" Caroline Gilbert sounded bewildered.

"Yes. I understand you went out with Mr. Geoffrey Hunt on Sunday evening, as well as on Tuesday?"

"Well . . . Yes, I did. As a matter of fact, Sunday was my first date with him."

"Would you mind telling me what you did?"

"Well . . . I don't see why not . . . Geoff picked me up at my place. We were going out for a drink. He hadn't told me before, but it was his birthday, and when I got into the car he said he hoped I wouldn't mind if he just dropped a present in at his twin brother's place in Hamilton Road. He had the parcel ready in the car with him, gift-wrapped."

Thanet's scalp prickled with excitement.

"Did he tell you what the present was?"

"Well, I said it was an exciting-looking parcel, and he said it was a leather jacket he'd bought when he was on holiday in Wales. He'd got it for himself, really, but it was new, he'd only worn it once. His brother happened to see it and really went overboard for it, so Geoff decided to give it to him for his birthday."

"Did you see his brother open the parcel?"

"No. I didn't go up to the flat with Geoff. He said he wouldn't be long, and he wasn't."

Thanet put his last question to her and rang off, well satisfied.

When Lineham arrived back, he was out of breath.

"I didn't tell you to *run* all the way there and back, Mike."

Lineham shook his head and collapsed into his chair, panting. "It suddenly dawned on me, sir."

"Told you it would," said Thanet smugly.

"Oh no, not our case, not who killed Steven Long . . . The other one."

"Mrs. Jackson, you mean."

Lineham nodded. "That's why you were on about the jacket. It was Steve's jacket, wasn't it? It was Steve who killed her. I've been working it all out, on the way back."

"I'm ninety-nine percent certain of it. I gather you hit the jackpot with Mrs. Bence. What did she say?"

"Steve was carrying a plastic bag. Blue. It was pretty full, bulging, in fact, so much so that the top edges didn't meet. A pretty sharp old bird, isn't she?"

"What did she see?"

"Enough. She's prepared to swear that the top item in Steve's carrier was made of gray leather."

Thanet nodded with satisfaction. "You'll be interested to hear that I rang Miss Gilbert while you were out." Thanet repeated the gist of the conversation.

"So Hunt bought the jacket in Wales!" said Lineham. "Of course. The red dragon . . ."

"Precisely."

"That just about wraps it up then, doesn't it?" said Lineham excitedly. "It all fits. On Sunday evening, his birthday, Steve goes around to see Sharon, is thrown out by Howells, and told in no uncertain terms never to show his face there again. He feels fed up, and decides to console himself with a few drinks. He has too many and ends up feeling very sorry for himself, so he decides to go to Chris's house, as it's usually to Chris he turns for sympathy. But the Mays have guests and Steve doesn't exactly endear himself to them by being sick all over their carpet, so Chris throws him out.

"Steve goes home, and hasn't been there long when Geoff arrives, plus present, the nice new gray leather jacket with a red dragon on the back that Steve had fancied so much when he saw Geoff wearing it. Quite likely, Steve asks Geoff if they could go for a jar together, to celebrate their birthday, but Geoff has got himself a new girl and doesn't want Steve along, playing gooseberry, especially as Steve is still sozzled and might not make too good an impression.

"So, when Geoff has gone, Steve is all alone again. He can't stand it. It's his birthday, he should be out there enjoying himself. So he puts on his new jacket and drives out to the Fox and Hounds at Coddington, hoping perhaps to pick someone up. He does. Marge Jackson. He's too drunk to see past the make-up and they go off in the car together." Lineham paused.

"I don't suppose we'll ever know, now, what went wrong, why he shoved her out of the car, but my guess is that at that point he may have had no idea she was so badly injured and so he would have got the shock of his life when some time on Monday, either on the radio or TV, he hears she's dead and the police are treating the case as murder.

"So on Monday night he stays holed up indoors, frantically trying to work out if there was anything to connect him with Marge's death. He may or may not have wondered if anyone had noticed the jacket, while he was with her. It is pretty striking, after all.

"Anyway, by Tuesday he was beginning to feel a bit safer, so after work he went to see Sharon, taking her a present, the gold bracelet he might well have intended giving her on Sunday, if Howells had been out. But Sharon refused to let him stay more than a few minutes and he went straight home afterwards, arriving in time to see the TVS news on *Coast to Coast*. There, to his horror, he sees an item about the murder of Marge Jackson, describing his jacket and saying the police want to interview its owner. He decides there's only one thing to do, dump it, and that's precisely what he does, in the skip where Quarry found it."

"And then?"

"He's still feeling a bit shaken, so he decides he'll go and try to make it up with Chris, apologize for Sunday night. But Chris refuses to let him in, so . . ."

"So?"

"So he went home and got himself killed," finished Lineham lamely. He sighed, shook his head. "That's where we come unstuck, isn't it?" He thought for a moment and added, a wide grin spreading across his face, "I'll tell you what though, sir."

"What?"

"Chief Inspector Hines won't half be mad, that we got there first."

"True," said Thanet. The thought afforded him considerable satisfaction.

"He'll say that the moment we realized there was a possible connection between the two cases, we ought to have been in touch with him."

"But it's all happened so quickly, hasn't it, Mike? All we were doing was going quietly along pursuing our own inquiries when, bingo! Suddenly it dawned on us . . ."

"That we'd solved his case for him!" finished Lineham solemnly.

"Exactly. Now, no one could blame us for that, could they?"

"Certainly not, sir."

The two men grinned at each other.

"All the same," said Thanet, "I'd hate to go to him too soon and have him prove that all this is merely a product of my 'convoluted mind,' as he put it. There's just one more piece of evidence I'd like to have, first."

"What's that, sir?"

"We ought to talk to Geoff Hunt again, make sure we haven't jumped to conclusions about the jacket."

"Mr. Hines'll say we ought to inform him now, and let him talk to Mr. Hunt."

Thanet's eyes opened wide in mock innocence. "But we're merely being conscientious and checking our facts before laying them in front of Chief Inspector Hines. I'm sure he wouldn't want us to present him with a lot of half-baked notions, now would he?"

Lineham grinned. "Certainly not, sir. We're going now?"

"Shortly. I've made an appointment for eleven thirty. But before we do, there's something you ought to know."

As he talked, Thanet was gratified to see Lineham's eyes stretch wide, his mouth drop open in astonishment.

twenty

Geoffrey Hunt's arrangements for his move were obviously running smoothly. A furniture van painted with the sign R. W. BECKETT, AUCTIONEER AND VALUER stood in the drive, and as Thanet and Lineham parked beside it two men carrying a large wardrobe almost as easily as if it were an empty cardboard box emerged from the open front door. The van was already half-full.

Hunt was in the hall, talking to a third man.

"I'm afraid we haven't come at a very convenient time," said Thanet.

Hunt waved a hand. "Not to worry. It's all under control. Everything's labeled. We'll go into the sitting room, we won't be disturbed in there. I'll see you later, then," he said to the foreman.

The big room looked like a saleroom itself. Furniture and rolls of carpet were piled up all around the edges and apart from a small area in front of the hearth most of the floorspace was taken up with packing cases, cardboard boxes and the thousand and one small objects considered by the civilized world to be an essential part of everyday life. It was obvious that in order to simplify today's operation Hunt had gathered together in here most of the stuff he had decided to keep.

"Sorry about the chaos," he said, "but it can't be helped."

There was only one armchair free of clutter, the one nearest the fireplace, and Hunt quickly disentangled two small upright chairs from the nearest pile and set them down in the little island of clear space. "The best I can do, I'm afraid," he said.

"Thank you, sir."

They all sat down, Hunt perching on the arm of the easy chair. A hint that he couldn't spare much time? wondered Thanet. Or a desire not to have the two policemen looming over him?

Hunt looked at him expectantly. "How can I help you?"

He looked tired, Thanet thought. There were hollows in the thin cheeks, as if the flesh had melted away, and his eyes seemed to have sunk back into the dark shadows of the eye-sockets.

"I can see you're very busy, so I'll come straight to the point. When we last saw you, you told us that on Sunday evening you went to see your brother Steven, to wish him a happy birthday. We know that you took him a card, because we saw it on the mantelpiece in the flat, but we understand you also took him a present. Could you describe that present to us, please?"

Silence. Hunt stared at Thanet, the tiny movements in the muscles of his jaw betraying the fact that he was clenching and unclenching his teeth. It was clear that he not only appreciated the significance of the jacket, but that he had not been prepared for this particular line of questioning. He was now torn between veracity, which would brand Steve as a murderer, and denial, which might well lead to even more trouble for himself, if it could be proved that he was lying.

The instinct for self-preservation won.

"It was a jacket," he said reluctantly, at last.

Thanet, fully aware of the power of silence, said nothing, waited.

Hunt shifted uncomfortably on his perch. "I bought it when I was on holiday in Wales. I only wore it once, and Steve saw it, took a real fancy to it." He shrugged. "So I decided to give it to him for his birthday."

"He was pleased with it?"

Geoffrey Hunt attempted a smile. "Delighted."

"Could you give us a more detailed description, please?"

A small pause. "It . . ." Hunt cleared his throat. "Er . . . it was a leather jacket."

"Color?" put in Thanet sharply.

Hunt blinked. "Er . . . gray. Yes, gray."

"Plain gray?"

"Yes."

"All over?"

Another silence. Then Hunt jumped up, began blindly to blunder his way through the jumble of furniture and household objects towards the patio doors. Lineham half-rose, but Thanet put out a hand, shook his head.

When he reached the tall expanse of glass Hunt stopped and shoved his hands into his pockets in a gesture of anger and frustration. "Oh, what's the point of trying to cover up any longer?" he burst out. "It's obvious, from the questions you're asking, that you know, anyway. And Steve's dead, the truth can't hurt him now."

Hunt swung around to face Thanet across the cluttered room. "Yes, it did have the design of a dragon's head, in red, on the back. And the very fact that I am aware of the importance of this information does show that yes, I did see the TV appeal on Tuesday and recognize the description and yes, I did go straight round to warn Steve not to wear the jacket again and that therefore yes, I suppose I am guilty of obstructing the police in the course of their duty, or whatever you call it . . ."

"Thank you," said Thanet. "And now, perhaps we could discuss this a little more calmly. Come and sit down."

Hunt threaded his way back and flopped down into the armchair. "In a way I'm glad it's out," he said. "It's been an awful strain, wondering if you'd find out."

"Tell us exactly what happened on Tuesday."

"Yes . . . Well . . ." Hunt passed a hand over his forehead, rubbed his eyes and shook his head, as if to clear it. "Like I said, I saw the TV appeal. There was no mistaking the jacket, they'd even done a drawing of it and you'd have recognized it anywhere. Anyway, it was the first item on *Coast to Coast*, and I didn't wait to see any more. I went straight round to see Steve."

"Arriving at his flat at about a quarter past six?"

"Something like that, yes."

Thanet sensed Lineham shift beside him. The sergeant was obviously thinking the same thing. Nowhere, in any of the reports, had there been any mention of a Scimitar parked in Hamilton Road. And such a distinctive car would surely not have escaped notice.

"You went by car?"

"Yes, sure," said Hunt impatiently. "How else would I have got there so fast?"

"Where did you park?"

"In the driveway of a friend of mine, in Beech Avenue."

"Why not in Hamilton Road?"

"Various reasons. For one thing it's often impossible to find a parking space, there're so many flats, and for another I don't like leaving the Scimitar there. Some vandal snapped off the aerial when I parked there a few months ago, so ever since I've left it around the corner in Beech Avenue."

"Your friend's name and address?"

Hunt told him, and Lineham wrote it down.

"Right, so you arrived at Steve's flat at about a quarter past six. He was in?"

"Yes."

"What was he doing?"

"Watching TV."

"He'd seen the appeal himself?"

"Oh no. No. I asked him if he had, but he didn't know what I was talking about. He'd only just got in, he said, and he'd missed the beginning of the program."

"So what did he say, when you told him about it?"

"At first he pretended he didn't know what I was talking about, but I said, 'Oh come off it, Steve. There's no need to put it on with me. If you'd seen the drawing of the jacket—*your* jacket, which *I* gave you—you'd know there's no point in trying to pull the wool over my eyes.' "

"What did he say?"

"He got very upset. Said he hadn't known she was dead, not until the next day, the Monday, when he heard it on the radio . . ."

Hunt was very pale now, and starting to sweat.

"Did you believe him?"

"Yes." Hunt's voice had the ring of conviction in it. "He told me all about it. He said he'd picked this woman up and they'd quarreled, and he'd . . . he'd made her get out of the car. He said she must have tripped and fallen, banged her head on something. She had very high heels on, he said. It was the only explanation he could think of, for what happened later. After he put her out of the car he didn't look back, and of course it was pitch dark, anyway . . ."

"He didn't tell you he'd almost strangled her, first?"

"No! I don't believe that!"

"Post-mortems do not lie, Mr. Hunt."

"I . . . I didn't know that. But if it's true, then there must have been a very good reason . . ."

"Have you any idea what it was?"

Hunt shook his head.

"So after he'd told you all this, what did you do?"

"I advised him to go to the police, of course. I said they—you'd—only find out in the end. He told me he'd picked her up in a pub, and it had been crowded. He'd been wearing the jacket and it's very striking. It was pretty obvious to me that someone would have been bound to notice it, quite a lot of people, probably. I told him it would be far better to own up himself, first, than wait until he was caught. All he had to do was tell the truth, and he'd come out of it far better in the end."

"Did he agree?"

"Yes. He said he could see my point. There were a few things he wanted to do first, then he'd go down to the police station and give himself up. I had a date, as you know, but I offered to cancel it, stay with him, but he said no, he'd prefer to do it alone."

"Then you left?"

Hunt nodded, then buried his head in his hands. "I should have stayed," he said. "If I had, then Steve would still be alive."

"Isn't he?" said Thanet softly.

Hunt became quite still and for a long moment there was silence. Outside, in the hall, one of the removal men could be heard shouting instructions, his voice unnaturally loud. Then, slowly, Hunt raised his head.

"What do you mean?" he said. "What are you talking about?"

"I think you know very well what I'm talking about, Mr. Long."

Thanet glanced at Lineham and nodded.

Lineham stood up. "Steven Long, you are not obliged to say anything unless you wish to do so but what you say may be put into writing and given in evidence."

The man was chalk-white, but still in control of himself. He attempted a smile. "I think you're becoming a little confused, Inspector, unless that was a slip of the tongue, just now. I'm Geoffrey Hunt, remember."

"No slip of the tongue, Mr. Long."

"This is preposterous! And would you mind telling me what I'm supposed to have done?"

"Why, murdered your brother Geoffrey, of course."

twenty-one

Steven Long stared at Thanet with such intensity that his thoughts were almost audible. *How much does he know? How much of this is guesswork?*

He gave a strange little gurgle of laughter, quickly choked off, as if a tiny bubble of hysteria had escaped against his will. "You're out of your mind," he said. "Crazy."

"Am I?" Thanet gave him a long, assessing look, then smiled. "It must have seemed the perfect answer, the perfect way out of all your problems: get rid of the one person who knew you owned the jacket; ensure that if by any chance we, the police, did manage to trace it to Steve, then Steve would be conveniently dead; and, best of all, step into Geoff's shoes, inheriting his money, his new job—which you were sure you'd be able to cope with—his new life, waving goodbye to all your own problems for ever. Truly a stroke of genius."

"No! No, I . . ."

"All you had to do," Thanet went on, implacably, "was kill your twin brother."

"I'm not listening to any more of this crazy nonsense!" said Long, erupting out of his chair. "I'm going to . . ."

"What?" interrupted Thanet. "Ring the police? Complain to my superiors? Is there really any point? You'll only be putting off the evil hour. Because sooner or later you'd still have to face it all, wouldn't you?" Thanet paused. "Aren't you in the least interested to hear what went wrong with your beautiful plan, Mr. Long?" He folded his arms and sat back in his chair. *If you're prepared to listen, then I'm prepared to tell you.* Long, he was sure, would find the lure irresistible.

He was right. Long hesitated for a moment and then gave an exaggeratedly nonchalant shrug. "My beautiful plan, as you call it, Inspector, does not exist. But I am interested in the twisted 'logic' that has led you to make such wild accusations." He sat down, crossing his legs and folding his arms in deliberate imitation of Thanet. "So go ahead. Let's hear this *beautiful* theory of yours."

Thanet noted the echoed mockery and reminded himself to be careful. Whatever else he was, Steven Long was no fool. At the same time Thanet was, he realized, enjoying himself. He relished a worthy adversary and besides, this was in many ways a unique encounter. In his work Thanet frequently found that during the course of an investigation he came to know the murder victim very well. Never before, however, had he actually met him, in the flesh.

"Well, you'll realize, of course, that we've spent a considerable amount of time talking to the other members of your family, and gradually a picture of you began to emerge. We learned, amongst other things, that you were very good at impersonating Geoff, 'taking him off,' as Debbie put it. We also learned that as a child you were naturally left-handed—and I had noticed, when we first interviewed you, that it was with your left hand that you grabbed for something you knocked off the table by the door there. We learnt that your case was typical in that when twins are separated, it is usually the mother who keeps the weaker, lighter-born twin, and that that difference in weight usually persists into adulthood—and I had noticed, when I first met you, that your clothes were rather loose. At the time I assumed that you had recently lost weight, perhaps through grief over the death of your adoptive mother, but later I began to wonder . . ."

Steve waved a dismissive hand. "There's nothing in all this. It's all guesswork. Admit it, Inspector, you're just clutching at straws."

"I haven't finished yet. Far from it. Now we come to the discrepancies . . ."

He paused, but Steve said nothing.

"There were several of these. One was to do with 'Geoff's' attitude to your separation from your wife. He was the only person in the family who told us that Steve hadn't really been too upset by that separation, and had no interest in getting her back. Everyone else told us a very different story. Steve, they said, had been pretty shattered by Sharon's departure and was still making a determined effort to get her back—to the extent of going to see her regularly and even giving her expensive presents. Of course, this discrepancy wasn't necessarily significant. As Debbie said, Steve might not have wanted to lose face in front of Geoff, and might have put on a show of not caring, so that Geoff could genuinely have believed that Steve hadn't wanted to get Sharon back . . . But I don't think that was so, was it, Mr. Long? I think you couldn't bear to reveal to someone as impersonal as the police what Steve's feelings towards his wife really were—because they were your feelings, and to you they were private, not to be bandied about in front of a lot of unfeeling coppers . . ."

Steve had again folded his arms in apparent insouciance, but Thanet could tell that his muscles were rigid. The fingers of his visible hand were white with tension, hooked deeply into the flesh of his upper arm. Briefly, Thanet experienced a twinge of pity for the man. There was no doubt that Steve still cared deeply for his wife, and the loss of her must have been the one great sacrifice he had had to make in the course of action he had chosen to take.

"Another thing that puzzled us was why Steve had apparently not driven to Chris's house, when he went to see him on the evening of the murder. We were pretty sure that his car had been in working order, and everyone agreed that Steve wasn't the man to leave his car at home without a very good reason, so we were bound to ask ourselves, what could that good reason have been? I'll tell you the answer we came up with in a moment, when I get on to events on the night of the murder. But meanwhile, this was something that nagged away at us—like the anonymous phone call."

"What anonymous phone call?" said Steve, sullenly.

Thanet sighed. "If you must persist in this charade . . . At ten twenty-five on Tuesday night we had an anonymous phone call, informing us that there had been a murder at number 3 Hamilton Road. It was a man's voice—your voice, Mr. Long."

"Nonsense. I was here, with Caroline."

"Not at ten twenty-five, you weren't. I checked. Oh, you were both here in the house, all right, but for approximately five minutes, at that time, she was in the bathroom. You had plenty of time to make that call."

"Speculation again."

"Maybe. But it all fits, doesn't it?"

Now that they were no longer talking about Sharon, Steve seemed more relaxed, and he shook his head in apparent disbelief.

"The point was, Mr. Long, as we later realized, that it was essential that 'Steve's' body be discovered while you still apparently had an alibi. You simply couldn't risk it not being found for perhaps a day or two. So you made quite sure, by informing us yourself. You wanted to make absolutely certain that you, as Geoff, would not be suspected of the murder. You had already gone to elaborate lengths to ensure this, earlier on in the evening . . . But I'll come back to that later.

"So, our investigation progressed. There certainly wasn't a lack of suspects. You've always had a knack of stirring people up, and just lately you seemed to have excelled yourself. And there was one person outside your family on whose life you had a disastrous effect."

Long's eyebrows rose in polite inquiry. He seemed fully in control of himself again now.

"Mr. Carpenter," said Thanet. "Ah yes, I see you recognize the name. Were you aware that his daughter's life support machine was switched off on Tuesday? You wouldn't have realized, but he spent most of Tuesday evening sitting outside your flat in his car, trying to get up the courage to kill you."

For the first time emotion flickered across Long's face, so fleeting that Thanet almost wondered if he had imagined it. What had it been? Remorse? Fear? Regret? Or had it been triumph, elation? Thanet wondered if he had perhaps been indiscreet in telling Long about Carpenter, thus handing him a defensive weapon. But no. Thanet was certain that his case was watertight and that despite Long's apparent coolness sooner or later the man was going to have to admit it.

"But despite a plethora of suspects, except for Carpenter I just couldn't bring myself to believe that any of them had hated you enough to kill you. The one person who had apparently had no motive and who appeared as white as the driven snow, was Geoff. Now this might sound very strange to you, Mr. Long, but that very fact made me look at him more closely. It is, occasionally, the most unlikely person of all who turns out to have committed a murder. But in this case everyone seemed to agree that Geoff had no possible motive.

They thought he probably felt very guilty at having had so much the best of the bargain, and they all agreed that you, Mr. Long, were bitterly jealous of him, even though you tried to cover up the fact by making jokes about it."

For the second time Thanet had caught Steve on the raw. Again so briefly that if Thanet had not been watching closely he might have thought that he had imagined it, a fierce flash of emotion sparked in the navy-blue eyes, like phosphorescence in a midnight sea. Then it was gone.

"If you've nothing better to do than listen to a lot of gossip . . ."

Thanet ignored him. "And I couldn't help thinking, now if it had been the other way around, if I had been investigating Geoff's murder, not Steve's, I could have understood it . . . I mean, it must have been truly galling for you, all those years, to see your twin getting so much more than you—not only materially, but in the way of affection, love . . . So that whereas Geoff would have had nothing to gain by killing Steve, this certainly wasn't true the other way around. Except that at that point there seemed to be no precipitating factor, no reason why Steve should suddenly have decided to kill his brother, after all these years . . .

"But there had, of course, been a precipitating factor, though I didn't realize it at the time—the murder of Mrs. Jackson and the subsequent publicity over the very unusual jacket her companion had been wearing the night she was killed—the very distinctive, expensive jacket that Geoff had given you for your birthday.

"And so we come to Tuesday night, the night of Geoff's murder. By this time you were in a very precarious state of mind. You'd heard about Mrs. Jackson's death, and you were naturally frightened that the police would catch up with you. You knew that Frank was likely to be on your tail the minute he found out about the fast one you'd pulled on him over the fake television deal. Chris had thrown you out on Sunday night and told you not to come back. And, worst of all, you'd just been finally rejected by Sharon, despite the gold bracelet you'd risked so much to give her.

"So, when Geoff arrived with the news of the television appeal over the jacket, you must have been feeling pretty desperate, and this was the last straw, especially when he insisted that you give yourself up. You argued, you lost your temper, you grabbed the ashtray, which ironically, Geoff himself had given you, and . . ." Thanet mimed the blow to the back of Geoff's head.

"Now you had to decide what to do. And this was the point at which the solution came to you. Why not change places with Geoff, leave all your problems behind you and grab the opportunity of starting a new life, in infinitely better circumstances? But first, you had to make sure that Geoff would not be suspected of killing Steve. You therefore had to appear as Steve to someone who knew him well, and at the same time provide Geoff with an alibi. You knew he had a date, he'd told you so, and you also knew he'd been out with the girl only once, for a couple of hours. Presumably he'd also told you where she lived. You were pretty confident you could pull it off, so you began by adding a touch of authenticity to the body by changing shoes with Geoff. You couldn't risk anyone who knew you noticing that those scruffy sneakers you always wore had disappeared. Incidentally, it was lucky for you that Chris didn't notice you *weren't* wearing them when you called on him. Then you stuffed the coat Geoff had been wearing into a large plastic bag, together with the ashtray and the incriminating jacket, and wearing your usual blue windbreaker you drove in Geoff's car to Chris's house. You had to leave the Scimitar out of sight, of course, which is why the neighbors reported you as leaving on foot. You left Chris at a quarter past seven and you then changed into Geoff's coat, and on the way to Caroline's house buried your own wind-breaker, the leather jacket and possibly the ashtray in a rubbish heap. You knew that the police would work out that there simply wouldn't have been time for you to get home and for Geoff to kill you and get back to Caroline's house by half past seven. Geoff would therefore be in the clear and you'd be home and dry. All in all, it was a most ingenious plan, and it almost worked."

Thanet paused and almost at once Long began a slow hand clap. "Bravo, Inspector. Bravo. You've missed your vocation. You ought to write detective stories."

"You like my reconstruction, Mr. Long?"

"Fascinating. There's only one thing wrong with it, of course. It's not true. Oh, I'll grant you that it has elements of truth, which is what makes it sound so plausible, but in essence it's a story, ingenious but with no foundation in reality. I am Geoffrey Hunt and nothing you can say or do will change that fact."

"Won't it?" said Thanet softly.

"No. There's no way you can prove otherwise."

"I'm afraid there's something you've forgotten, Mr. Long."

"Oh?" There was an edge of uneasiness in the mono-syllable.

"Do you remember, when you were a child, you had to go into hospital?"

Long frowned. "How can I, Inspector?" he said irritably. "I haven't been into hospital in my entire life."

"It was after an unfortunate incident with your step-father, in the garden. You were four years old at the time. You suffered concussion and a broken leg, and you were in hospital for some time."

"What are you trying to say?"

"I'm saying that I've checked, and the hospital still have the X-rays they took at the time. The nature of that fracture was such that it would most certainly show up in an autopsy, many years later. The post-mortem on your brother's body showed no such fracture. The leg bones were intact, had never been broken . . ."

Something was happening to Long's face. The light of combat in the eyes was fading, the hard, fierce lines of cheek and jaw slackening as the inescapable truth of what Thanet was saying sank in.

"I presume that you would be willing to undergo some X-rays, Mr. Long?"

Steve buried his face in his hands.

Silence.

Thanet and Lineham exchanged triumphant glances.

Then Long stirred, sagged back in his chair and gave a long, defeated sigh. "OK, you win. I'd better make a statement."

Astonishing, thought Thanet. Already Long's accent had reverted to the slurred glottal stop, the Kentish vowel sounds.

"In that case, I think we'll transfer ourselves to the police station."

Long heaved himself wearily to his feet. "OK." His face hardened. "But you might as well get one thing clear from the start, Inspector. This isn't going to be a confession. I may have changed places with Geoff, but I didn't kill him."

twenty-two

"Chief Inspector Hines, please."

"One moment, sir."

Thanet gripped the receiver tightly. *Let him be out.*

Etiquette demanded he make this call, but Thanet wanted to take Steven Long's statement himself.

"Sorry, he's slipped out for a bite to eat, sir. Can I take a message?"

Relief. "Just tell him I rang, and I'll try again later."

"Right, sir."

Thanet returned to the interview room. Long was insisting on making a statement about Marge Jackson's death before talking about the switch with Geoff. He wanted, he said, to get it over with. Thanet and Lineham had already arranged that, providing DCI Hines was not available, Lineham would begin the questioning.

After Geoff's birthday visit on Sunday evening, Steve had roamed restlessly around the flat for a while, drinking some cans of beer he had picked up on the way back from Chris's house. He was feeling very depressed, all the more so because earlier on his hopes had been high. Encouraged by the birthday card Sharon had sent him and knowing that Howells often played rugby on Sunday afternoons, he had counted on finding Sharon alone, and had taken along not only the birthday cake but the gold bracelet in the hope of softening her attitude towards him. Instead, he had been forced to leave, disappointed and humiliated.

After attempting to console himself with a succession of double whiskies he had gone to Chris and his wife for comfort, but once again things had gone wrong and he had succeeded only in antagonizing them and being told not to come back.

By this time he had been desperate for company and although in the normal way of things he wouldn't have been particularly pleased to see Geoff, he had appreciated the fact that his twin had remembered his birthday ("Not that he could very well have forgotten it, it was his, too") and had been disappointed at Geoff's refusal to go out for a drink with him, because of the date with Caroline.

So when Geoff left he had felt abandoned by the world. There was no one he wanted to see, except Sharon, and no one, apparently, who wanted to see him. And it was his birthday. So in the end, he had decided to go and see if he could pick up a girl.

He had tried several pubs without luck before ending up in Coddington, where he had struck lucky ("if you could call it that, she was forty, if she was a day") with Marge Jackson. By this time he was past caring what the woman was like. All he wanted was some warmth, some closeness, however artificial, to another human being. So when Marge suggested leaving he had agreed readily enough.

They had driven to a quiet place she knew, a layby off the minor road which runs through Coddington Woods. And it was there that horror struck.

It had been obvious for some minutes that Steve was approaching the part of the tale he dreaded telling. His speech had become more hesitant, his face the color of tallow.

Until now Lineham had had to do little more than make encouraging noises.

"We were kissing, see, and, you know, getting down to it, when . . ." Steve broke off, shook his head in disgust, his face contorted.

"When what?" said Lineham.

Thanet wondered what on earth was coming. Surely Steve wasn't so innocent that any sexual ploy used by a prostitute would produce this degree of revulsion?

A complex succession of emotions chased each other across Steve's face—puzzlement, confusion, bewilderment. "I still don't know why it got to me like that. I . . ." Steve gulped, tried again. "One of my cuff buttons had caught in her hair and suddenly . . . suddenly it all came off, and she was . . . she was bald."

So Marge Jackson had been wearing a wig, thought Thanet. Comprehension flooded in. Lena May, Steve's mother, also habitually wore wigs. What if she, too, suffered from partial or total hair loss? If so, there had perhaps been some traumatic incident in the past when Steve, as a child, had witnessed his mother's "hair" come off, an incident that, though long forgotten, could have triggered off Steve's exaggerated response in the car that night.

Thanet glanced at Lineham, but the sergeant was showing no reaction. He had no doubt known about Mrs. Jackson's baldness all along, but had no reason to mention it to Thanet.

"I'm still not really sure what happened next," said Long. "One minute there we were, getting down to it, like I said, and the next . . . It was just like if a bomb had exploded nearby."

"Try to take it step by step," said Lineham. "Her wig came off, then . . . ?"

"I jerked away from her and she must have realized

why. I suppose her vanity was hurt or something because suddenly she just threw herself at me, screeching and swearing and hammering away at my chest with clenched fists." Steve shook his head. "Ever since I heard the news on the radio I've tried and tried to remember exactly what happened next, but it's just a blur. That noise she was making . . . It went through my head like an electric drill and I just wanted to shut her up, to stop her. I think I managed to get hold of both her wrists with one hand, while I tried to put the other over her mouth, but I couldn't because she kept twisting her head from side to side. So I transferred my grip to her throat, just for a few seconds, to cut off the air. But I knew I couldn't keep it up, it would be dangerous, so, very quick, before she knew what was happening, I reached across, threw open her door and shoved her out. Then I chucked her . . . her wig after her and drove off, fast. I didn't wait to see if she was all right, I just wanted shot of her. I suppose I should have checked she was OK, but all I could think of was getting away. I didn't mean to kill her, I swear I didn't."

"Nevertheless, she fractured her skull and lay there all night, unconscious. She was still alive, just, when they found her next morning but she was dead on arrival at the hospital."

"Oh God . . . If . . . Do you think, if I'd waited, taken her to hospital straightaway . . . ?"

Lineham consulted Thanet with a glance.

Thanet shook his head. "We don't know. All we know is that she is dead, and from what you say it would seem likely that you were responsible."

"But I told you, I didn't mean to . . ."

"Intentions have very little to do with it at this stage, I'm afraid. Anyway, as I've already explained to you, we don't know a great deal about the case. Detective Chief Inspector Hines is in charge of it and I've no doubt he'll be along to see you as soon as I can get in touch with him. Meanwhile, my prime concern is the death of your brother. So if you don't mind I'd like to move on, now, to Tuesday evening."

It seemed that Thanet's theory as to what happened on the night of Geoff's murder was substantially correct—with the crucial difference that, according to Steve, he was innocent of Geoff's murder.

Geoff had arrived at Steve's flat between a quarter and twenty past six. *Coast to Coast* was on TVS.

"Did you see the beginning of the program?"

"No, I've only just got in. Why?"

"What the hell have you been up to, Steve? That woman who was murdered in Coddington on Sunday . . ."

"What about her? What're you talking about?"

"Oh come off it, Steve, there's no point in trying to pull the wool over my eyes. Look, a man was seen with her, and there was a description of the jacket he was wearing—a gray leather jacket with a red dragon on the back . . . How many gray leather jackets with red dragons on the back d'you think there are around here?"

"Oh God . . ."

"There was a sketch, too. Every five-year-old in the area would recognize that jacket if he saw it now. Where is it?"

"Oh, God. Look, Geoff, she wasn't dead when I left her, I swear . . ."

"Never mind that for the moment. I said, where's the jacket now?"

"On the back seat of the car."

"If anyone should see it . . . Go and get it. This second. Then we'll decide what to do."

Leaving the door to the flat ajar Steve had hurried off downstairs and along the passage to the back door. The car was parked at the back of the house and this was the quickest way to get to it. There was an outside light, but the bulb must have gone because it didn't come on when Steve depressed the switch and it took him a moment or two to adjust to the darkness.

He picked his way cautiously across to his car, and then, in his haste to open the door, dropped his keys. It had been raining earlier and there was a puddle alongside the driving door, so he had to grope about gingerly in the water and then dry the keys before finding the right one by touch and inserting it in the lock. Then he had grabbed the jacket, bundled it up under his arm and hurried back upstairs. He had seen no one, either on the way down or on the way back, though he thought that as he came in through the back door he had heard the front door close. He had been away perhaps five minutes, in all.

By now Thanet had guessed what was coming.

"As I came up the stairs I noticed my door was open wider than I'd left it. I thought the draft coming up the stairs must have done it. Until I went inside . . .

"I couldn't see Geoff at first and I thought he must've gone into the kitchen. I walked a few paces into the room and then I noticed the ashtray on the floor . . ."

"Where was it, exactly?"

"Halfway between the back of the settee and the door, and a bit to the right."

Thanet nodded. "Go on."

"It usually stood on the sideboard. It was a present from Geoff, he'd brought it back from Italy . . . I couldn't think how it'd got on the floor, but naturally I picked it up—well, you would, wouldn't you? And then I saw there was blood on it, and on the carpet, too, underneath. It didn't register at first, what it was, but the second it clicked, I went further into the room, looking around, and . . . and there was Geoff, lying face down on the rug in front of the settee. Well, you didn't have to be a genius to see what had happened . . . I went and felt for a pulse, but there wasn't one and when I half-rolled him over and saw his eyes open like that, staring . . . Well, it was obvious he was dead.

"I just sort of collapsed into a chair and stared at him. I couldn't believe it. I'd only been away a few minutes and . . . Then it dawned on me. *Whoever had killed Geoff must have thought it was me.* After all, here he was, alone in my flat, looking just like me . . . It wouldn't have occurred to the man who killed him that it could be anyone but me. So someone out there wanted me dead, and when they found out it was Geoff who had been killed, they'd probably have another go.

"That was when I had this brilliant idea. Geoff was dead now, nothing would bring him back. Why not change places? Like you said, it seemed a stroke of genius. I was really browned off with my life, everything seemed to have been going wrong lately, and if I stepped into Geoff's shoes, I'd be able to make a fresh start. In fact, I'd be sitting pretty. Geoff's mum was dead, and I knew Geoff was moving to Staffs next week, for his new job with Scimitar. I was pretty confident I could step into his shoes, for a while, anyway. If it turned out the job was beyond me, too bad. They could fire me if they wanted to, and no one'd still be any wiser I wasn't really Geoff. And in the meantime I thought if I lay low for a few days, kept away from his old friends on the excuse I was too busy packing and so on, no one need ever know. I'd get out of the mess I was in, over that woman on Sunday night, and also, which seemed just as important, I'd fool the character who'd done Geoff in into thinking I was dead . . . I must've sat there for a good ten minutes, working it all out, trying to think of all the snags. And in the end I thought, I'll give it a go. What have I got to lose?"

A flicker of pain crossed Steve's face at this point and Thanet knew he was thinking about Sharon.

"And I'd have everything to gain. By now I knew exactly what I was going to do, and I got on with it. I swapped my own stuff for Geoff's, keys, wallet and so on, and changed shoes with him. We've always taken the same size, and like you said, I was afraid someone might notice if he wasn't wearing my sneakers. I never wore anything else. Then I . . . Well, you've already worked it all out, haven't you? It was just like you said, back at the house. I did wonder whether to leave that bloody jacket in the flat, and let them work out that Steve was the man they wanted in connection with Marge Jackson's death, but somehow I couldn't. Although I wasn't going to be Steve any more, I didn't want Steve blamed for a murder he hadn't done. So I decided to dump it. The ashtray was another problem. I didn't dare leave it there, because I'd got some of the blood on my fingers, and I was afraid the police would be able to tell I'd handled it after I'd apparently been killed. So I decided to dump that, too. Apart from that . . . well, like I said, you had it all worked out."

And Steve looked at Thanet with grudging admiration.

"You were taking a bit of a risk going out with Caroline. Weren't you afraid she'd realize you weren't Geoff?"

"I had to do it. I needed that alibi. And Geoff had only been out with her once. I thought I could pull it off, and I did."

"How did you know where she lived?"

"A bit of luck. She lives next door to a girl we both fancied at one time, and when Geoff came round on Sunday, he just happened to mention it, as a bit of a coincidence."

"How did you know he had a date with her last night?"

"I didn't. I was just banking on it. I could tell, on Sunday night, that Geoff was pretty taken with her, and knowing he was moving in a week or so, I guessed he'd have arranged to see her again soon. If not, I thought I could always spin her some tale of not being able to wait so long before seeing her again. As I say, I was pretty sure I could pull it off."

There was a knock at the door. Detective Chief Inspector Hines was on the phone.

Thanet and Lineham exchanged glances. *Now for it.*

"All right, Sergeant, we'll take a short break. Arrange for Mr. Long to have a cup of tea or coffee, will you?"

Thanet went up to his office to take the call. He didn't want any distractions.

"Thanet here."

"Hines. You rang earlier."

"Yes. Things have been moving rather fast here, sir, and, well, I thought you'd like to know we've got your man."

"What d'you mean, got my man?"

"The man who killed Mrs. Jackson, sir."

"He turned himself in, you mean?"

"Not exactly. But he is definitely the man you're after."

"What the hell are you talking about, Thanet? You're surely not trying to tell me *you've* arrested him?"

"Well . . . Not exactly, sir. But we have cautioned him and brought him in."

"You've WHAT?"

Thanet winced and held the receiver away from his ear as Hines started bellowing down the phone.

"What the devil d'you think you're playing at, Thanet? How DARE you interfere in my case like this?"

"Well, it wasn't exactly your case, sir. You see . . ."

"What d'you mean, 'not my case'?"

"Well, we were . . ."

"I don't know what you're babbling about, Thanet, but get one thing straight. I'm going to have your guts for garters. I'll be right over."

And the phone was slammed down. Thanet grinned at it and gave it a pat, as if it were a particularly obedient dog.

Lineham put his head around the door.

"What did he say, sir?"

"He wasn't exactly over the moon, Mike. Come on, let's go back down to Long. As soon as Mr. Hines gets here, we're not going to get a look in."

Long was sunk in gloom, tea untouched.

"Detective Chief Inspector Hines will be here shortly, Mr. Long. But before he arrives, just tell me this. Give me one good reason why I should believe your story that someone else killed Geoff while you were out of the room, and that the idea of changing places only occurred to you *after* he was dead?"

"Because it's true! I swear it is!"

"Maybe, but there's no way of proving it, is there?"

"There's no way of proving I did kill him, either."

"True. At present, anyway. So what it's going to come down to is whether the jury would believe your version or mine. What do you think, Mr. Long? Do you think they'll take the word of a man who, on his own admission, half-strangled a woman and then drove off, leaving her to die, and a couple of days later seized the opportunity of stepping into his dead brother's wealthy shoes and deceiving everyone—wife, family and police alike —into thinking that he himself was dead?"

Long stared up at Thanet, obviously assessing the truth of what he had just said, and then slumped back in his chair, as if acknowledging defeat.

"As a matter of interest," he said, "would it have been more sensible to have left the ashtray where it was?"

His tone was casual. Too casual?

Two could play at that game. Careful not to betray his quickened interest, Thanet shrugged. "Difficult to tell. I can quite see why you decided to take it away with you. On the other hand, we might have found one or two nice clear prints which could have led us straight to the murderer. So on balance, I'd say that looking at it from your point of view, at the time it was obviously sensible to remove the ashtray, but that now you've been found out, if you could wave a wand and magically whisk it back from wherever it is, you would be wise to do so. But as that's impossible, I think it's a waste of time talking about it. I think you'd be wiser to concentrate on . . ."

"But it's not," interrupted Long.

"Not what?" said Thanet, innocently.

"Not impossible."

Thanet pretended enlightenment. "Are you saying you didn't actually dump the ashtray in that skip, along with the jacket and your windbreaker?"

"That's right." There was a hint of triumph in Long's voice now, and the beginning of a smile in his eyes.

"So . . . ?"

"I just couldn't make up my mind, see, whether it would be better to get rid of it or not. So I hid it where I thought it would be least likely to be found."

"In one of the packing cases full of china, I bet," said Lineham.

Long looked crestfallen. "How did you . . . ?"

Thanet grinned. "You can't do this job for long without getting rather good at that kind of guess. Which packing case?"

"The one marked 'FRAGILE. HANDLE WITH CARE.' "

"Keys?" said Thanet, holding out his hand. By now the men from the auctioneers would have finished, the house would be locked up.

Long handed them over and Thanet gave them to Lineham, taking him into the corridor outside. "Get Carson on to it right away. Tell him—no, on second thoughts, I'd prefer you to do it yourself. You know what we're looking for. As soon as you find it, take it personally to forensic and stress the urgency. I'll give them a ring myself, in the meantime. In view of this rather tricky situation with Hines, it would help if we could get our own case cleared up quickly."

"Like, yesterday," said Lineham with a grin.

"Quite."

"You think Long's telling the truth, then?"

In the distance there was a sudden commotion. Hines's voice could clearly be heard demanding to know where Thanet was.

"Not now, Mike." Thanet gave Lineham an encouraging little push on the arm. "Off you go."

Lineham resisted. "You'll be needing some moral support."

"Mike! I can handle it. Go on, hurry up, or you'll get tangled up with Mr. Hines and you'll never get away."

Lineham capitulated. "I'll be as quick as I can."

"Thanet!" Hines had spotted him, and such was his single-minded concentration on the object of his wrath that he passed Lineham without noticing him. He charged along the corridor like an angry bull, head down, feet pounding. Thanet could almost see the angry little puffs of hot breath issuing from his nostrils.

"Well?" he roared. "This had better be good, Thanet, or . . ."

Thanet had no intention of enduring a flood of abuse from Hines out here, where every word would be public. During Hines's advance he had opened the door of an empty interview room and now he backed into it. Hines charged in behind him and Thanet shut the door.

". . . or you'll be sorry you ever heard of Marge Jackson."

"Won't you sit down, sir?" Thanet was all courtesy.

"No, I bloody well won't sit down. I don't want a chair, I want—I *demand*—an explanation."

"And I'm quite happy to give you one. Please . . ." Thanet indicated the chair he had pulled out.

Hines glared at him suspiciously. "Very well," he said, sitting down with a thump and folding his arms belligerently. "No one can say that I'm not a reasonable man. But, as I said, it had better be good."

Thanet launched into his explanation of how he had

come to suspect a possible connection between the two cases.

Hines listened intently, his little piggy eyes glittering with a dangerous light. At the end he grunted contemptuously. "If that's the way you work, Thanet . . . A load of airy-fairy notions and half-baked guesswork . . . Anyway, that's beside the point. The point is that the second, *the very second* you suspected that your case might be impinging on mine, you should have informed me. As your superior officer, it should have been up to me to decide how to proceed."

He stood up with a jerk that almost toppled his chair over backwards. "You haven't heard the last of this, by a long chalk. I shall seriously consider making a formal complaint. Now, where's Long? I think it's about time *I* had a word with him."

"In interview room 3, sir."

Hines opened the door, glanced along the corridor and bellowed, "Draycott?"

The sergeant hurried towards them, almost at a run.

"We're going to interview the suspect," said Hines. And with one last venomous glance at Thanet he and Draycott disappeared through the door of interview room 3.

Thanet took a deep sigh of relief and felt in his pocket for his pipe. He was sorry for Long. He wouldn't wish a long session with Hines on to his worst enemy. Then he hurried up the stairs to his office. With luck he could persuade Specks, in forensic, to rush through the tests on the ashtray. He sent up a fervent prayer that they would provide him with some good, sound evidence.

twenty-three

All six houses in Benenden Drive were individually designed, generously proportioned, and set in extensive wooded grounds of an acre or so.

"At least five bedrooms, wouldn't you say?" murmured Lineham as he swung into the graveled drive of "Smallwood" and parked neatly beside the porticoed front door.

"We're not estate agents, Mike."

Manicured lawns stretched away on all sides, bordered by well-tended flowerbeds, and at the far end of the garden beneath a stand of deciduous trees a man was busy raking up fallen leaves and piling them into a wheelbarrow.

"Full-time gardener too, by the look of it," added Lineham, undeterred by Thanet's mild rebuke.

Thanet did not reply. He had been notified that morning that Harry Carpenter was insisting that he was well enough to go home and that the hospital intended to discharge him. Thanet imagined him now, drifting like an aimless ghost through the empty rooms of the big house that he and his wife must have bought—perhaps even planned and built—with such pride. Carpenter was a self-made man, and this spacious neo-Georgian house would have been for them a symbol of all that he had achieved. Thanet shook his head sadly as he and Lineham climbed the short flight of steps between the white pillars.

The door was opened by a dowdy middle-aged woman wearing an old-fashioned crossover apron and carrying a duster. She looked worried.

"May we speak to Mr. Carpenter, please?"

"Who shall I say?"

Thanet introduced himself and presented his identification card, which she studied carefully before handing it back.

"You can't be too careful, these days."

"Quite right," said Thanet as she stepped back and gestured them in. "How is Mr. Carpenter?"

She hesitated.

"It's all right. We do know what's been happening to him, and that he only got back from hospital this morning."

She shook her head, her mouth turned down, and with a glance at the door on the left drew them away to the far side of the hall. "To tell you the truth I'm ever so worried about him," she said in a low voice. "Ever since he got back he's been sitting in there not saying a word. He didn't so much as touch his lunch . . ."

"You've been with him long?"

"About eighteen months."

"Since before the accident, then."

"Yes." She shook her head again, mournfully. "You'd hardly believe this is the same house. When I first came there was people in and out all day long—Mrs. Carpenter knew loads of people, and Chrissie's friends were forever coming and going. There'd be a dinner party at least once a week and always people here for lunch and tea on Sundays . . ." She sighed. "It was a lot of work, but

223

I enjoyed it. But now . . . Ever since Mrs. Carpenter died . . . And then Chrissie, on Tuesday, poor little scrap . . . The place is like a morgue." She clapped her hand to her mouth. "Oh, I'm sorry. I didn't mean . . . Anyway, the point is, I've never seen Mr. Carpenter quite as bad as this."

"You really are worried about him, aren't you?"

"Well, before Chrissie died he never lost hope. He kept on saying he believed she'd get better, that he had to believe it, or go mad. He did everything a human being could do, in the circumstances. He got one of them coma kits, so as to see how to go about it, and he'd sit up hour after hour in the evenings, trying to put together the things he thought were most likely to get through to Chrissie—the voices of her friends, the whinny of her pony and the sounds of him feeding, trotting, being groomed . . . oh, all sorts of things, I can't tell you. And he'd spend hours at the hospital every day, talking to her, playing her all the tapes . . ." The woman was almost in tears by now. She took out a handkerchief and blew her nose. "If there was any justice in the world," she said, "Mr. Carpenter would have been rewarded for all that effort, all that faith, and Chrissie would be home and running about by now . . ."

"You were obviously very fond of the family."

"Oh I was. I am. They're really nice people. I've worked for a lot of families, and I know what employers can be like. But the Carpenters—they were always so kind, so appreciative . . . You don't find many like that around these days, I can tell you."

Especially self-made men, who've probably had to claw and struggle their way up, thought Thanet. Carpenter, then, was that rare creature, a man with sufficient determination to get to the top and the ability to retain his humility when he got there. It seemed unfair that the personal hell he had had to endure for the last year should have been his reward.

"It's so unfair," said the housekeeper, echoing his thoughts. She glanced at the door across the hall again. "To be honest, the state he's in, I'm surprised they let him come home from the hospital. I don't think he's safe to be left alone, I really don't."

"You don't live in?"

"Yes, we do. Ron—that's my husband, he's the gardener—and me've got a self-contained flat in the house, but that's not the point. I can't keep an eye on him all the time—what about at night? He's alone for hours then. He could do anything."

"You mean, commit suicide?"

She nodded, lips compressed.

"You really think it's a serious possibility?"

"You'll see for yourself . . . I'm very relieved you've come, I can tell you."

The poor woman wouldn't be so relieved when she knew why, thought Thanet as she led them across to the door she had been looking at, and knocked. "Mr. Carpenter?"

No reply.

She tried again. "Someone to see you, Mr. Carpenter."

This time there was a faint response and she opened the door, ushered them in.

The room was obviously Carpenter's study. It was luxuriously furnished—Persian rug on the parquet floor, heavy velvet curtains, antique mahogany kneehole desk, opulent swivel desk chair, floor-to-ceiling bookshelves laden with leather-bound volumes, a set of Jorrocks hunting prints. For Carpenter, dust and ashes all, now, thought Thanet.

A coal fire burned in the hearth and before it, slumped in a green leather wing chair, was Carpenter. Had he chosen this room because it held the fewest memories of his wife and daughter? Thanet wondered.

"Good afternoon, Mr. Carpenter."

"So you've come at last." The man's speech was slow,

almost slurred, as if he had just woken from a long sleep. "Thank you, Mrs. Epps." And he nodded, dismissing her.

Thanet waited until the door had closed behind her, then said, "You've been expecting us?"

"I knew you'd get around to it, sooner or later, when you'd eliminated all the other possibilities." He paused. "You didn't believe me yesterday, did you?"

"We weren't sure what to believe. You were very . . . confused."

"I know." Carpenter eased himself up a little straighter in his chair. "Well, I'm not confused now—not, at least, over the part that matters. Do sit down, Inspector . . . Thanet, was it?"

"That's right. And this is Detective Sergeant Lineham."

When they were seated, Thanet said, "Are you saying that what you told us last time wasn't true?"

"To be honest, I'm not sure exactly what I did tell you, last time. Tuesday was still a blur in my mind, then. I wasn't even sure if I had killed him, until you told me he was dead. But when you did . . . Well, I was suddenly certain, then, that I had. But I couldn't remember the details, so I just told you what I thought must have happened, as I'd imagined it happening, over and over again, while I was waiting for it to be time for me to go and see him, on Tuesday."

It looked as though they needn't have bothered to rush through the tests on the ashtray after all, Thanet thought. Carpenter was obviously bent on making a full confession. A clear set of prints had in fact confirmed what Thanet suspected—that it had been Carpenter, the most likely suspect of all, who had delivered that fatal blow to Geoff's head, thinking him to be Steve.

"One moment, Mr. Carpenter. In view of your confusion yesterday, I think it would be advisable to caution you again." Thanet glanced at Lineham and nodded.

But Carpenter was waving his hand dismissively. "You

226

needn't bother. I remember it quite clearly, and in any case it doesn't matter. I'm not going to deny anything, now or later. I killed Long, it's as simple as that. And I can't pretend I'm anything but glad."

Thanet wondered what Carpenter's reaction would be when he discovered that he had murdered the wrong man.

"Do you want to tell us about it?"

Carpenter nodded. "It'll make it more real. Until today it's all been so . . . fragmented, in my mind. At times I've even wondered if it was all a dream . . ."

"But you don't think so any longer?"

"No. When I woke up this morning, I had a clear memory of what had happened, for the first time."

There was little that was new in Carpenter's story. Thanet had already worked most of it out for himself.

Carpenter had arrived in Hamilton Road at around a quarter past six. He thought that Long would probably be home from work by then. He knew where Long lived, even knew which was his flat, because at one point during the long months of waiting for Chrissie to regain consciousness he had gone to Hamilton Road with the intention of venting his anger and grief upon the man responsible for her condition. But Long had been out, Carpenter had come away unsatisfied, and the impulse that had driven him there had not returned—until Tuesday, after Chrissie's death. On that occasion his purpose had been much more deadly. Quite simply, he had been bent on murder.

"I'm sorry, may I interrupt for a moment, there?" said Thanet.

"Of course."

"How, exactly, did you intend to kill Mr. Long?"

"You may not believe this, Inspector, but I really hadn't thought. I suppose I imagined I was going to choke the life out of him with my bare hands, or something like that . . . Sounds crazy, doesn't it? The truth is, I *was* crazy, I suppose. I was just in a daze of grief and misery. When I got home from the hospital after my daughter . . . When I got home from the hospital I took a couple of Valium . . ."

"What time was that?" said Thanet, sharply.

Carpenter frowned. "I'm not sure. Mid-afternoon, I suppose. Why?"

"When we picked you up you'd obviously been drinking heavily. Whisky. Did you have anything to drink before you went to Hamilton Road?"

"I'd certainly had a few, I admit."

"A few? What time did you start drinking, do you remember?"

Carpenter frowned.

"Around five, I should think."

"Thank you. Go on . . . You were saying that you got there at around a quarter past six."

"Somewhere around then."

He had just pulled up when in the light from the streetlamp he saw Long come running along the pavement and turn in to the driveway of number 3. Because of the combined effect of tranquilizers and alcohol his reaction was slow. Long had disappeared into the house before Carpenter had really registered who it was.

Thanet and Lineham exchanged glances. *That was Geoff. Steve was already home.*

Carpenter had taken one final long slug of whisky before getting out of the car and entering the house. As he came into the hall a door slammed at the back of the house, but he had paid no attention and had made his way up the stairs to Long's flat. The door was ajar and Long was sitting on the settee, with his back to him. As Carpenter pushed the door open with his elbow Long turned his head, revealing himself in profile, and said, "You really are a bloody fool, you know." The words were a match to gunpowder. All Carpenter's despair, suppressed by force of will throughout the long months of hope of Chrissie's eventual recovery, erupted now in an explosion of anger against the man he saw as the murderer of his wife and child. With just enough sense left to realize that in his condition he was no match for a much younger and presumably fitter man, he had looked around wildly for a weapon. The ashtray had been to hand and he had grasped it, staggered forward the necessary couple of paces and brought it down on Long's head with all the strength he could muster. Long had toppled forward and sprawled on the hearthrug. Carpenter had not waited to check that he was dead. Having done what he had set out to do, all he wanted now was to get away. Dropping the ashtray he had retreated back down the stairs and returned to his car.

His story told, Carpenter lifted his hands and dropped them in his lap with a gesture of finality. "And that's it, Inspector. After that, I can remember practically nothing."

But it wasn't quite as simple as that, thought Thanet. Now they were coming to the really difficult part.

"When you went into the room and the man said, 'You really are a bloody fool, you know,' you assumed he was talking to you, personally?"

"Yes, I did . . . Oh . . ." Carpenter broke off and stared at Thanet, obviously taking his point. "I suppose he couldn't have been. He didn't actually turn his head far enough around to see who I was."

"Quite."

"I was pretty drunk, of course, and it simply didn't occur to me that he could have been addressing someone else. There was no one else in the room."

"But the door was open, you remember. Didn't that strike you as odd on a cold November evening?"

Carpenter shook his head. "I can't say it did. I'm sorry, Inspector, but I really wasn't thinking logically . . . You're implying, of course, that he was expecting someone."

"Expecting someone *back*, actually."

Thanet's tone must have conveyed to Carpenter something of his reluctance to proceed beyond this point, because Carpenter looked at him sharply and said, "You're working up to telling me something, aren't you, Inspector. What?"

"I'm sorry, Mr. Carpenter. There's no way I can diminish the pain I'm going to cause you, when I tell you . . . He was expecting his *twin* back."

"His . . . twin?"

Carpenter's face went blank as he stared at Thanet and realized the implication of what Thanet had just said.

"Oh, my God," he whispered at last. "You're not trying to say . . ."

"I'm afraid so. You killed the wrong man."

twenty-four

Thanet put an arm around Bridget's shoulders and gave her a brief hug. "Good luck, then."

The South-East regional heats of the Junior Chef of the Year competition were about to get under way.

The Fletcher Hall at the Black Swan, Sturrenden's premier venue for wedding receptions, Ladies' Nights and the glossier public functions, had been transformed for the occasion into something resembling the Domestic Science room of a well-equipped comprehensive school: gleaming electric cookers (by courtesy of the South-East Electricity Board), each with its surrounding island of work surfaces and basic cooking equipment, were spaced out along one side. Chairs for the audience waited expectantly, with reserved notices for the judges in the front row. It was now half past nine and doors would open to the public at ten thirty. The competitors had all arrived and were left to unpack their ingredients and equipment. Pairs of anxious parents were drifting towards the door, the Thanets among them. Ben was not there, having been picked for the school football team for the first time, to play in an away match.

231

"She looks quite cheerful, don't you think?" said Thanet, with one last backward glance over his shoulder.

Joan took his arm and smiled. "If practice makes perfect, she should be able to get through the whole thing blindfolded."

"She's never done it with an audience before, though. It's quite different."

"She'll be all right." Joan gave Thanet's arm a little shake. "Don't worry, darling. I think you're more nervous than she is."

"And you, of course, couldn't care less."

She grinned back at him. "I just hide it better, that's all."

"What on earth are we going to do for the next hour? It's too early for coffee."

"It's a beautiful morning. Let's walk down to the river."

"Why not?"

It was still too early for the Saturday morning crowds to have arrived and they both enjoyed the novel experience of a leisurely stroll along Sturrenden's picturesque High Street. At the bottom, near the river, it widens out into a broad, cobbled area called Market Square, and it was in a tranquil little Victorian cul-de-sac nearby that the Linehams lived.

"Oh, by the way," said Joan, glancing in that direction. "I forgot to tell you. I ran into Louise yesterday afternoon and they've got a reprieve."

"You mean, Mrs. Lineham didn't get the house?"

"That's right. Apparently the vendor had agreed that Mrs. Lineham could have it provided no one came along with the ready money before the negotiations were too far advanced. Mrs. Lineham, of course, has to wait to sell her own house. Anyway, she was unlucky. Some people who've been living abroad turned up, cash in hand, so to speak. So that was that."

"What a relief, eh? Perhaps it'll compensate a bit for the disappointment over the promotion."

They strolled in silence for a few minutes and then Joan said, "You didn't have a chance to tell me properly what Superintendent Parker said, about Mr. Hines's complaint."

After Carpenter's arrest yesterday, there had been much to do. Thanet had managed to get home to supper and tell Joan the gist of what had happened, but it had been difficult with the children about, and she had long been in bed and asleep when he eventually got home in the early hours. He had been determined to clear up as much of the paperwork as possible in order to be free this morning.

"Ah, yes. Well, it was most impressive, really. I'm still not sure how he did it, but he somehow managed to reprimand me and compliment me at the same time. And he persuaded Hines to let the matter drop. Reading between the lines I got the impression that he'd hinted that it was Hines who'd come off worst if he pursued the matter—be made to look a bit of a fool. And of course Hines wouldn't enjoy that one little bit."

"Odious man," said Joan, with feeling.

"Not my favorite policeman, I agree."

They had reached the bridge now and they descended the long flight of stone steps to the paved walkway along the river bank. It was another perfect late autumn day: bright sunshine, cloudless sky and crisp, cool air still tinged with a breath of early-morning frost. There was no wind, and the bare branches of the cherry trees hung in motionless contemplation of their mirror-images in the water below. A pair of swans and a gaggle of assorted ducks converged on the Thanets, eyeing them hopefully.

"We should have brought some bread," said Joan.

"We didn't know we'd be coming down to the river, did we?"

"Luke, last night, after you'd gone back to work, I was thinking about the case . . . How did Steve react, when he knew his plan had failed? Was he angry?"

"Strangely enough, no. Initially I think he felt defeated, fed up, and then he was, well, just resigned, I suppose. It was as if, all along, he never really believed he could pull it off."

"That fits. Nothing's ever gone right for him, has it? By now it would be surprising if he didn't automatically expect things to go wrong. What about his family? How did they feel, when they heard the news?"

Thanet grimaced. "I don't think they knew what they felt, especially as they heard at the same time that he was under arrest for the murder of Marge Jackson. To be honest, I think his mother and two brothers would have been relieved if he'd stayed 'dead.' I don't think any of them cares tuppence about him. Sharon, of course, is a different matter. I think she's genuinely fond of him, but finds it impossible to cope with him." Thanet shook his head. "It's difficult to tell how she feels. I don't think she really knows, herself. Relieved . . . Appalled . . . Sorry for him . . . Of course, as far as he's concerned, the one good thing about having been found out is that, theoretically at least, he now has a chance of edging his way back into her life."

"I still find it difficult to believe that she identified the body as Steve, when it was Geoff. Oh I know you'll say they were identical twins, but even so . . . her *husband* . . . And she still insisted that it was Steve, even after you'd put to her the possibility that it might be Geoff."

"Yes, but you've got to remember that people in that particular situation don't look very carefully. They are in a highly emotional state, and they see what they *expect* to see. They *expect* the dead body to look different from the live person they knew. And in this instance, Sharon had been told that her husband had been found dead in his flat, therefore she *expected* to see Steve's body in the mortuary. So she did. Why on earth should she think it was his twin brother? Even after I suggested the possibility, it would have seemed a very bizarre notion to her."

"Yes, I see what you mean . . ."

They walked in silence for a minute or two and then Joan said, "What I don't see, though, is how you made the connection between the two cases."

"Ah, now that's much more difficult to explain. But I'll try. You remember the night we sat up late, talking? Well, afterwards, I found it impossible to get to sleep, so for a while I read that book Doc Mallard lent me. Then I just lay there, thinking—trying to relate what I'd been reading to Steve and Geoff, and going over everything that had happened during the day. And suddenly it all just . . . coalesced."

"But how? Why?"

"It was simply a matter of a lot of apparently unrelated little facts coming together and making sense. As I say, I'd been thinking of Geoff and Steve, and how Geoff was the only person in the family who had even bothered to send Steve a birthday card. And I suppose it crossed my mind to wonder if he'd given him a present, too. Then I was thinking about the murder weapon, the ashtray, and wondering where it was, thinking it had probably been dumped somewhere, like the jacket in Hines's case. And I thought about the jacket itself, with that very unusual design on the back, the red dragon, and suddenly I remembered that when I'd gone to Geoff's house, in amongst all the stuff he was in the process of packing, I'd seen two brand-new Welsh blankets, still in their polythene bags. I recognized them because of the distinctive pattern that's woven into them—if you remember, your mother brought one back when she went to Wales on holiday last year. And suddenly I thought, of course! The red dragon—the national emblem of Wales! What if the jacket had been bought in Wales? What if

Geoff had bought it, at the same time as the blankets, and had given it to Steve, as a birthday present? *What if Steve was the murderer of Mrs. Jackson!*

"It seemed such a wild idea that at first I didn't know whether to take it seriously, but the more I thought about it, the more I came to believe it could, just possibly, be true." Thanet grinned. "I didn't tell you, but I sat up half the night, in the kitchen, thinking about it. Because once I'd decided it could be true I started to work out how it might affect our investigation, and I realized at once that it could provide a missing link. Up until then we could see no reason why Geoff should have murdered Steve, or vice versa. But now, if Geoff had given that jacket to Steve, and had seen the television appeal, if that was why he went to see Steve early on Tuesday evening—to persuade him to give himself up . . . If Steve had refused, then lost his temper, killed him and then changed places with him, to save his own skin . . ."

"An awful lot of 'ifs.' "

"I know. That's why I didn't want to tell you who I thought the murderer was, yesterday morning. I wanted to check one or two things first—whether or not Geoff had in fact given Steve the jacket, and whether or not that leg injury that Steve had had as a child was the kind to show up in an adult. If so, I knew I had him. The body that was supposed to be Steve's had no such injury. But the more I thought about it, the more convinced I became that I was right, and Steve had taken Geoff's place. There were various things which backed up the idea."

Briefly, Thanet explained about Steve's left-handedness, about the weight difference, and about Steve's reputed ability to mimic Geoff. "Debbie, Frank May's wife, had told me that Steve had made them laugh by 'taking Geoff off.' "

"Ah, I did wonder," said Joan. "I must admit I thought it a bit unlikely that Steve, who'd had to leave school at sixteen, would be able to imitate convincingly the vocabulary and speech patterns of a graduate." She spotted a crust of bread lying on the grass, a leftover from the previous day's largesse. She stopped to pick it up, then broke it into several pieces and tossed it into the ever-hopeful little flotilla of ducks that had been cruising along, keeping pace with them. For a few moments there was flapping, squawking bedlam.

"Pity we haven't got any more," she said.

"Do you think ducks like lemon flummery?" said Thanet. "We could always pop down after the competition's over."

They both laughed. "I'm not sure Sprig would appreciate that," said Joan. "And talking about the competition, what's the time?"

Thanet consulted his watch. "Ten o'clock. Better be getting back."

They turned, unconsciously speeding up a little.

"No," said Thanet, picking up the thread of their conversation again. "I think—well, in fact I know—that you're underestimating Steve. The IQ of twins is very similar, and the findings in the book were quite positive. There might be some personality differences owing to dissimilar environmental influences, but there was still an astonishing resemblance between identical twins brought up apart, in terms of voice, habits, mannerisms . . . I'm not saying it would have been easy for Steve to step into Geoff's shoes, but he had a better chance of succeeding than most, especially as the adoptive mother was dead. He had a lot to lose if he was found out, remember, and I should think the thought of a murder charge would be enough to make anyone give the performance of his life . . .

"No, I think the impersonation was feasible, but a

strain. It was interesting how quickly he reverted to his own accent once he knew that I could actually *prove* he was Steve. Where I went wrong was in jumping to the conclusion that if Steve had taken Geoff's place, then he was also the one who killed him."

Joan frowned. "He may not have actually killed Geoff, but he was still to a large degree responsible for his death, wasn't he?"

"What do you mean?"

"Well, if Steve hadn't been involved in the death of Marge Jackson, and Geoff hadn't seen the TV appeal and gone along to warn him that the police were looking for him, Geoff would still be alive today."

"True . . . However sorry you feel for Steve because of his rotten childhood, there's no denying that he has, as you once said yourself, a kind of destructive power. Look at all the people whose lives he's damaged . . ."

Joan nodded. "And the ones who have actually *died*, because of him. Mrs. Carpenter, her daughter, Mrs. Jackson, Geoff . . . It's terrifying, really. Perhaps it's as well society is going to be protected from him, for a while, at least. How long will he get, d'you think?"

"Difficult to tell."

"I suppose he'll plead not guilty to the murder of Mrs. Jackson and get away with manslaughter?"

"Probably."

"So, seven years, perhaps?"

"Something like that, I should think. With possibly another twelve months on top, for obstructing the police—in deliberately misleading us over the identity of the body and then compounding the deception by pretending to be his brother . . ."

"What about poor Mr. Carpenter?"

"That's a bit tricky. The trouble is that however many excuses you might make for him, the fact remains that he went to Steve's flat with murder in his heart and actually killed someone. That it happened not to be the person he thought it was probably won't make a scrap of difference. Premeditated murder is premeditated murder.''

"Quite. I suppose the only way he could hope to get away with less than a life sentence would be by pleading diminished responsibility.''

"Yes. His counsel might well pull it off. He'd emphasize the long strain Carpenter had suffered . . .''

"The shock of Chrissie's death, that day . . .''

"And he'd stress the fact that although Carpenter freely admits he intended killing Steve, he didn't actually equip himself to do so—he didn't take a gun or any other weapon with him. So the defense could argue that the threats were really empty ones and Carpenter hadn't really intended to do more than have a stand-up fight.''

"There's the drink and drugs angle, too,'' said Joan. "Everyone knows by now that a combination of tranquilizers and spirits is disastrous, and that self-control is diminished to the point of nonexistence.''

"On the other hand, it won't help Carpenter that all the while he thought it was Steve he had killed he showed no remorse whatsoever.''

"How did he react, when he found he'd killed the wrong man?''

"He was absolutely shattered. Appalled that he'd killed an innocent bystander . . .''

"And furious that Steve had escaped, after all?''

"No, I don't think so. I think that by then the first flush of his anger against Steve after Chrissie's death had worn off. I certainly don't think that at that point he would have been prepared to go off and kill Steve in cold blood . . . That was why the fact that he'd killed someone else by mistake was so horrifying to him. He's not by nature a violent man. His counsel will stress this fact, and rely upon it becoming apparent during the course of the trial . . . I should think Carpenter will probably end up with five or six years."

"You liked him, didn't you?"

"Yes, I did. And I couldn't help feeling sorry for him. I suppose I couldn't help identifying with him, in a way, wondering how I would have felt, if it had been you who had been killed, Sprig who had died that day . . . I'd like to think that under no circumstances would I ever commit murder, but the fact is that we can never tell how we would react, in extremity. Most of us are never pushed beyond our limit of tolerance . . ."

Joan shivered. "Thank God."

They had almost reached the hotel now. A steady trickle of people was flowing through the doors of the Fletcher Hall, which had an entrance on the street. Joan pressed Thanet's arm. "Look, there's Doctor Mallard and Mrs. Field."

The new, benevolent Doc Mallard had spotted them and raised a hand in greeting. The Thanets joined him and Luke was duly introduced to the woman who had wrought this wondrous change in his old friend. She seemed, as Joan had said, absolutely right for him, a plump, smiling little woman with calm, kind eyes as blue as forget-me-nots and laughter lines around eyes and mouth. She was neatly dressed in a navy-blue coat and flowered silk scarf. Thanet thoroughly approved and greeted her warmly. He was amused to see that the little doctor was blushing.

"Kind of you to come," said Thanet.

"Oh, not at all. Fly the flag for Bridget and all that. And Helen's very interested in cooking, aren't you?"

"Very."

"Writes cookery books, as a matter of fact," said Mallard, with shy pride.

"Oh, *that* Helen Fields!" said Joan. "Bridget would be fascinated. She'd really love to meet you."

"And I'd be delighted to meet her. I'm always interested in young people who are keen on cooking."

"Keen isn't the word," said Thanet. "The amount of practice she's done for this competition . . ."

Chatting, they moved into the hall and seated themselves where they would have a good view of what Bridget was doing without being disconcertingly close.

At ten thirty sharp the competition got under way. The proceedings were briefly explained to the audience. There were ten competitors, of ages ranging from nine to sixteen. Each had brought his own utensils and ingredients, had decorated his own table, and would have an hour and a half to prepare two dishes, a main course and a pudding. Presentation was important, but taste would be the main decider. The judges were a cookery writer, the owner of a famous London restaurant, and the editor of *Food and Wine* magazine. The winner and the runner-up would go on to the National Finals in London, in April.

Time flew. The contestants settled down to concentrated activity, apparently oblivious of the audience. Delicious smells filled the air, mouths salivated. At last it was over and the judges moved from table to table as the youngsters stood by, ready to answer questions on their handiwork. The Thanets strained to hear as Bridget, two bright spots of color burning in her cheeks, responded to the inquiries put to her.

Finally, the judges retired to the far end of the room to confer. Tension mounted as the young cooks and their anxious parents awaited the verdict. Thanet's mouth was dry and he and Joan exchanged supportive glances. At last the announcer approached the microphone, accompanied by the chairman of the judges. A cathedral hush immediately fell upon the room.

After the usual inordinately long preamble about the high quality of the food produced by the contestants and a string of compliments on their talent and originality, the judge at last raised the piece of paper upon which every eye had been riveted.

"I shall announce the results in reverse order. The runner-up is fifteen-year-old Karen Cunningham of Benenden, for her Smoked Haddock with Cream and Egg Sauce, and Hazelnut Roll."

Applause. Karen came forward, obviously delighted to have won through to the finals.

There was an electric silence as the remaining nine contestants stood rigid with hope and fear and their parents agonized with them. Thanet felt sick.

"And now the result you are all waiting for . . ."

Come on, come *on*, urged Thanet silently.

"The winner, for her Pork Chops with Mint, which she tells us is an old recipe published in the *Daily News* in the excellent series that appeared during the winter of 1928–29, and for her Lemon Flummery, exquisitely decorated with the white horse of Kent, is thirteen-year-old Bridget Thanet of Sturrenden."

Thanet felt as though he would explode with relief, delight and pride as Bridget stepped forward, eyes shining. No achievement of his own had ever affected him quite so profoundly. He and Joan clutched at each other's hands and exchanged exuberant smiles before turning to receive congratulations from Doc Mallard and Mrs. Field.

Released by the judges at last, Bridget pushed her way through the crowd towards them, acknowledging the compliments showered upon her from all sides.

Thanet put an arm around Joan as they smiled down into their daughter's radiant face, and they all linked hands.

It was a moment of pure joy.

ABOUT THE AUTHOR

DOROTHY SIMPSON, winner of the prestigious Silver Dagger Award, is the author of seven Luke Thanet mysteries, most recently ELEMENT OF DOUBT, LAST SEEN ALIVE, CLOSE HER EYES, and SUSPICIOUS DEATH. A contributor to *Ellery Queen's Mystery Magazine* and *Alfred Hitchcock's Mystery Magazine*, she lives in Kent, England.

THE MYSTERIOUS WORLD OF AGATHA CHRISTIE

Acknowledged as the world's most popular mystery writer of all time, Dame Agatha Christie's books have thrilled millions of readers for generations. With her care and attention to characters, the intriguing situations and the breathtaking final deduction, it's no wonder that Agatha Christie is the world's best-selling mystery writer.

☐	25678	SLEEPING MURDER	$3.50
☐	26795	A HOLIDAY FOR MURDER	$3.50
☐	27001	POIROT INVESTIGATES	$3.50
☐	26477	THE SECRET ADVERSARY	$3.50
☐	26138	DEATH ON THE NILE	$3.50
☐	26547	THE MYSTERIOUS AFFAIR AT STYLES	$3.50
☐	25493	THE POSTERN OF FATE	$3.50
☐	26896	THE SEVEN DIALS MYSTERY	$3.50

Kinsey Millhone is . . .

"The best new private eye." —The Detroit News

"A tough-cookie with a soft center." —Newsweek

"A stand-out specimen of the new female operatives."
  —Philadelphia Inquirer

Sue Grafton is . . .

The Shamus and Anthony Award-winning creator of Kinsey Millhone and quite simply one of the hottest new mystery writers around.

Bantam is . . .

The proud publisher of Sue Grafton's Kinsey Millhone mysteries:

- ☐ 26563 "A" IS FOR ALIBI $3.50
- ☐ 26061 "B" IS FOR BURGLAR $3.50
- ☐ 26468 "C" IS FOR CORPSE $3.50
- ☐ 27163 "D" IS FOR DEADBEAT $3.50

Special Offer
Buy a Bantam Book
for only 50¢.

Now you can have Bantam's catalog filled with hundreds of titles plus take advantage of our unique and exciting bonus book offer. A special offer which gives you the opportunity to purchase a Bantam book for only 50¢. Here's how!

By ordering any five books at the regular price per order, you can also choose any other single book listed (up to a $5.95 value) for just 50¢. Some restrictions do apply, but for further details why not send for Bantam's catalog of titles today!

Just send us your name and address and we will send you a catalog!
